THE FALL IN LOVE CHECKLIST

A NOVEL

SARAH READY

CROWN

W.W. CROWN BOOKS

An imprint of Swift & Lewis Publishing LLC

www.wwcrown.com

ISBN: 978-1-954007-00-0 (eBook)

ISBN: 978-1-954007-01-7 (pbk)

"TEN STEPS TO FALL IN LOVE"

What if you made a list of all the crazy things you've dreamed of doing, but have been too scared to try...and then did them? Every. Last. One.

Unassuming, nice-girl Dany has always done what other people expect. She keeps her dreams buried beneath boring cardigans and beige upholstery. Until the day she's diagnosed with breast cancer, her fiancé dumps her, and she loses everything.

Now Dany is going to do the unexpected – survive and thrive.

She has a ten step checklist and a sexy new landlord determined to tag along. Suddenly, Dany's life goes from ordinary to wildly unexpected. But when everything turns upside down again, Dany has to decide, is number ten on her list *the end* or just the beginning?

1

Dany

*M*y mother said nothing should stop my wedding, not even a pair of misbehaving breasts.

It's funny the things you remember when coming out of anesthesia.

So, it's done.

My breasts are gone. The girls. My boobs. Chopped off for misbehaving.

Farewell, dear friends. Goodbye. Adios amigas. Ciao. Auf wiedersehen. Adieu. I imagine they'll be chucked out with the rest of the surgical unit's biohazards: gallstones, colon polyps, cellulite. My grandfather got to keep his old pacemaker, do you think they ever let you keep your breast tissue?

I try to open my eyes, but the harsh light hurts and the room spins. I close them again.

There's beeping and distant voices. The sounds of a hospital running. The fluorescent light shines through my closed eyelids.

I drift back into a warm sleep.

Sometime later, I wake up again. Try to open my eyes. Can't. Still, I smile. *I did it.* I made it through the mastectomy. It's going to be okay. My throat tightens and I swallow down the urge to cry. It's all going to be alright now. The doctors said *it* was confined to the breasts, and now that my breasts are gone, everything's going to go back to normal. It'll be okay.

It will, I tell myself. My chest tightens. *It will.*

I fight down my doubts. In the last weeks, since my diagnosis, fear and doubt have sprouted like weeds in July. I can't stop them from growing. Weeds will always grow. But I can smother and cut them out like a ruthless gardener.

Everything is going to be okay. *It is.*

I drift back into that groggy dizzy state.

I dream about my fiancé. Shawn. He should be here soon. And my mother. But not my father. He didn't want to see me like this. That's alright. I don't want him to see me like this either.

But it'll be alright. It's gone now. Gone.

The dry hospital air tickles my nose. I'm cold beneath the scratchy thin blanket. I stretch my sluggish arms and legs. My chest *hurts.* I flinch and hold still. The cocktail of pain medication and anesthesia takes over again, and I float back into numbness.

Shawn will be here soon.

The overhead lights send little stars sparkling through my eyelids and I drift into a nice dream about my wedding. The sparks of the fluorescent are the twinkle lights lining the aisle. The machine beeping is the trilling of a harp. The sharp medicinal scent is the perfume of roses. I pull in a breath.

My dream wedding is three months away. I'll be better by then.

I will.

I'll wear the strapless ivory silk mermaid gown. There are

freshwater pearls sewn in the bodice and the train. Shawn will stand at the altar, waiting for me. We'll be married. Start our lives. I'll have everything I've ever wanted. A perfect family and home. Shawn as the head of The Boreman Group, and me as his wife. Everything I could ever want.

I pull out of my wedding fantasy. The grogginess of anesthesia is still thick. My thoughts feel like molasses. Sticky and sweet.

I hear someone shift next to me.

"Shawn?" My voice cracks and I don't know if I managed to say his name or not. I reach up and try to feel my chest. *Ouch.* I flinch. There are bandages. Ice packs. The IV pinches the back of my hand. I flop my wrist back to the hospital bed.

Suddenly, I feel his presence, a warm maleness. I squint my eyes. He's there, sitting on a metal folding chair. He's partially blocked by a curtain. It's a tight space. My vision's fuzzy. My brain's moving too slow. But, I know one thing...

"I love you," I say.

I do. We're perfect for each other. His business pedigree and my social standing check all the boxes. Our relationship is built on affinity and respect. The perfect combination. I'm not interested in five husbands, like my mother. One will do. And Shawn fits. He's solid. Reliable. Efficient. He wants a wife who can be an elegant hostess and an asset to his business. I check his boxes too.

I got The Diagnosis two weeks ago. Those weeds of fear whispered that everything would change. That I wouldn't survive. That Shawn would leave me. But Shawn told me he'd be here for it all. That nothing would change. Another mark in his favor. I don't want anything to change.

"Tell me you love me," I say. I need to hear it.

Nothing.

I reach. Grab for his hand.

When I find it, I nestle my palm in his. Pull him toward me.

His warm, strong grip reassures me. I sigh in pleasure.

He'll tell me he loves me now.

I squeeze his hand.

Nothing.

The long pause makes my skin itch.

"Please," I say.

Another hesitation.

Then he clears his throat.

My heart thumps. I swallow in trepidation. Something's wrong. Although my foggy mind can't quite grasp *what*.

"Is it awful?" I ask.

"No," he says.

I hang onto that word and squeeze his hand. The room spins like a wobbling top near to falling over.

"I thought I might not wake up," I say. Although, it's not so scary now that I'm holding his hand.

His breath hitches and I hear the metal chair scrape the tiles as he scoots closer.

His thumb gently strokes the back of my hand. His touch vibrates over my body.

"Did they say they got it all?" I ask. Then I chide myself. *Of course they got it all. We're going to get married. Everything's okay.*

"I don't know," he says.

There's something odd in his voice.

I tumble back into a floating mist. I brush my loose hand over the air above my chest. It feels suspended in jelly. I move my hand up and down. No breasts. No boobs. Ding dong the boobs are gone. I giggle and shake my head. It feels wobbly on my neck.

His thumb, rubbing my other hand, is doing something to my insides. I want to press up against him.

"You feel so good."

I hear a sharp voice across the room. Not Shawn.

Did I say that out loud? My mother would've been mortified. I should be mortified. I'm not. What's in these drugs? Who else is in this room?

Shawn clears his throat. I've made him uncomfortable.

Was my mother here? A thought bubbles up. What had she said yesterday? Oh, right.

"Do you still think I'm beautiful? My mother said you might not."

I hear a low growl. Shawn never growls. Never.

"Honey, you're the most beautiful woman I've ever seen."

My body warms. I try to scoot closer to his deep voice. I want to feel the low rumble of it down to my toes. I imagine his voice licking over my skin. I like this version of Shawn.

"She said you might get scared off. That some men run."

Another low growl. I think he's angry at my words. His hand tenses in mine.

"Some men are fools. I've never been a fool."

"I'm going to marry you. I'd marry you tomorrow if I could." Suddenly, a swell of emotion rushes through me. I want to marry this man more than anything in the world. There's a desperate urgency there that I've never felt before. Blame it on the drugs, the mastectomy, whatever, it's there.

He drags his free hand across my forehead and pushes my hair away from my face.

A warm fuzziness settles over me, but a niggle of foreboding is there too. I run my fingers over his hand. The back is covered in a light dusting of hair. And his finger pads have calluses. A slow chill slides down my spine.

Shawn has smooth hands and no calluses. None.

Plus, in no way does Shawn have a southern drawl. Or a low rumbly growl. And he has never in his life called me *honey*.

I slit open my eyes. The room tilts and rolls and the bright light momentarily blinds me. I blink. The man holding my hand slowly comes into focus.

He has dark brown wavy hair. A five o'clock shadow. Deep-set gray eyes. A full bottom lip with a kissable dent in the middle. He's wearing a flannel and jeans with steel-tipped boots. And he's looking at me intently. Holding my hand. Like he's used to taking what he wants and never letting go. You can tell a lot about someone in the way they hold your hand. His grip is firm and confident. Reassuring. Possessive.

Nothing like the casual, loose hold of my fiancé.

Because he's *not* my fiancé.

He's not Shawn.

2

Dany

I pull at my hand. He doesn't let go.

"Who are you?" I ask. The room tilts and jars until it finally settles and crashes. The fog sweeps away.

I yank at my hand again.

"Let go." I pull again.

My brain doesn't know him, but that doesn't stop my body from wanting him.

He clears his throat. "You, uh..." He stops, and I can see thoughts flashing behind his eyes, but I can't decipher what he's thinking. Finally, he lets go of my hand. My lips wobble.

"Why are you in my room?" My eyes open wide, as another fact hits home. "And why are you pretending to be my fiancé? What's wrong with you?" My cheeks heat. Where's Shawn? Why isn't he here? Why isn't my mother here? I look toward the door. What's going on?

My body has never gone haywire for a man, and I don't know why it has to start now.

He winces. "It's not your room," the man says.

I swing my head back to him.

"Ouch." That hurt. Then, what he says sinks in. "Pardon me?"

He gestures behind him. "It's not your room. You're in a shared recovery suite. I was on the other side of that curtain."

I look around. The hospital room comes into sharp focus. Bland pea green wallpaper. Generic painting of a woodland scene. A television. IV poles and medical apparatus. Curtains. And three hospital beds. All occupied.

On my right a balding man with papery skin and thick blue veins snores. To my left is a pretty, sleek-haired teenage girl with a bandage on her nose. She stares unabashedly at me. Her expression reminds me of a mischievous otter I once saw at the zoo. She's peeking at me from the bed behind the man. The one on the metal chair who held my hand.

I clear my throat. Mortification washes through me.

"It's a shared room," I say.

"That's right."

"You're here with her."

He nods. "I'm here with her."

"Hi," the girl says. She waves at me.

I close my eyes. My mind has almost completely cleared and I'm rapidly coming back to my senses. I attempt to shake off the attraction I felt for this man. It was misplaced. He is *not* my fiancé. I only felt that spark, okay, flame, because I thought he was Shawn.

I snap open my eyes and look him square in the face.

"I'm sorry," I say. "Please forget what I said."

He shakes his head. "Don't be sorry. I'm Jack." He holds out his hand to shake. I don't want to take it.

For some reason, it feels dangerous to take his hand again. *Jack.*

What if, when I touch him, that ember sparks into flame

once more? Even when I know he's not Shawn? No. I don't want to find out what could happen.

"Daniella. There you are."

Oh thank goodness. It's Shawn.

He hurries into the room and steps in front of Jack's hand, effectively blocking him out. Shawn sends him a peevish look.

I let out a relieved exhale. Shawn's here. He's wearing his usual Tom Ford suit and Ferragamo shoes. He's immaculately groomed. Even his fingernails are perfect half-moons. A sharp contrast to the flannel-clad, rough-hewn, southern-drawling Jack.

"I've been looking everywhere. They didn't tell me they moved you to the third floor."

"You're here," I say. Tears start to fill my eyes. I blink them back. Everything will be okay now. Shawn's here and I'm going to be okay and everything will be fine.

Jack looks between me and Shawn. Frown lines form on his forehead. His gray eyes narrow. I want to tell him to go away. I don't like him witnessing this moment. My mind's mostly cleared from the anesthetic and I'm embarrassed about what I said to him.

"Did you speak with the surgeon? What did he say?" I need to know. I have to know that I'm in the clear. That everything can return to normal.

Shawn clicks his tongue against his teeth. Something he does when he's annoyed.

"I have no idea. I was on the phone with the office. I'm grinding non-stop on that multi-level parking bid." He sighs and kneels at the edge of my bed. Then, he finally really looks at me. His face leaches of color.

"Jeez," he breathes. He grimaces and his mouth twists like he wants to spit out a mouthful of milk that has unexpectedly curdled and soured on his tongue.

My chest twists. I wince. My hands flutter above my

bandages. Suddenly, I feel naked and vulnerable. The gauze and hospital gown don't feel like enough cover. I tug the paper-thin hospital blanket over my torso.

"Okay?" I ask.

Shawn glares around the shared room. The sleeping man. Jack and the girl. He stands stiffly and scowls at the chair Jack is sitting on not two feet from my bed.

"Excuse us." He pointedly looks at Jack. "Could you move?"

Jack gives me a long, measuring stare.

"Certainly," he says in a slow honeyed drawl.

I turn my head.

My mouth is dry. I try to swallow the lump in my throat.

Shawn grabs the curtain on the ceiling runner and yanks it closed. I can no longer see the others. No sleeping blue-veined man. No mischievous otter girl. No Jack. I shake my head. Shawn's here. I smile up at him.

"Thank you for being here," I say.

It'll be okay now. Shawn's just shocked. It'll pass.

He's efficient in everything he does. He'll get me home, help me recover from the surgery. Then, we'll be married. This cancer thing is a quick blip. That's what Shawn said. Plus, the doctors think this surgery will take care of it. No problem. No worries. I cut down the anxiety that tries to rise. It will be *fine*.

Shawn runs a hand through his blond hair. My mother always said his angelic good looks were the perfect counterpart to my English rose beauty. He starts to talk, then stops. Looks down, then up again.

I shift nervously.

"What is it?" I ask.

"I can't do this," he says.

I stare at him. I'm not sure what he means.

"God, look at you," he says. "Look at you."

I look down at myself. There's dried blood. Some sort of

ointment. Bandages. An ugly blue gown. An IV taped on. My hair is in a limp bun. I don't know what my face looks like.

"Is everything okay?" I ask.

He's pacing the few feet of space at the end of my bed.

I try to sit up, but a tight stabbing pain stops me. I sink back down and take shallow breaths until the pain passes.

"What am I doing?" Shawn mutters.

My mouth is horribly dry and his pacing is starting to worry me. "May I please have a glass of water?" I ask. My voice is small.

He sighs. "Look. Daniella. I can't do this. I'm not up for this. All this." He waves his hands at me.

I try to swallow. Can't.

"It's okay. You don't have to. I made casseroles to last for at least two weeks. And I sent your suits to be dry cleaned. The house cleaners were in, I had the carpets done..."

I drift off. The expression on his face is pained.

There's a hard thud behind my rib cage.

"Shawn?" I ask. It comes out as a croak.

He flinches.

"Look. I don't love you." He glances at the gap in the curtain, like he wants to be anywhere but here.

His words crash around me, but I can't catch ahold of them. Like I'm trying to clasp water and every time I close my hand it shoots away.

"What?" I ask.

I shake my head. He keeps on.

"It's not the cancer, it's me. The cancer has nothing to do with it. I don't love you and I don't want to marry you."

He says the last in a rush. Then he stops pacing and stands at the bottom of the bed, staring at me. There's a desperate pleading look on his face.

"You...but..." I swallow.

I finally catch his words.

And I know he said he doesn't love me, that he doesn't want to marry me, but what comes out is, "But what about the casseroles?"

The fifteen casseroles I baked and froze. Who's going to eat them? There's taco casserole, tuna casserole, hamburger casserole, tater tots casserole...

"Look. I'm sorry," he says.

I look. And look. A heavy weight bears down on my chest and settles in.

"I've known for a while now. It's obvious. We don't fit. To be honest, Daniella, you're boring. Other women have interests. Passion. They're alive. You never argue, you're never spontaneous, you don't have any opinions, you think barbeque sauce on chicken is taking a risk."

"A risk?" I ask. My throat is burning dry. I'm so thirsty.

"Look. Think of it from my perspective. Would you be attracted to someone who doesn't have any career ambitions, or hobbies, whose idea of weekend fun is bleaching the whites, dusting the china, and going to a charity brunch? Look, it's not the cancer. See? I don't want to be saddled with a hothouse flower the rest of my life."

A sharp jagged pain runs down my side. Spots start in my vision and I realize that I need to breathe. I suck in a hard breath. It hurts, like shards of glass.

"May I please have some water?" My throat is killing me.

Shawn shakes his head. "Daniella. Did you hear anything I said?"

The room is tilting again and there's a ringing in my ears.

"Daniella?"

I nod. "Yes?"

"Look. I'm sorry. I can't do this right now. I have to go. They need me at the office." He sends me one final unhappy look, then turns and leaves.

3

Dany

I stare at the swinging curtain.

I close my eyes, then open them.

The curtain's still shifting back and forth. It has fish on it, like a seafood casserole curtain.

I stifle a hysterical sob.

Maybe I'm still in surgery. Maybe I'm having post-anesthesia hallucinations. Maybe I'll wake up and Shawn will say that he's decided to whisk me away for a whirlwind wedding and a tropical honeymoon. In Fiji. Or Turks and Caicos.

The curtain shrieks on its runners as it slides open.

The man, Jack, has a small plastic cup of water. He holds it out to me.

I stare at the white cup in his dark hand. I just look at the darn cup. I can't turn away. I follow the curve of his fingers, the line of his wrist and the muscle of his forearms up to his biceps, his shoulders, his face. I look into his gray eyes. I didn't dream this. I see the reality of it reflected in his eyes. In the plastic cup he's holding out to me.

It hits me then.

Everything at once.

I had a double mastectomy. My fiancé doesn't love me. He dumped me. And three strangers witnessed it all.

Tears burn in my eyes.

"Here," he says. His voice is gentle.

He puts the water on the stand next to me.

His eyes are full of, I don't know, knowledge, understanding, something...

And that something makes me ashamed. I feel naked and ugly. I don't want him to look at me like that. With what...pity? Anger rises in my chest. And I'm glad for it, because anger is a thousand times better than tears.

"You deserve better—"

"Please go," I say.

"I'm sorry—"

"Go away. Please." Because even when humiliated, I still say please like a lady. Even that makes me angry. I've always been kind, good, done everything right, and what has it brought?

This.

I grab the cup of water and swallow. It slides down my burning throat and cools the fire.

"Thank you. For the water," I say.

He gives me a smile, there's a dimple in his left cheek. "You're welcome." His politeness hurts. "And you deserve better."

I lash out, like a wounded animal.

"My fiancé's a good man. He's merely confused and scared. We're getting married in three months." My voice is firm. Shawn will come around. I have to believe this right now. I'm hanging on by a thread. I won't let myself think otherwise. He doesn't believe those things he said. Shawn loves me. Or at least, he has respect and affinity for me. And isn't that what all good relationships are built on?

Something like disappointment shows on Jack's face.

I turn my head away. I'm not wrong.

The teenage girl on the bed clears her throat.

I look over.

"Not that it's any of my business, but your fiancé's a total dick."

"Sissy," Jack says in a low voice.

"Seriously. It's awesome he dumped her. Now she knows what kind of loser he is. Better now than in the future. She can move on with her life. It's all good."

I shake my head. It's not all good. None of this is all good.

"Seriously," she keeps on, "your life's better without him. Wouldn't you rather be on your own, rocking life, loving your bad self, than be 'loved' by the dick?" She air quotes the word *loved*.

No, my heart cries, *I wouldn't.*

"Sissy, enough with the D word," says Jack.

"Whatever," she says. "We're growing here. You can't make popcorn without some banging around."

"Sissy," says Jack.

"Who has popcorn?" the older man in the corner says. He props himself up on his veiny arms.

"No one," says Sissy.

"But is there casserole?" asks the man.

"Dude. Seriously. You did not just go there," says Sissy.

I consider burying my head under the scratchy hospital pillow. If I did, maybe they'd all go away.

Before I can, my mother rushes in, her gold bangles clanking and the scent of Chanel No. 5 chasing her.

"Oh, darling, darling," she says. She bends over and quickly air kisses my cheeks. "I ran into Shawn. What did you say? What did you do? The poor man said the engagement is off.

He's in a state. A state. I told you this could happen. I told you."
Her hands wave in the air like small nervous birds. The heavy
bejeweled rings glitter in the lights.

"Hello, mother."

"You look absolutely awful. Awful. Poor Shawn. It's hard
when you care too much. No wonder he was in a state. No
wonder. You didn't do your hair. Your nails. No polish. You look
awful. Awful, Daniella. Can you imagine how that made him
feel?"

"Awful?" I ask.

Sissy snickers. *Dick,* she mouths at me.

Jack clears his throat. My mother turns to look at him.
Clearly, she's surprised. She didn't take the time to notice that
this is a shared room.

"Ma'am," he says.

She tilts her chin and sizes him up. I've been her daughter
long enough to know that she's estimated his net worth within
one half of a percent and deemed him unworthy in less than
three seconds flat.

She turns away. "Excuse us, if you please." She snaps the
curtain shut. "I saw the doctor. The biopsy will be back soon.
You're moving to a private room for three nights. Oh, darling.
Poor Shawn. Poor, poor man. Didn't I tell you to reassure him?
Don't worry. He'll see reason. Your father especially wants this
marriage."

"Mother," I say. I'm tired. Suddenly, I'm exhausted. "He
broke the engagement because...he said I bore him."

She stops her fretting and looks at me. "You bore him?"

I nod. "Do you think I'm boring?"

"Darling. What I think doesn't matter."

She does.

"You'll get him back. Five years together is nothing to
sneeze at." She starts to tear up. "Don't worry, darling. I know
just the thing. A makeover. We'll get through this little hiccup.

It's the cancer, of course. Some men aren't cut out for illness. But it'll be over soon and then we'll have a wedding. A beautiful wedding. Lots of tulle. Remind me to order more tulle. Rose pink. Not carnation pink, carnations are vulgar."

She pats my hand again. I take in a lungful of her perfume.

"Regardless, a makeover is just the thing. Add a little shine and glamour. Men don't actually care about personality. It's the packaging that matters. We'll glitz you up. No matter what's on the inside, your outside will be the opposite of boring."

I close my eyes. Maybe I could go back under anesthesia?

"Darling?"

"I'll speak with him when I get home." I say. "I'm sure he'll have changed his mind. He hates casserole, apparently. It was a misunderstanding."

My mother squeezes my hand. "Didn't I mention? Shawn sent your things over. Said it'd be better if I took care of you during the recovery. But, darling, you can't stay. Your father and I are having a sort of second wind to our marriage. Lots of hanky panky happening. Lots of middle-of-the-day whoopie. We did it on the fax machine the other day. The fax machine. I'm sorry, sweetheart. You must, you absolutely must find another place to convalesce." She looks down at me and tsks at my limp hair.

I hear fake gagging from the other side of the curtain. My friend the teenager is vocal in her opinion of my life.

"Mother," I say. There's pleading in that one word. After college, I stayed at my father's company as the donations coordinator, and my few friends from school left for jobs in New York or Chicago. The only person I'm close with in Stanton is Shawn. I isolated myself without realizing it. I made a life that circled entirely around him. The realization hits hard.

"You look awful, darling," my mother repeats. "You really should take better care of yourself. How can anyone love you if you don't take care of yourself?"

"I don't have anywhere to go," I say. I choke on the realization.

She tsks. "Don't be selfish. Your father and I deserve our special alone time. You only live once."

I stare at her. Shocked.

"But I had major surgery, I was just..."

"You'll find something. Don't fret, it creates an unbecoming wrinkle on your forehead." She smooths my hair down.

I don't know what to say.

And that's when it finally, truly hits. I'm post-surgery. Maybe cancer free, maybe not. I've been moved out of my home. Dumped. No fiancé. No wedding. My parents don't want me to stay with them. I have nowhere to go. No friends to depend on. No doting family. Nowhere to lick my wounds in peace. This isn't a misunderstanding. It's a disaster.

4

JACK

I pretend not to watch as the attendant rolls Daniella from the recovery suite. We don't speak. No good-byes. Why would there be? We're two strangers who met in a hospital room and shared...nothing.

Lie.

"Jack's in looove," says Sissy. "L-U-V looove."

I scrub my hand over the back of my neck.

She has that special kid sister knack. She can sense exactly what you'd like to hide, or bury, or never admit to anyone and wave it in the open.

It doesn't matter that we only met six months ago and we're both new at this sibling thing. She's a natural.

"Oh ho ho," says the man in the corner. "This show needs popcorn. I haven't had this much fun in years. Rarely get out of the house, don't ya know? I'm starving."

I walk over to the man and hold out a wrapped breakfast bar. "I've got a granola bar. You allowed to eat?"

"No," says the man. He grabs it and cradles it in his lap. "Thanks, son."

"You're welcome," I say.

I walk back to the folding chair by Sissy's bed.

"Looove," she starts in again.

"Yeah right," I say.

She smirks. "I could see the back of your neck all blotchy red. And that dopey look on your face. Dude, it's love."

I sigh. Unlike most guys, I believe in love at first sight. I believe in it, and I don't want it. I thought I could avoid it, but it came and slammed me like a wrecking ball. I'm still reeling.

But I promised myself that I would never make someone suffer because of my love. That's all that can come from it. Suffering.

"She sure was a pretty princess. Good thing she got dumped by the dick. The field's totally clear now," says Sissy.

"Sissy," I say. My go-to reprimand.

"Yeah, yeah."

"The field's not clear," I say. She grins at me, like I admitted to her theory of looove.

But if, and I repeat, *if,* I gave in to my desires and pursued her, our relationship would never work out. One, her fiancé just broke their engagement. I'd be a rebound at best, or a way to make her ex jealous, or a confidence-boosting one-night stand. Two, her fiancé mentioned cancer, she might think I was pursuing her out of pity or some other misplaced emotion. She would never trust my motives—that a guy could fall in love with her at a time like this. Three, and most importantly, every time I love someone, they leave or die. End of story.

"Remember the day we met?" asks Sissy.

"Sure," I say. "It was only six months ago."

"You had a dopey look then, too. Not a lovey dopey look. But an *I'm a big brother, must protect* kind of look. I was freaked out until I saw it. Then I knew I'd be okay. You're a good bro."

I shake my head. "Your scheme's not working. You're still going to boarding school next fall."

"Seriously. Come on," she says.

I fold my arms over my chest. "It's for your own good," I say.

"Bull."

She lies back on the hospital bed and turns on her side away from me.

"Got any water?" the man asks.

I get up and pour him a cup.

"Thanks, sonny," he says.

"Anyone here with you?" I ask.

"Nah. Better on my own. You get it. I can tell, you're a lone ranger at heart. Like me."

I study him, a man nearing his eighties, all alone. He has no one to love and no one to lose.

"Yeah," I say.

I go back to Sissy's bedside and think about the day we first met. It was six months ago.

It took me about three seconds to realize I'd do anything for her. She stepped out of Dad's rusted Bronco with a scuffed Jansport backpack. It was filled with all her possessions in the world. In her arms was a ratty stuffed elephant with one eye missing and its trunk half fallen off. I watched as she nervously tugged on its trunk.

She and Dad had been living in the back of his SUV. For years. Her nose was crooked and broken in three places. Her left eye was black and blue. *"She's been getting in fights on the road. I've got a new opportunity in Mexico. Can't have her around. You gotta take her, son. She's your half-sister, don't you know?"*

I hadn't known. Fury swept through me. She was fifteen and I'd never heard of her existence. What had her life been like, travelling the country with my scheming drifter dad?

This was only the third time in my life that I'd seen him. I'd never come away with a good impression. His eyes were constantly shifting and he could never look me straight on.

"I told you, pops. I'll be good on my own," she'd said. Her chin tilted up and she looked at me with haughty pride. But there was uncertainty there, and a challenge. She was challenging me to care. I recognized the look because I'd given it to my dad, once, long ago. He'd not risen to the occasion.

I sighed and she unconsciously hugged her stuffed elephant against her chest.

Dang.

That was it. I was sunk. Hard and fast.

"Take your bag inside," I'd said.

She did. Then I gave my dad the five thousand dollars he hinted at and requested that he not stay the night but leave for Mexico right away. And never come back.

That protectiveness I feel for Sissy, the sibling love, I'll do anything for her.

Even send her away. Because if she gets hurt because of my bad luck, I'll never forgive myself.

I let out a long, heavy sigh.

A nurse in thick-heeled white shoes hustles into the room. She stops at Sissy's bedside. "Ready for discharge?"

Sissy looks up. "Seriously ready," she says.

An hour later we're in the driveway at home.

"I'll be back after my meeting. You'll be okay?"

"You worry too much," says Sissy. She starts to smile, then stops. She reaches up and touches the bandages. "Hurts to smile."

I frown.

"Take the painkillers they gave you. Have a nap."

"Yeah, yeah," she says.

She looks out the truck window at the dusting of early spring snow. Then, she blows on the glass and traces a smiley face in the fog.

"Anyway, I can't. I've got two papers due and an exam on Monday. Plus, I'm running for student body president. Big campaign to plan."

"You're taking over the world," I say. She's gone from a jumpy scrapper to a driven young woman intent on ruling the world. Sissy is as subtle as a bull and has the drive of a runaway train.

"Out with the old, in with the new me," she says. It was her New Year's resolution. She wanted to shed the last of her old life, and that included fixing the visible breaks and scars on her nose.

"Text me if you need anything," I say. I chuck her on the arm.

She holds back a smile. "Good luck at your meeting. If they don't approve your project I could dig up some dirt and blackmail them, or pull a con that involves—"

"Hey, I got this. Where's the faith?" I hold up my hands. She probably would find a way to blackmail the committee. She learned quite a few questionable practices from our dad.

"Yeah, yeah," she says again. "Still. Offer's open."

"Go on. Get out of here."

"K. But don't forget, I'm going to look up that cute girl from the hospital. The tragic pretty princess that got dumped by the dick. She *loooves you*. Jack and Pretty Princess sitting in a tree."

I pull at my collar.

"Get out of here, Sissy. You proved your point."

She laughs and I level her with a long look. But I can't help the edge of my mouth quirking up.

"Bye, bro."

She walks across the driveway and lets herself in the house.

As I pull out, my thoughts return to the woman in the hospital.

Daniella.

I don't know her last name. I don't know anything about her. Except that I fell hard. After one look.

Dang.

I'm not completely sure why she was in the hospital recovery suite today, or why her creep of a fiancé dumped her, or why she lets her mother railroad her like that. I only know that my instincts are telling me I have to see her again. It's the same feeling I get when I find a building that I know I have to have. I *always* get those buildings. And then the renovations are like a relationship. I choose my buildings when something in me recognizes them as a kindred spirit. It's like that. But not. Maybe because the feeling is a thousand times stronger. I've never had that with another person.

I blow out a long breath as I pull into Stanton City Hall.

I clear my mind and prepare for my presentation. Winning this project is what's most important. My entire future hinges on this meeting. Nothing can go wrong.

5

JACK

*E*verything's gone wrong.

I worked for more than a decade toward my goal of building an affordable, safe, sought-after housing community in Stanton and I'm about to fail.

I click through my slide show on the conference room wall. All of my artist representations of Rose Towers Community are on the projection screen. I have the plans completed, the funding set, everything in place, except the approval of the Downtown Development Committee.

The eight members of the committee sit behind a long table. The chair, Mr. Atler, was my biggest supporter. With his backing, I expected my bid to pass. He leans over and whispers to Ms. Smith. She's co-chair and in the seat next to him. She scribbles something on her notepad and shows it to him. He scowls and looks at me. The committee member on the end is frowning. Another is staring out the window, not even pretending to pay attention.

I rally and continue my presentation.

"As you can see, the community will have a circular walking and jogging path, a playground, an outdoor pool, grills and picnic tables, and a large open grassy area for recreation." The pictures on the wall give a bird's eye view. The land is currently overgrown and fallow. The warehouses have been empty for twenty-five years. But the buildings have character and incredible potential. I glance at the faces of the board again to gauge their reaction.

Only a few of them are paying attention. The second I stepped into this room I knew the attitude toward me had turned. The committee's no longer supportive. They're ambivalent at best and antagonistic at worst.

But why?

"The buildings will retain their character and historic appeal, but include modern amenities," I say in a confident voice meant to disguise my confusion.

I click through lifestyle images showing the kitchen, bath and laundry in the units. The images are polished, appealing— but for some reason that I can't fathom, I've lost the committee.

The mood in the room isn't with me.

I make one last effort to sweep them up in my vision. My passion.

"For more than a decade, I've renovated homes in Stanton. My passion is taking unlivable, discarded spaces and converting them into homes. In renovating the warehouses to residential, the city of Stanton will open up a new market of living space. The city will show that it cares about the quality of life of its people and its families. Right now, there's a housing shortage for the working class and middle class. It's reached crisis levels. Throwing up new developments and bare-boned apartment buildings with paper-thin walls isn't the answer. No matter a person's income level, they deserve a well-built, solid family home with character, architectural beauty, and a feeling of security, safety and community. By giving a city livable homes, you give it a heart. Which is why I ask that you vote to approve my bid for Rose Tower."

I close the presentation. The dimmed lights turn back to brightness. I scrutinize the faces of the board. I lobbied hard before the meeting today to make sure I had enough votes. They denied the other contenders. There are no other open proposals that I know of. This should have been a win.

This project is more than business for me, it's the culmination of my life's passion. I grew up in a housing development, with cold, drafty walls, mold, rot, and petty crime. I want to give kids and families more than what I had.

Mr. Atler, the Chairman, leans forward. "Mr. Jones. Thank you. While we appreciate your vision, we have reservations."

My shoulders tense. As of yesterday, Mr. Atler was my main supporter. Now, his arms are folded over his chest and he's leaning back in his chair. Classic closed-off posture. Defensive look on his face.

Something changed in the last twenty-four hours, and it's not to my benefit.

I roll my shoulders back. "Let me address those reservations," I say.

Ms. Smith, the co-chair and a lawyer at a prominent law firm, speaks. "This committee was formed last year with the directive to act in the best interest of the city of Stanton. The *best interest*. Am I clear?"

Her lips are pursed. I scan the faces of the board. All closed off. None friendly.

"No. I'm not clear. My proposal will do exactly as you say— provide the city with an income for decades, bring life to downtown, increase foot traffic, revenue, revitalize the riverfront. Rose Tower will bring untold benefits to the community. I'm sure Mr. Creston, the donor of the property and a known philanthropist, would agree."

A quiet debate begins amongst the committee members. It quickly becomes clear that another party has entered the field and money, a great big sack of money, is at stake. And, the amount apparently, is much more than what my project will bring.

"I move to deny the Rose Tower bid," Mr. Atler says.

"I second the motion," Ms. Smith says.

I'm speechless. Completely speechless.

A vote is called and my vision is unanimously voted down.

"Thank you for your time, Mr. Jones. Meeting adjourned."

And that is how a ten-year dream is crushed in ten minutes.

The committee files out. I'm left standing at the front of the room. I look at the empty chairs and the vacant table. It's done. It's all over.

Mr. Atler and I are alone in the room. He stands and starts to make his way out. When he looks my way, he shakes his head.

"Dratted business. You understand. I've always been an admirer of your work. What is it fifty, sixty properties rehabbed now?"

"Sixty-two," I say. Each one is meaningful.

"Yes, yes. Charitable of you. Anyway, Jones. We received another bid. Too good to refuse."

I step forward. I can't let this go. I can't let this be the end. The Creston warehouses are perfect for my project, there's not another spot within sixty miles that fits as well.

"What can I do to convince you otherwise. Can I file an appeal? Bring more funding? What do you need from me?"

He shakes his head. "There's nothing. We'll be wrapping this up at the next quarterly meeting." He looks at his watch. I'm losing my chance.

"There's got to be something. Anything. Come on, Rick. You believe in this too." I put my hand on his arm, trying to recapture our connection.

He sighs and rubs at his eyes. "I'm retiring next year. Can't wait to hit the golf course every morning. I'm too old for these political machinations. You hear me?"

I nod. He's thawing.

"Cindy, my wife, she thinks well of you."

"She's a lovely woman."

He scrubs his eyes again. "She nearly had my head last night when I told her we'd have to vote you down. Renovation is a pet project of hers. She's HGTV mad, thinks she's a fixer-upper diva. Couch pillows, fluffy throws, quartz countertops. Do you hear me, Jones?"

"Yes?" Honestly, I'm not clear what he's getting at.

"Good, good."

"I'm to make an appeal?"

"Criminy, no. You'll be shut down again. I'll vote you down myself."

I shake my head. Confused.

"It's not me who's blocking you. It's the Richie Riches of Stanton, the power players. The committee's in their pocket. They've decided the warehouses should go to another party. Line their bank accounts a little more. If you can convince them that you're the better bet, then you'll get your project."

"The Richie Riches?" Stanton is a small city, with a population of a few hundred thousand.

Rick shakes his head ruefully. "The Drakes, to start. Get them on your side and the rest will fall in place."

My mind works out questions and plans. The name Drake sounds vaguely familiar.

"Any other advice?"

He shakes his head and holds out his hand. I take it and give a firm shake.

"My wife will be happy if you get your project through. She wanted to pass on some wallpaper suggestions for the entries. A happy wife makes a happy life. I'll walk you out."

We head down the hall to the front door of City Hall.

At the parking lot Rick gives a last bit of advice. "The final vote for the warehouse bid is at the next quarterly meeting. I'd have made my play before then if I were you."

"Thanks."

I hold up my hand in farewell.

Inside, my mind is spinning.

I failed. Failed miserably. But I have a direction and a glimmer of hope. Find the Drakes and convince them to fall in love with my dream. Heck, I'll convince them to fall in love with me if I have to. I head off, ready to get in bed with the Drakes and make them fall in love.

6

Dany

I'm discharged after three nights in the hospital. My mother holds the wheelchair handles as she confirms the instructions from the nurse.

"Drakes don't get cancer," she says for the seventeenth time this morning, and possibly the nine hundredth since the diagnosis. "We just don't."

She sends me a look. She made it perfectly clear that cancer is *beneath* the Drakes.

"I don't know where Daniella went wrong. Possibly the hamburger phase she had in second grade. I warned her. I told her, Drakes *do not* eat hamburgers. Or candy bars. There were some candy bars that year too."

The nurse hums a non-answer. She's a no-nonsense black woman in blue scrubs. She points back to the printed pages on wound care. There are instructions on how to remove the bandages and care for the drains—those delightful little tubes that send out all the oozy fluid from the surgical site. The ooze was red at first, then pink, now it's the color of apple juice. There are instructions for showering, for medication, for activity level. There are pages upon pages of instructions. I nod and try to listen. But I'm distracted. There's a room with an open door that's diagonal from the nurses' station. It has coral-colored trim around the door and light salmon linoleum floors. There are plants, a white and fuchsia orchid and a blooming bird of paradise. A flood of sunlight spills across the floor from the large window. All this color is almost a vulgar contrast to the dull green and blue and gray everywhere else.

I crane my neck and make out a group of women, sitting in plushy lounge chairs. An older woman in a purple track suit is talking and gesticulating widely. The rest of the women are roaring with laughter. I'm stunned. What could be so funny? So wildly amusing? I've never heard so much noise, so much laughter in a hospital. Or anywhere really.

"What is that?" I ask. I point to the room.

My mother bats at my hand.

"Don't point, darling," she says.

The nurse looks over. She scratches her chin. "That's the girls."

Another round of laughter erupts. My mother sniffs.

I don't know why, but I'm drawn to their laughter. It's so uninhibited and unapologetic. It reminds me of the first time I saw kids doing somersaults at the park. I stood in awe, then rashly joined them. I rolled down the hill, my stomach flipping in joy as I sped down. I was free. Until my nanny found me and scolded me for the grass stains on my dress. I haven't felt that joyful rolling since. Except that colorful room reminded me so much of it.

I shift in the wheelchair and crane my neck to see inside better.

My mother sends me a pointed stare. I ignore it.

"What are they doing?" I ask.

The nurse doesn't answer.

My mother clears her throat. "As I said, thank you for your care. We won't be back. The cancer is cut out. Gone. Drakes don't get cancer. As I said."

I wonder if my mother remembers that I wasn't born a Drake. Probably not. I assumed the role so well.

We receive the final paperwork, my prescriptions, follow-up instructions, when the drains can come out, when the staples can be removed...enough information to direct a military campaign, but finally, finally my mother begins to wheel me out.

"Someone else can push me," I say. My mom is five foot two and all of one hundred pounds.

"Don't be silly, darling. What would they say?"

"Of course," I say. Which is absolutely always the right response.

The wheels squeak as the wheelchair glides down the hall. I hunch my shoulders down, then adjust my posture as the stitches pinch my skin.

When we get close enough to *the room* I send a quick furtive glance at the plaque on the wall.

It reads, *Chemotherapy Lounge.*

Shock punches me and I recoil. I don't want to go anywhere near that room. Laughter or not.

The women cackle again.

I wrap my arms around myself.

"Are you cold, darling? Would you like a shawl?"

"No, Mother. I'm fine."

"Of course you are, darling. Of course you are."

She lays a beige cashmere shawl across my lap.

The smell of antiseptic chases us through the halls and clings to my skin. At the entry, Karl, our driver, opens the door to the Jaguar.

"Good to see you, Miss Drake. Mrs. Drake."

He gives me a polite smile.

"Thank you, Karl," I say. I slide into the leather seat, careful not to pull on my stitches.

My mother glides in next to me.

"Now that this ghastly illness is over with, let's discuss the future," she says.

She takes my hands as the Jag pulls out of the parking lot and into traffic.

"Shawn has jumped ship," she says.

"He's merely scared. A small misunderstanding." I attempt to pacify.

My mother pats my hand. "Exactly. I'll consult with the plastic surgeon. Perhaps you should go to New York, rather than Stanton Medical. Yes, I think that's best. A makeover. I just love makeovers. Why didn't you marry Shawn years ago? I told you to. I warned you."

"Of course," I say.

I think about Shawn. About our home. It's a beige sided new construction executive home that his parents gave him as a college graduation gift. It came with the promotion to President of The Boreman Group, his family's business. I always wanted to paint the walls different colors, burgundy, ice blue, saffron, maybe sage green, but Shawn said a beige interior was more refined. For five years, I've been cocooned in beige.

At least my childhood home isn't beige. It's white. All white.

"And why are you still working? At least you took a break for this blip. What would they say? You know Drake women don't work. They marry powerful men who work. It's your job to run a household, be a hostess, sit on charity boards. Darling, why didn't you marry years ago? You've wasted your life. Don't wrinkle your brows. You know I'm right."

I sigh. "You know why. Shawn wanted to wait until he turned thirty. He said it's passé to marry before then."

"Well, far be it from me to naysay, but your father's not impressed."

My chin falls to my chest. My father. I've always craved his good opinion.

When I was three months, my biological father left. As my mom tells it, he was her one true love, and she rues the day she ever laid eyes on him. He got the Russian model, my mother got me and a one-hundred-thousand-dollar divorce settlement. Dad number two left after one year and my mom received a cool million from the prenup. There was another after that. And another. When I was six, I'd already had four dads and my mom had climbed up the prenup ladder to independent wealth. Enter my current father. My mother told me that he wouldn't leave us if I acted like a lady. She wanted this marriage to stick. At the engagement party my mother introduced me. I curtsied and lisped *"how do you do?"* My father-to-be was charmed and declared me his English rose. From that point forward I learned that in the world of the Drakes, I was to play the part of the lady, and if I played my part well, I'd be loved.

And I've been well loved and cared for. From age six to twenty-four.

Unfortunately, English roses don't get breast cancer.

It's messy. And gross. And makes people uncomfortable.

My mother pulls out her phone and opens her calendar. "I'm making a reminder to call the plastic surgery group in Manhattan. The Hollywood set uses them, not that I follow their vulgarity, but still, if it looks good on the silver screen..."

I watch out the window as we pull into the drive.

There, a half mile down the gently rolling, weeping willow-lined driveway, is my childhood home—Rolling Acres. It sits like a diamond, nestled in emerald green lawns. It was built in 1881, after Thaddeus Drake, my father's great-great-great-grandfather, made his first million. It's a palatial white rectangular mansion with long, tall windows and a dozen chimneys. Wide marble front steps sweep up to the front door.

When I was little I imagined it was the palace in a fairy tale. It filled me with wonder.

"Welcome home, darling. You may stay a few days." She sighs as she looks me over. "A week or two at most. Oh, darling."

I lift my sagging shoulders.

Karl opens my door and my mother helps me out of the car. We walk up the front steps, then my mother opens the heavy wooden door and I step into the white marble entry. Our shoes echo on the stone floor. I look up at the domed ceiling and columns and grand staircase. The thirty-two steps never seemed such a great distance to climb before today. I ignore my clammy palms as we climb the stairs and then walk down the wide hallway.

My bedroom is one of seven on the second floor. When we reach it, I open the door. The room is the same as I left it five years ago. White walls. White bedding. White carpet. Three hundred square feet of clean, white, colorless, pristine...room. Looking at it makes me unreasonably sad. And tired.

"I'm going to lie down," I say.

My mother hesitates at the door. Finally she puts her hand on my arm and squeezes. Words of meaning have never come easy to her.

"I'll have chef send up a dinner tray," she says.

Which I know means *I love you*.

"Thank you," I say.

My mother closes the door. I listen to the soft rustling of her satin skirt until the sound fades. Then I step away from the door and look around the empty room. Nothing to do now but move forward. I pull out my phone and look at the screen. It's a picture of me and Shawn at his parents' house. We look happy. We *were* happy.

Before I can think better of it, I tap his name.

He answers on the third ring.

"Daniella," he says. His voice is short.

"Hi, Shawn." I silently push for him to say something. When he doesn't, I continue. "I'm out of the hospital. My mother said you sent over my things." My heart thuds inappropriately loudly in my ears.

I hear a voice on the other end of the line and Shawn mutters something in return.

"I'm glad you're okay," he says.

There's another short silence. My legs start to shake. I walk to the bed and sit down on the edge.

"Look, I don't want to make this awkward and rehash what I said yesterday. Can we let this drop?" he asks in a tight voice.

I lean forward and take a deep breath. *No, we can't,* I want to scream, *what are you thinking?*

Instead, I say, "I thought...I thought you may have changed your mind. I'd like to come home. To you."

He says nothing, so I whisper, "I know this was a shock. It scared me too. But I'm better now."

Silence. And I hear in his silence how pathetic my request sounds. How sad and small.

"Daniella. Please don't make a scene."

My breath is sharp and short. I've never in my life made a scene. The white room swims around me. I grasp the comforter with my free hand and the white fabric bunches in my hand.

"What can I do to fix this?" I ask.

He sighs, long and low. "I don't know."

"So, there's something I can do?"

"No, that's not what I said."

"But you don't know one hundred percent that things are over."

The voice sounds again in the background, high and thin. *Who is that?*

"We can still get married. We don't have to cancel the wedding. You still love me, I know—"

"I have to go," he says.

"Can I see you? Can I come home?"

"No. Maybe. No. Look, Daniella, you are home. Please don't make this hard."

He hangs up and I'm left holding a silent phone to my ear. I pull it away and stare at our picture on the screen. A peculiar stinging sensation rushes through me and I can't believe he's done this, I can't...I can't...the feeling threatens to erupt, and I shove it back down. My phone screen goes blank and I see my reflection. Pinched mouth, wide eyes. I smooth my face into the picture of calm.

A thick lump sits in my throat. But I won't cry.

I can fix this.

I survived the mastectomy. I can get Shawn back.

For a moment, my world feels like it has broken, and all the glass pieces are reflecting a different reality. One where, even though I am kind, and good, and give all my love to others, they don't love me back. They hurt me. It's a world where I have no one. I always expected that if I was nice, if I smiled and nodded and agreed, if I gave and helped and loved, that I would be loved back. Was I wrong?

I shake my head.

No. I can't have been.

So, what now? I can't go home to Shawn and I can't stay here. I need a place to live.

I work through my contact list, all my friends in and around Stanton are friends of Shawn too. They can't help.

I don't know any work colleagues well enough to ask.

Finally, after two hours of texting and calling, I admit defeat. No one wants a post-surgery, post break-up disaster sleeping in their guest room or on their living room couch.

Okay.

If my mother means it, and I really can't stay here, then I'll rent an apartment.

It'll be fun.

Shawn will come around soon. I'll get him back and I'll get my life back. There's nothing in the world that can stop that from happening.

7

_____

Dany

*T*wo weeks pass. I rest. I get my drains removed. I have physical therapy. I start to feel almost myself again. My mom hints that I need to find another domicile. My dad hints how much he'd like Shawn as a son-in-law. Shawn ignores my calls.

On a dry but blustery early spring Tuesday, I call about an apartment.

It meets my single criteria—available immediately. Surprisingly, there's a severe shortage of housing in Stanton.

The landlord says to swing by at ten. There's something familiar about his voice. But I ignore the niggle. Last night at dinner the tension with my mother and father was palpable. They must be desperate to enjoy solitude during their "second wind."

The taxi pulls up to the house on Rose Street five minutes before ten. Karl, our driver, asked if I needed a ride, but I want to do this on my own. I pay and step out of the back seat.

The front yard is a postage stamp. Tiny. And full of scraggly brown winter grass and overgrown bushes. An empty wooden porch wraps around the front of the house. I take a minute to look my fill.

The house is a little bungalow with peeling yellow paint and rotting wood around the windows. There are weeds clustered at the foundation. I can't help feeling that it's a sad little place. It's in a neighborhood of teeny Cape Cods and bungalows, all bunched together and lined up closely to the road. This house is the most tired, though. The others are well maintained.

I wrap my coat closer and burrow into its warmth. Maybe this was a mistake. I look at the house again. The torn screen door on the porch flaps in the cold wind. Its hinges squeak as it bangs against the wall.

My heels click on the sidewalk as I walk to the front door. I watch my step on the stairs. I'd hate to fall through a rotted board. I reach up and ring the bell.

It chimes a little old-fashioned melody.

No answer.

I ring again. It echoes inside.

I shift uncomfortably. I feel a little queasy. To be fair, I skipped breakfast. My stomach gurgles. I'm tempted to turn around. I could call a taxi and go home, back to my mother. But no. I'll get my life back on track on my own.

"Door's open," I hear a man's rich drawling voice. "Come on in."

I frown. Who leaves front doors unlocked? Who lets people in without knowing who it is? I turn the old brass doorknob and slowly open the door.

I step into the dim interior.

"Hello?" I call.

The interior of the house is a construction site. The brown carpet is partially torn up, the avocado wallpaper is half peeled off and hanging in grotesque curls, there are saws and hammers and drill thingies and...I think I'm in the wrong place.

"Hello? Mr. Jones?"

I step over a pile of debris.

"In the kitchen," he calls.

I walk down the hall toward his voice. Again, it sounds familiar. Not only from the phone call, but from something else. Stanton is a small city, maybe we've met?

I make it to the kitchen and let out a surprised huff.

"It's beautiful," I say.

I'm talking about the stained-glass window over the large farmhouse sink. The window is maybe four feet across and four feet tall. It's clear beveled glass with panels of colored glass showing scenes from a garden. Yellow roses, white lilies, purple hyacinth, butterflies and green grass. I can almost smell the grass—fresh mowed springtime. The sun is shining through the window and little rainbows are glinting on the white marble countertops. I smile at the farmhouse sink. There's a hand-painted wheelbarrow in a flower garden.

"Mind giving me a hand?"

I startle at the man's voice. "I'm sorry. I was admiring the view."

He chuckles and the sound reminds me of warm honey dripping over freshly baked buttery biscuits. My mouth starts to water.

I peek around the kitchen and realize he's on his hands and knees. His head is buried in a cabinet and his backside is... goodness. My mouth stops watering and goes dry. His backside is gorgeous.

"Admire away," he says. I choke a bit when I realize what view he must think I'm talking about. "But while you look, do you mind giving me a Phillips head?"

"Pardon me?" I say. What's a Phillips head?

He cranes his neck around and stares at me from the darkness under the cabinet. Prickles form along my skin. I feel an electric pulse and I'm itchy and uncomfortable. I shift under his hidden gaze. Then I wonder, is Phillips head another term for *head*? Is he propositioning me? My face heats.

"A Phillips head. There's a connection here that I need to screw."

I gasp. "I'm sorry, I came here about the rental. Not..." I clear my throat. Not about *screwing*.

He mutters something under his breath. He backs out of the cabinet and stands. As he turns, I take a step back. And another. He fills the space. Absolutely fills it.

I ignore the electrical feel lighting in my body. I ignore the rainbows from the glass window shining on him. I ignore the halo of light surrounding him and the thought that he was sent from heaven just for me. Not a chance.

"You," I say.

Dark brown wavy hair. Gray eyes. Full, smiling lips. A dimple in his left cheek. I know this man.

I hold up my hands, warding him off. He witnessed the most mortifying moment, the most pathetic moment of my life. To be honest, he made me feel like a fool. Embarrassment washes through me.

"Me?" He smiles and looks down at himself then shrugs. "Give me a minute, honey. I need to screw something real quick."

My mouth falls open then I snap it shut. *Not me, he won't.* "Just because I said I'd marry you"—I hold up a finger—"while I was under heavy medication, mind you, does not mean I'll screw you, or give you a Phillips head, or do anything else your opportunistic mind comes up with. I'm here about the rental. But *not* any longer."

"Wait a minute. *What?*"

I hurry from the kitchen. I hear him coming after me. My embarrassment becomes righteous anger. I turn around to face him. Our faces are inches apart in the cramped space of the hallway. The light is dim again and I blink until he comes into focus. His lips. They are so close to mine. I shake my head and look into his eyes.

"I think we have a misunderstanding," he says in a low, slow drawl. It reminds me of the way he spoke to me in the hospital. My body itches to move even closer to him. I scowl.

"There's no misunderstanding. I will never give you a *Phillips head*, or a *screw*, and I will never, ever *marry you*. I was post-surgery, you cretin. I was here about the rental." I put my hands on my hips and try to look firm. Because, sad to say, when I emphasized the words "head" and "screw," certain images entered my mind. Images I *liked*.

He's trying to respond. He starts. Stops. Runs his hand through his hair. When he does I can smell wood chips and oil and leather. I start to take another breath, then stop myself. This man is not Shawn, he's exactly the opposite of Shawn. Which means, he's the opposite of what I want and need. My heart falls in my chest and gives a sad little ping. I don't want to think about why.

"Pardon me, I'll be going now," I say.

I can't live here. Because, one, it's under construction. I don't do construction or fixer-uppers or whatever. Two, this man witnessed me vulnerable and pathetic. I don't do that either. And three, every time he's near I feel antsy and confused and forget about Shawn and start thinking about other things and...no. Just, no. I liked my life the way it was, and this situation here is not going to help me get it back.

"Goodbye," I say. I step into the living room. My eyes fill with hot tears and my vision blurs.

"Watch out," he says.

I look down, worried I'm about to step in something. But down was the wrong way to look. My head smacks a wood plank and I stumble back and then fall on my butt. Sticky, gooey cold liquid soaks through my pants.

I cringe and scramble back like a crab. A plastic tray sticks to my butt. I lurch back and smack against a roll of old carpet.

"There's a two by four. And a paint tray." He leans down next to me. "Are you alright?"

I shake my head. He looks me over and something shifts in his eyes.

"You're bleeding." His mouth tightens into a firm line.

I look down. A splotch of blood seeps through my white linen shirt. "It's okay," I say. I'm trying really hard not to cry. "I guess it stretched the wound when I fell. Don't worry about it. I'll call a taxi and..." I make to stand, but the tray sticks to my pants. Pathetic, vulnerable, idiotic, weak...can I add anything else to the list of things I am around this man?

"Here. Let me help," he says. He gently pulls me up. Then my eyes widen as he reaches around. His hand trails in the air over my back. I can feel him, even though he's not touching me. He peels the paint tray from my pants. Then he scoops me up.

I squeak and wave my arms.

"Cretin. You can't just pick up—"

"Don't wobble. You'll hurt yourself."

"What are you..." I trail off.

It's the oddest thing to be picked up by a strange man and held against his warm chest. He's wearing a soft flannel shirt that rubs against my check. The heat coming through his shirt warms me and I hold myself still so that I don't give in and melt against him. He carries me up the stairs and nudges open a wooden door. It opens to a large renovated bathroom. There's white mosaic tiles, a clawfoot tub, a towel warmer, a polished and shining antique dresser with a copper sink.

He sets me down next to the bathtub.

"Thank you, I'll manage from here," I say.

He clears his throat. "I'll set bandages and clean clothes

outside the door." Beneath his tanned skin I think I see the faintest reddening in his cheeks.

"Thank you. I appreciate it. I'll call my driver. He'll be here in a few minutes." I need him to know I'm not some pathetic discarded woman all alone in the world.

"Of course, Miss..." He pauses.

I realize he doesn't remember my name.

"Miss Daniella Drake." I hold out my hand. Yes, I'm covered in paint and a little blood and I'm starting to feel woozy, but good breeding always wins.

He quirks an eyebrow. "Are you a relation of John Drake?"

"My father."

Something strange flashes in his eyes.

"Ah," he says.

"Do you know him?"

"No." He runs a hand through his hair again. "I'll let you be." As he closes the door he pauses, then, "A Phillips head is a type of screwdriver. In case you were wondering." His eyes fill with laughter.

Mortification washes over me.

I clear my throat, then nudge the door shut and lock it.

I may not know anything about construction or tools, but I do know one thing.

There is no way I can live in this house or anywhere near *him*.

8

JACK

$\mathcal{T}$he chance of a lifetime just fell in my paint tray, and I'm not letting her get away. I rush to the medicine cabinet and pull out gauze and antibiotic, then grab a pair of jeans and a T-shirt from Sissy's closet. I hold the jeans up, maybe a few inches too long, but they'll do.

A plan is rapidly forming in my mind. All the pieces are clicking together.

I don't believe in coincidence. Everything happens for a reason. And there's a reason Daniella Drake's here and I think I know what it is. The universe wants my proposal to go through. The stars have aligned so that I can help hundreds of families. Rose Tower will get built.

Rick Atler said I needed to woo the Drakes for a chance to get my project through. Well, there's a Drake taking a bath in my tub and I'm going to woo the ever-loving heck out of her.

I brush aside my misgivings. I won't let myself fall for her. I won't share my feelings with her. This isn't about love anymore.

It's about absolution. Two decades in the making, but finally I'll have absolution.

Daniella and I may not have had the most fortunate first meeting, or second meeting, and I'm fairly certain she doesn't like me all that much, but none of that matters. Not one bit. I grimly set the clothes and medical supplies down outside the bathroom door.

I saw her judging me and looking me over with ladylike disdain. She made her disapproval pretty clear as soon as she opened her eyes in the hospital, and again this morning. She's all prim and proper, with her pearl buttons cinched up to her throat and her diamond-studded ears.

I hear her splashing around and muttering to herself. I give a small smile. She sure is wound tight.

I feel a stab of discomfort at the thought of misleading her. I push it aside.

I'm not fully sure why she was in the hospital. None of my business. I'm not sure why her weasel fiancé dumped her. Again, not my business. Even her overbearing mother is none of my business. The only part of this that's my business is convincing her to rent my room. She came here with that purpose in mind, and now it's my job to close the deal.

I'll get her to sign the rental agreement, then I'll figure out how to woo her. Not to get her to fall in love, or hurt her. I'd never. But woo her. Befriend her. Give her what she needs, for one small favor in return. She may even have fun. And right now, I think the one thing she needs in her life is a little more fun.

I hear the door open and watch as she looks around the hall. I put a reassuring, friendly smile on my face.

"Everything alright, Miss Drake?" I ask.

She turns and the light from the bathroom spills over her. The T-shirt hangs loosely on her and I focus on the creamy skin of her neck. A lock of gleaming hair curls against her collarbone.

She clears her throat and I shoot my gaze back to her face. Her mouth is a tight line.

"Fine, thank you. I'll have the clothes dry cleaned and returned as soon as possible."

She pulls at the T-shirt and jeans. They swamp her. Sissy must be at least four inches taller.

"Since you're still here, I could show you the unit. No point in wasting a trip out."

"No, I've decided against—"

"It's down the hall." I lead the way, hoping either curiosity or good manners will make her follow. "The apartment takes up most of the second floor. It has a bedroom, a bath, and a living room. The kitchen downstairs is shared with the owner. Originally, the apartment was for my sister, but she decided to take the downstairs bedroom instead." I open the door. "After you, Miss Drake."

"Fine." She gives me a cool smile and steps in.

I watch her rather than looking at the apartment. I've seen it. I haven't seen her reaction. I want her to like it. I tell myself that I want her to like it because she needs to like my work if she's going to help get my project through. It's not because I'd like to hear that little hitch in her voice again, like she had in the kitchen when she said it was beautiful.

She walks forward and her shoes click on the hardwood floor. Her fingers trace over the blue linen couch and settle on the chunky sea glass-colored throw. She looks at the modern painting over the fireplace, splashed with dozens of bright colors. She sniffs. I wonder if that sniff means she doesn't like color. I hold my tongue. This room is opposite the beige and white outfit she's wearing. She doesn't say anything as she walks to the bedroom. The walls are periwinkle, there's a vase of fresh daffodils on the nightstand, and a purple Amish quilt on the bed. I used a lot of girly colors in here. It was before I realized Sissy preferred decorating in black with a highlight of gray and a bit more black.

Miss Drake is quiet. So quiet that I'm worried she's too polite to say she hates it. Her small shoulders are tense. She hasn't turned around.

"I can paint it beige if you don't like the colors," I say. "Or white. Beige and white." I need her to live here. I need to *woo* her.

"No," she says quickly. "No."

My stomach twists. She doesn't like it.

"Could I do anything to make it more to your taste?" I ask. I recognize the feeling in my gut. Desperation. She's going to walk.

No absolution.

No *her*. That bit hurts more. Don't ask me why.

She turns around. There are tears in her eyes. I take a step back, stunned.

"Miss Drake?"

She sniffs and gives me a wobbly smile.

"It's perfect," she says.

There's a hard thud in my chest. I can't stop looking at her lips, at the small curve that shakes between hesitation and happiness. My hand lifts and I realize that I was starting to reach for her. I lower my hand.

Her forehead furrows. "Thank you for showing me. But I can't take it."

"Why not?" I ask.

She clasps her hands in front of her. She looks tired. I'm an idiot, she recently had surgery. Has or had cancer.

"Here, come sit on the couch." I lead her to the living room and help her sink into the plush couch. She lets out a small sigh.

"You're the perfect tenant. Move in today. I'll bring up your stuff. You can rest. Recover."

Her eyes flash.

I hold up my hands.

"Apologies. None of my business."

There's an awkward pause. Then she asks, "How's your friend?"

"My sister," I say. "She's doing good."

She nods and we sit in silence. She's studying the painting on the wall. "I've never seen so many colors in one room."

I don't know if she thinks that's good or bad.

"What are your reservations about renting? I can try to relieve them."

She folds then unfolds her hands. It must be a nervous gesture. They're fine boned and pale. Her nails are painted a soft beige. She has delicate hands. I'm a large brute next to her. She's like a nervous deer at the edge of the woods, afraid of the meadow. How am I going to convince her to stay? Convince her to get to know me enough to love my work as much as I do — then have her convince her father that my project is the best. Can she even do that?

She lowers her head and I study the line of her neck. She looks so tired.

The light from the window lands on her hair. Individual strands flicker between coppery red and gold. The fire flashes before my eyes. That blistering fire that roared through my childhood home.

My lungs clench at the memory of scalding smoke. Burnt flesh.

I can't do this.

I change my mind. Scrap all the plans that formed after Daniella told me she was a Drake.

I can't.

No matter how much I need this project to go through. I can't.

I won't be wooing Miss Drake.

My breath tightens. Am I going to let her walk away? A part of me wants her to stay. I could still show her fun, I could still be her friend.

She turns to me and narrows her eyes. Like she can hear my thoughts.

"Do you live here too?"

"Downstairs," I say. I swallow tightly as I imagine her living above me. Her on top and me on the bottom.

She folds her hands and sets them in her lap.

"Mr. Jones, may I be honest?"

"Call me Jack," I say.

She nods. "Jack."

My body responds at the way her prim accent rolls over my name.

"You," she says.

"Hmmm?" I ask. To be honest, a lot of the blood is moving away from my brain and heading somewhere else. Hadn't I decided I wouldn't be wooing her? Parts of me aren't listening.

"You are my reservation," she says.

Blood rushes back to my brain. "What do you mean, *me*?"

"You're a player. An advantage-taker. You see a downtrodden woman and all you can think about is taking advantage of her."

I flinch. "That's not true." Okay, it's somewhat true, in an upside down sort of way. But she doesn't know that. And I changed my mind.

"Oh really?"

"Really."

She stares me down. "Don't look at me like that," she says.

"Like what?"

"Like in the hospital. With pity."

"I'm not. I don't—"

"Yes, you do. I was there in the hospital, too. I saw your face."

"What?"

"Exactly. That look. So, *Jack*, what did you like best in the hospital? The part where I made a fool of myself over you? Or the part where I looked pathetic with my fiancé? Or that bit where I was pitiful and desperate? Or how about the moment where my mother decided the reason I was dumped is because I'm inadequate? You've had a front row seat and now you want to have a *screw* for the after show. Because pathetic women are easy. Is that it? Well, I'm not in the market for your kind of rental agreements."

Wait. *What?*

She stands up. Her back is ramrod straight and her cheeks are full of color. I stand too. I may have wanted her help so I can bring affordable housing to the city's families, but I'm not a creep.

"I don't know where you got this impression from. But I'm a decent guy. Heck, even a nice guy. I might not be a Rolls Royce-driving pencil neck like your fiancé—"

"Pencil neck?"

"—and I might not have a bulging bank account and a stick up my butt to match."

"Excuse me?" Her eyes narrow.

"You're excused," I say. I narrow my eyes back. "Get your head on straight. I'm trying to rent a room, not seduce you."

She scoffs, and I lean toward her.

"You know what part I liked best the other day?" I ask.

She purses her lips and doesn't answer.

I lean even closer until our noses are almost touching.

"I liked the bit when you were a human being instead of a charm school robot. I liked those two minutes when you were nice. And hell, I admit it, I liked that bit when you got dumped by pencil neck because that meant you were *available.*"

She gasps. Her mouth hangs open but no more sound comes out and I am this close, this close to kissing it shut.

But she ruins the effect by stepping back and putting on her armor.

"I rest my case. Good day, Mr. Jones. You won't be hearing from me again."

She leaves the apartment and I follow her down the narrow hall. This is it. It looks like I won't be seeing her again and for some reason that makes chest hurt.

"Right," I call after her. "Next time you need a good screw, don't call me."

She stomps down the stairs. "Go ahead and take your Phillips head and shove it where the sun don't shine, mister."

The front door slams behind her. I stop at the bottom of the stairs and look around the living room. What just happened?

"Woo her," I say. "Befriend her. Don't insult and infuriate her."

Unbelievable. I just ruined a decade's worth of work. I'm done for. It's all over. And strangely, that doesn't even feel like the worst part of all this. I won't be seeing her again.

"Bro," I glance up. Sissy stands in the doorway of her bedroom. She's laughing at me. I glare at her.

"Wasn't that the chick that *loooves* you?"

"That chick," I say, "is from one of the richest families in the state. She was also probably the only chance I had of winning the Rose Tower Project."

"And she just told you to shove a screwdriver where the sun don't shine?" Sissy starts to laugh.

Ah, the pleasure of having a little sister.

I narrow my eyes. "Why are you home?"

She shrugs. "It's possible that I was suspended."

"For?"

"Sooo...I may or may not have allegedly broken into the school records room and published documents concerning the discrepancies in budgetary allocations between the boys' and girls' sports funding—"

I hold up my hand. "When do I have to go in?"

She bites her pinkie nail. "Tomorrow morning."

"How is this going to convince me to not send you to boarding school?" I ask.

"Dude. Unfair. Also, I'll be worse at boarding school. And I'll keep running away to come back here. Over and over. I'm not going."

I cross my arms over my chest. "It's for your own good."

"Bull. You promised Dad you'd look after me."

I clench my jaw. "I'm looking after you by sending you to boarding school."

"That's not the real reason you want me to go and you know it."

"Sissy."

"You're scared. Nope, don't deny it, you are."

"It's for your own good."

"I'm the only family you've got that's—"

"I have a family."

"—still alive."

I flinch and turn aside. From the corner of my eyes I see her shoulders slump.

"Sorry, Jack," she whispers.

"It's alright." I avoid her eyes and stare at the closed front door. "Dad's alive."

She shrugs.

"I'm not trying to punish you, I want what's best. I can't give you everything you need. This school has an Ivy League acceptance rate of twenty-five percent. Think about that, you can't get that kind of future in Stanton."

"I don't care about that," she says.

"You will."

"Bull. You're scared to let anybody in, even someone as amazingly awesome as me. Someday you're going to admit that when you push people away it's the same result as them leaving you. It just sucks sooner."

I shake my head. "We're going to have to agree to disagree on this one."

It looks like she's about to go back to her room, so I address the reason she's home in the middle of the day.

"I want you to write a letter of apology."

"No way. What they're doing is wrong. You have no idea. They're taking the booster money from the girls and giving it to the boys. It's bull."

"It's life."

"Then life is bull. Dad wouldn't make me write a letter."

"I agree. Dad would've helped you break in and then blackmailed them."

She nods. "Good old Dad."

"Not a good example to follow."

She tilts her head and gives me a considering look. "You know, Dad wouldn't let the Rose Tower deal fall through so easily."

"I'm not either. I'm handling it." Sort of. I just need a new plan.

Again, she shrugs. How do teenage girls put so much meaning in a shrug?

"Well, when your big screwdriver plan doesn't come to fruition, let me know. I'm good at finding dirt and—"

"No, thank you. I'd like my little sister to stay out of jail and grow up to become a productive member of society."

"Society is boring."

I rub the spot between my eyebrows. There's a headache coming on.

She continues, "Anyway, it's obvious the committee is doing

some back door dealings and general shadiness. There's no other reason for them to have dumped your project when it was all in the bag."

"It's called politics. Besides, when did you become a conspiracy theorist?" I ask.

She shrugs. "Yeah, yeah. I'm going to my room. Remember, I'm good at breaking and entering."

"Didn't hear that," I say.

"Someday you'll admit you love having me around," she says.

I sink back to the couch and let out a long sigh. For her sake, I hope not.

9

Dany

Three weeks after the surgery I'm in an exam room at the hospital. The drains are gone. The staples are gone. The cancer...

The paper gown scratches my skin and I want to itch the scar on my chest. My mother stands across the room. She looks between me and the doctor. I look down. The vinyl of the exam table is cold against my bare legs. Why is it that everyone else gets to wear clothing during these conversations? The doctor wears a long white coat, buttoned-up shirt and pleated khakis. My mother is in her Burberry coat and Donna Karan wrap dress. Me, I'm in cotton underwear and a blue paper gown that opens at the front. I try to fold the edges more closely together so that I'm not so exposed.

"What do you mean it's not gone?" my mother asks. Her voice drips ice.

The air conditioning kicks in and the edge of the paper

gown flaps open. I flash the room. Did anyone notice? No? I pull it tighter. It crinkles and scratches my skin.

"The cancer spread beyond the breast tissue..." he says.

A rushing noise fills my ears. I took a boat tour of Niagara Falls once, I couldn't hear anything but the thundering of water on water. This is the same. I look between the doctor and my mother. Their lips are moving. My mother is pointing a long thin finger at the doctor. He flinches back, then puffs up and starts talking again. The waterfall noise is carrying me along. I shake my head. Their muffled voices start to come back as the roar fades.

"We need to start chemotherapy immediately. The course will last..." The doctor's voice fades out again.

My entire body is numb. It's like I'm sitting outside of myself. Like I'm perched on the exam table next to my body watching everything happen. I can't feel anything. Not the scratchy paper gown. Not the cold of the air conditioning. Not the pinchy scar on my chest. Not panic. Not fear. Not anything.

They turn to look at me.

The doctor says something.

I shake my head. "What?" I ask. My voice echoes in my ears.

"...this week," he says.

I blink. There had to have been more to that sentence.

"Pardon me?" I ask.

"I'd like to start treatment immediately. With the aggressive nature of the..."

I'm going to be honest, nothing the doctor says is sticking with me. None of the words he's using are familiar. None of the sentences make any sense.

The cancer was gone.

It was *gone*. Wasn't it?

Plus, the sound system is playing eighties megahits.

My heel swings in time to the guitar and beats against the metal table legs.

My one and only secret, that one thing in my life I hide from my parents, Shawn, my friends, the whole world, is my obsession with eighties rock. There's something about it—it's unapologetic, loud and brash, alive, so *alive*. When no one is around, I'll plug in my headphones and imagine I'm dancing and free. I never listen to eighties music where people can see me or sense my enjoyment. And I've never danced. Never. Even when I'm alone.

This is the first time I've ever heard eighties music in my mother's presence. I focus on what the doctor is saying. I get the gist. The tone says more than the words.

"How long?" I ask.

The doctor clears his throat. "The cycle length of adjuvant chemotherapy for your case may last anywhere between four and six months. The goal of course is cure. We base our cycle length on evidence-based medicine utilizing clinical trial data and—"

"Not how long is the treatment. How long do I have to live?"

The music is winding up. It's the hit about counting down the seconds until she's gone. What kind of sicko plays this song in the cancer wing anyway? Doesn't anyone else sense the irony? Or is that the point?

I'm not numb anymore. Feeling has come back. Denial mostly. If I run, run away far and fast, this might not happen.

"Daniella," my mother gasps. But she doesn't say anything more. Her mouth closes in a tight firm line. Then her shoulders straighten and she turns to the doctor.

"How long?" she repeats. Her left hand starts to shake. She clenches it and the shaking stops.

Oh Mom.

"A few months, a few decades. Daniella may have a normal life span. It depends on how she responds to treatment. The mortality rates vary based on stage..."

His voice drones on and Latin terms blur into indecipherable medical-ese. I guess the scientific terms are a way for doctors to distance themselves from the crushing emotional news they have to deliver every day. It's easier to say, "You have a neo-blasto-cystic goober blob on your transverse pectoral wing ding to which we can apply cryostistic protocols in an evidential procedure" than to say, "I'm sorry, you have cancer and will probably die soon."

The song playing over the sound system ends on a drastic crescendo. The entire conversation of *the cancer isn't gone and you have to start chemo and you might not make it* took less than five minutes.

I stand. The paper gown hikes up and I push it down. "Thank you, doctor, for your time." I hold out my hand for him to shake. He hesitates then comes forward. His hand is cold and strangely soft. His grip is loose.

An eighties love ballad gears up on the speakers. There's a burning sensation spreading through me. An acrid taste like day-old bitter coffee settles in the back of my throat. I try to swallow it down but it's lodged there.

His hand falls away. The syrupy chords play on.

"Go ahead and get dressed. I'll send in a nurse to walk you through what to expect." He leaves. The door closes with a sharp snick.

"I loathe this song," I say. "Loathe it."

"Darling. Get dressed," my mother says. Her voice is high and brittle. On the verge of breaking.

She turns her back and I slip out of the gown. There's a small sink and mirror on the wall. I stare at my chest. The faded bruises. The six-inch-long incision scars. The still-swollen puffs. I look at my face. My eyes. They're haunted.

I turn away from the mirror. I have the sudden urge to hurl the metal instruments on the wall at the glass. Let it shatter into a thousand pieces. My fingers itch to grab the reflex hammer.

"Daniella, what's taking so long?"

I startle. I'm still in my underwear. The paper gown is a ball in my hand. I hold it so tightly that my fist is white and cramping. I could tear the gown. Rip it apart. Shred it.

A knock sounds at the door.

"Just a moment please," says my mother. "Daniella?"

I take a breath and loosen my fingers.

"Of course," I say. With monumental effort, I take a mental weed-whacker and ruthlessly slice all the weeds of fear that just sprouted into ten-foot-tall monsters. I leave a wasteland inside.

Then, I gently fold the gown and set it on the exam table. I put on my post-mastectomy supportive camisole, my cashmere sweater, my wool pants, my dress shoes.

The nurse comes in. She describes the treatment. I listen carefully, hearing nothing, then thank her for her help. As I walk down the carpeted hospital hall next to my mother, I have a vision of walking down the aisle at my wedding.

Before the cancer, that's all I wanted. A wedding. A marriage. A life.

I make a decision. I'm going to survive. I'm going to live long enough to get married. Walk down a different kind of aisle. I'm going to survive. It's not the end.

10

Dany

A few days later, I start my chemotherapy cycle.

I've been poked and prodded. Blood samples taken. More oncologist visits. Blood pressure. Pulse. Temperature. Height and weight. Explanations of what to expect, et cetera, et cetera.

I sped from denial to anger lightning quick. The oncologist referred me to a therapist, Ms. Dribett. She told me anger was good. It would motivate me to change and heal. She said I was moving along the stages of grief. Soon I would experience pain or guilt. Then depression. Or all of the emotions again and together or out of order.

I told her as politely as possible that I wasn't going to experience her stages. Because soon this would be over and I'd go back to my life. No stages necessary.

Ms. Dribett wrote something on her legal pad and told me that my response was common. A natural part of the denial stage.

At the end of the session I thanked her, and again promised that she shouldn't worry. There would be no guilt, no depression, none of that. I wouldn't let cancer define me. It was merely a small thing that happened, not the whole of me, or even a sliver of me. I would be past it in a flash and everything would return to normal.

On the day I start treatment I'm led to the chemotherapy lounge by a plump, chatty nurse.

It's the room with the laughter. The four women receiving treatment stare as I'm led to my chair.

The nurse pokes around with a needle until she find a good fat vein to insert the IV tube. That's where they'll pump in the chemo. Apparently, I'm going to be here for hours.

"What are you here for?" asks a woman in her late thirties. She's wearing an oversized T-shirt with dancing cats. "My name's Matilda."

"I won't be here long," I say. I give her a polite smile and turn to the nurse. "Do you have any magazines?" I ask. I'm acutely aware of the other women staring at me.

The nurse sets down a wide selection of magazines on the tray next to me. "Buzz if you need anything. I'm around the corner."

"Thank you," I say.

I look at the magazines as she walks away. I like the spring flowers on the cover of the gardening one.

I don't want to talk to the women around me. I'm not going to be here long enough to make friends. I'm already making a list in my head of all the things I need to do. Research cancer treatments, holistic diets, exercise plans, alternative therapies. Anything. Everything. Also, go talk to Shawn. Again. In person this time. If I can get him back, then I'll be that much closer to my life plan. Somehow, I know that if I can win Shawn back and have my wedding then I'll also beat this cancer. They're connected. Logically, it's crazy, but I know it's true. Win love back, beat the cancer.

"My name's Geraldine."

I look up at the woman in chair across from me. She smiles and goes on.

"You may call me Gerry since we're chemo pals. Looks like they hijacked your hooters. They didn't Frankenstein me like they did you. No cutting away the bits over here. You look appalling by the way." I can't turn away from Gerry. She has to be in her late seventies. She's wearing a lime green sequin track suit, pink heels, and has a beehive updo. "Matilda over there." She points to the woman in the cat t-shirt. "She's the nicest." Matilda gives a shy smile and waves. "The knitter on the end is Sylvie."

I obediently look at the woman knitting an orange pumpkin hat. Her fingers are moving quickly as she pulls the yarn. She glances up at me. "I have to finish this hat. My grandbaby is due in June."

"Oh, congratulations," I say.

She smiles and I imagine her as a grandmother, lovingly peddling knitted sweaters with matching hats, or handing out chocolate chip cookies and milk. She has on a cardigan that I bet she knit and a soft-looking scarf. She's maybe mid-fifties, her hair has only a little steel gray. A young grandmother.

"Sylvie will probably die before the baby reaches one year old. But that's life," says Gerry.

"Rude," says the final woman.

"Truth is rude," says Gerry. She points to the woman that spoke. "That's Cleopatra. She's grumpy today because she's constipated." I study Cleopatra. Her face is wrinkled and pinched up like a prune. Her hair is jet black and sticks up in a violently curling pixie cut. I can't place her age, she's dark skinned and anywhere from fifty to seventy.

"Constipated Cleopatra," says Gerry.

Sylvie laughs and then clucks her tongue. "Phooey, Gerry, you made me drop a stitch."

"Fix it then," says Gerry. "Also, don't think the rest of us aren't constipated too. We simply handle it better. It's either that or the runs. One or the other. Or both at the same time, consta-runs. You'll see."

"Oh," I say. For lack of anything better. I blindly reach for one of the magazines and open it. The IV feels strange in my vein. There's a sharp cold sensation spreading from the needle.

"Gerry, it's your turn today. I've been waiting all week to hear more about David," says Matilda.

"Humph," says Cleopatra.

Matilda leans toward me and explains.

"To pass the time we agreed that anytime we're at chemo together, one of us will tell a love story. A real romance from our own life. I love romances." Matilda beams. "Last time, Gerry told us about David."

"Bah," says Cleopatra. I get the distinct impression that she doesn't approve of much.

Matilda leans forward and says in a single rushed breath, "He asked Gerry to marry him, but her father said no. David worked on their farm and loved Gerry for years, but he never told her until one day Gerry fell off her horse and he saved her. He picked her up and carried her home and he kissed her, and then Gerry knew—"

"I knew that I loved him," says Gerry. Her blue pencil-lined eyes sparkle and a slow smile spreads over her bright pink lips. "And that he was the man I was going to marry."

I want to ask how long ago this was. One thing stops me. I don't want to be friends with these women. I think that if I get close to them, then somehow I'll be admitting that I'm like them. Or that I'll be here long enough to hear the end of their stories. It won't happen.

"Go on," says Matilda.

"Bah. This David character never existed, I'll bet my appendix," says Cleopatra.

"Appendixes are expendable, dear. Bet your colon," says Sylvie. She winks at me. I look away.

Gerry scowls. "Well, I'll tell you about David. Or we can watch my colonoscopy video again. I put it to music. That thing was pleading for a soundtrack. I've got it on my tablet."

"Eek," says Matilda.

"Oh boy," says Sylvie.

I smother a strangled laugh. Music dubbed over a colonoscopy?

"Humph," says Cleopatra. "Fine. Tell us about David."

"Please," says Sylvie.

"Go on, Gerry" says Matilda.

Gerry shifts in her seat and spreads a knitted blanket, courtesy of Sylvie, maybe, over her lap. She poses like a grand dame about to give a royal announcement. I pretend to read the magazine but really, I'm listening.

"My father, a well-off cattle farmer, refused David's suit. He decreed that no dirt-poor migrant worker would ever marry his daughter. He said David was not even fit to brush the dirt from my horse. He fired him."

"No," whispers Matilda.

"That's because Daddy knew David only had one thing on his mind. Like a stallion chasing a mare in heat," says Cleo.

"Have you seen a stallion's equipment? That mare is one lucky lady," says Sylvie.

"No interruptions," says Matilda.

Sylvie cackles wickedly and my image of a sweet, innocent grandmother is wiped away.

Gerry continues. "David left that very day. My heart was broken. I snuck out of the house to say goodbye. We met in the peach grove. I gave him a lock of my hair and promised to wait for him. He promised me that one day, he'd be back. The richest, most educated, most worldly man, in not only Stoutsberg but the whole darn world. He swore that soon he'd be worthy of me. I thought he was already, but he wouldn't run away with me. Instead, he picked a peach. He cut it up and fed me the pieces, then kissed the juice from my lips."

"Innuendo, dear?" asks Sylvie with a hopeful glint.

"Humph. Purple prose blather," says Cleo.

"No interruptions," says Matilda.

"And then he handed me the pit, and said, 'Geraldine. My heart. Plant this, and before it bears fruit, I'll be back to marry you. Our children and their children's children will eat peaches from our tree.'"

Gerry settles back into her chair and closes her eyes. Everything is silent except the clicking of Sylvie's needles.

Finally, Cleopatra grunts. "Fine, have it your way. Did your imaginary randy stallion come back?"

"Did he?" asks Matilda.

I flip a page in my magazine and pretend to be absorbed in how to prune perennials.

Of course David came back. That's how all these fake love stories end, with the lovers getting their happily ever after. I agree with Cleopatra. This David character isn't real.

"Well?" says Matilda.

I tilt my head to hear Gerry's answer.

"No. He didn't."

"What?" I say. I'm shocked out of my feigned indifference.

"Humph," says Cleopatra. "Looks like you had to find someone else to eat your peaches."

Sylvie chokes on a laugh.

Gerry nods. "Sure enough. Five years after David left, I saw an article in the newspaper. An American boat named *The True Love* had been shipwrecked off the coast of Russia. There were no survivors. The next week, I boarded a steam liner. My peach tree was growing and I was convinced David was still alive. And that's all for today."

"Wow," says Matilda.

I take a quick peek at Gerry's hand. Her left ring finger has a thin gold band. Does that mean she found David? Or did she marry someone else? It doesn't matter, I chide myself.

"What about you, girl? What's your name? What's your story?" asks Gerry.

After a moment of silence I look up. The question was directed at me.

"Dany," I say.

"That's a boy's name," says Cleopatra.

"I think it's lovely, dear," says Sylvie.

"Thank you," I say. "I don't have a story. I met my fiancé when I was a freshman in college. He checked all the boxes and I checked his. He proposed. Our wedding is in a few months..." I stop. "He, uh...we're postponing...just a bit."

"The wanker gave you the cancer kiss-off didn't he?" says Cleopatra.

"What's the cancer kiss-off?" This from Matilda.

I don't know what it is, but I have an idea.

"No, he didn't. He merely needs some time. He's over-whelmed."

"What a wanker," says Cleopatra.

Sylvia clicks her tongue, "I believe the kids call them jerk-offs."

"Wanker has a better ring," says Gerry. "Wanker," she annunciates.

"Wanker?" asks Matilda.

My cheeks burn.

"He is not," I say loudly. I'm shocked at the forcefulness of my voice. My hands shake as I smooth them over my pants and settle back in the chair.

"He's not," I repeat. My lips press tight against unexpressed emotion. Shawn is the key to getting my life back on track—beating all this and being okay again. Loved.

Sylvie looks at me with sympathy. Cleo stares at me with a disbelieving expression.

How dare they judge my life?

I swipe at a stray tear.

"Pardon me, but I'm not like any of you. I don't want to be your friend. I don't want to tell stories. I don't want to bond over chemo chats. I'll be out of here soon and I'll go back to my life. My fiancé will get back together with me and everything will go back to normal. I'll get out of here. I'll forget all of you. And everything will be back to the way it was before any of this happened. You're all just part of a bad dream that I want to go away. So leave me alone. I don't want to be one of *the girls*." I pick up the magazine and hold it in front of my face. My hands are shaking and I feel dizzy and ill.

"Rude," says Cleopatra.

"Fiddlesticks, dropped another stitch," mutters Sylvie.

My face is burning behind the magazine. I want to get up and walk out, but I'm attached to the IV and this infernal chair.

The silence is thick and awkward.

After a few minutes, Sylvie clears her throat. "A piece of advice, dear. Cancer is a wake-up call. Whatever you're doing in your life at the time of diagnosis, you should start doing the opposite. Because whatever you had going before...it wasn't working."

I don't lower the magazine. A single tear falls down my cheek.

Nothing was wrong with the life I had with Shawn. *Nothing.* I clench my jaw at the little voice inside me that whispers otherwise. *What about the coldness between you?* it whispers. *What about how you never show your true self?* it says.

I close my heart to the voice. My life was perfect before. Perfect.

And I don't need their friendship or their sympathy.

"When I get out of here, my husband Steve and I are going to take a second honeymoon," says Matilda in a soft dreamy lilt. "We always talked about taking one. But life got so busy we never got around to it. He used to come into the kitchen while I was doing dishes. He'd pretend that my rubber gloves were silk and that I was a princess at a ball. We'd waltz in the kitchen. We haven't danced in years. I'm going to dance on my second honeymoon. I love to dance." Matilda's voice is soft and I can tell she's smiling.

I've never danced with Shawn. Not once. I frown. Maybe I've been too passive. I can take a more active role. Tomorrow, I'll go and confront Shawn. I'll set him straight. The wedding is still on. The cancer will be over and done with in no time. Everything will be wonderful.

Everything.

11

JACK

$\mathcal{I}$ grip my sister's purse, and stand outside the changing room in some poofy dress shop. Sissy has a date to the prom. I grind my teeth. My little sister is going to the prom so some football-playing meathead can—

Sissy swings open the door and steps out. She's in a miniskirt dress thing. Too mini. Really, too mini. I have images of beefy football player hands sneaking up.

"No," I say.

She stops mid step. "But—"

"No."

She scowls at me. "This is the fifth dress I've tried on—"

"And they've all been terrible."

She rolls her eyes. "This is ridiculous."

"What's ridiculous is *Bert*,"

"It's Bret."

"*Bret*," I say, "getting all handsy on my sister."

"He did not."

"I saw you on the porch."

"Are you kidding? Mind your own business. I'm fifteen. I'm allowed to have a boyfriend."

She scowls at me. I raise my eyebrows. "Next dress. Floor length. High neck is preferable."

"Seriously. Why are you such a caveman?"

"I became one when Dad dropped you at my door." I lower my brow and put on a caveman voice. "You, sister. Me, big brother. Must protect."

She rolls her eyes, then laughs. "There's only one more dress. But if you don't like it I'm getting the black one. No matter what you say."

I flinch as she closes herself back in the changing room. The black one had a V-neck that reached her belly button.

"Why am I here?" I say as I scrub my hand over my face. That's a rhetorical question. I'm here because Sissy came to me this morning, nervous and unsure of herself. The girls at school told her that anyone who is anyone buys their prom dresses from Madame Bovary's, Madame Butterflies, Madame whatever this place is called. I'd not seen Sissy unsure of herself since the day she was dropped at my place.

She wasn't even unsure when the surgeon took off her bandages and there was still swelling and bruising on her face. No. She handled it like a champ.

She's only unsure when it comes to meatheads and prom.

I drag my hand across my face again and let out a long sigh. I want to do better for Sissy than play the overprotective brother. Unfortunately, she needs more than I can give.

Maybe she's right, maybe I am scared.

I need some fresh air. I turn toward the front door of the little shop. But instead of a clear path, I'm bulldozed over by a tower of dresses.

"Ack." A small squeak sounds from beneath the dress mountain.

I steady the woman under the pile.

"You alright?" I ask. My hands linger on the soft skin of her arms.

"Pardon me, would you please remove your hands from my person."

"Huh?" I ask. My hands linger on the warmth of her smooth skin. Sissy would be proud. My descent to official caveman is complete.

I recognize the rounded vowels and the upper crust accent of that voice. I even recognize the current flowing between us.

She stiffens, then peeks her head over the dresses.

"You," she says.

I clear my throat. "Me."

She takes a step back. I frown down at my hands, still hanging in the air where she was standing.

"Did you find yourself a place to live yet?" I ask. Because, clearly, I'm looking for trouble.

"Thank you. I have a place to live," she says. Her eyes narrow on me. "I live with my *fiancé,* if you recall."

Then her face flames red. I don't know about her, but I'm remembering the excellence of her so-called fiancé.

"I was hoping you'd remedied that situation," I say. Meaning she'd forgotten about the pencil neck that didn't deserve her.

She gives a regal nod. "I apologize for inconveniencing you the other day. I was exploring options. Which is no longer necessary, as I live with my fiancé."

I nod in agreement. Something's odd here.

"Let me help you," I say. I take the pile of clothes from her. "Celebrating something?"

She has a load of sequin and lace items to try on. She ignores my question. I hang the dresses in the second changing room. "Thank you," she says. Then she closes the door.

Sissy opens hers and I turn to her.

"Well?" she asks.

I let out a long relieved sigh. The dress is shiny and navy blue. The neckline is at her collarbone, the hem is halfway to her knees. Her hands flutter over the dress then nervously smooth the material. She bites at her lip and looks at me questioningly.

I don't see my funny, con-artist-in-training little sister, I see the woman she's going to become. I'm speechless.

"You don't like it?" Her shoulders slump. She starts to turn around.

"It's perfect," I say.

She turns back. "Really?"

I nod. There's a smile spreading across her face and suddenly I feel on top of the world.

"Bart has no idea how lucky he is."

"Bret. His name is Bret." She rolls her eyes.

"Yeah, exactly. Let's get ice cream."

She laughs and goes back in the changing room to throw on her jeans.

I lean back against the wall. While I stand there, I try not to stare at the closed door of the changing room Miss Drake is in. Daniella.

Like she heard me, her head pops out of the door. She looks around. Her eyes wide. Then she spies me.

"Pardon me," she says.

I look behind me.

She sighs. "Mr. Jones."

I point to myself.

She widens her eyes. "Yes."

"What?" I say, and then, "Why are we whispering?"

She crooks her finger and motions me to come in the changing room. "I need your help."

To say I'm stunned is an understatement. I look around the shop. There's no one nearby. Okay, we've all heard about changing room hookups. I'm not opposed to having one if offered, but my sister is in the room next door for crying out loud.

I take a few steps to the changing room and let myself in.

The space is three foot by three foot. I bump into Daniella and she quickly steps back. Her calves hit the padded bench.

"Sorry," I say.

Her shoulders shake and she sniffs. I look down at her tilted neck and the bare line of her shoulders. Her skin glows in the soft light.

"Are you okay?" I ask.

Her shoulders shake again. I take a small step back and try to see her downward-tilted face. She's not laughing. As she looks up, I realize she's crying. A large tear falls down her cheek. Then another. I'm confronted by my complete inadequacy. I don't know how to help her. I don't even know what's wrong.

I deflect to humor. Because, when in doubt, make a joke.

"My sister's in the next stall over. If you want to do the dirty we need to hurry."

She stops mid sob and her eyes flash. Thank god.

"You're so vile."

I feel better. I'd take her anger over tears I can't help any day.

"Hey, you invited me to the party."

"Sorry," she says. "Sorry." She forcefully wipes the tears from her cheeks. "I, um...I can't zip the dress."

She turns around. The zipper hangs open and the curve of her back is exposed. At the base of her spine are two small dimples. I stare at them. I have the urge to place my mouth over them and suck.

"Can you please zip it up?" she asks in a tight voice.

"Alright." My voice is gruff.

She stands stiff and still as I slowly pull up the zipper. It makes a low growling noise as I drag it along her back. I watch as goose bumps form. Her skin glows pink and smooth. I let out a breath and the hair at the nape of her neck ruffles in the current.

We're so close I can feel the warmth radiating off her. The magnetic pull of her. She sways back toward me. I lean my head down. She smells like flowers. Like the freshness of first spring blossoms peeking up through the snow. I close my eyes and draw in a deep breath.

My fingers find the base of her neck. The zipper reaches its end.

Suddenly, I'm imagining this moment in reverse. I'm pulling down the zipper and Daniella's not stiff, she's pliant. She's not whispering, she's screaming.

The backs of my knuckles brush against the feathery softness of her curls.

"Thank you," she says. She steps to the side and turns around. Her cheeks are red and her eyes are bright. Not with tears.

"My pleasure."

She smooths the fabric down and looks in the mirror. It's a lacy black dress with a low neck and a short skirt.

"Do you like it?" she asks.

"I like the zipper," I say.

She looks at my reflection in the mirror. Her eyes narrow. "I'm not interested, Mr. Jones."

I shrug. "You win some, you lose some." My heart is doing flips, but in the mirror my face looks impassive.

Apparently, the universe is bent on torturing me by dangling in front of me the one thing I can't have. Miss Daniella Drake. I can have friendship, flings, meaningless relationships, and maybe, please maybe absolution, but not love. But goodness, do I want her. Like fire wants wood. But the thought of fire extinguishes my enthusiasm.

She studies me with a slightly annoyed expression.

Probably because I irritate and insult her every time we're thrown together.

"Thank you. I appreciate your help. Since the surgery, it's hard to lift my arms above my shoulders. Zippers are the worst. I do physical therapy but...I'm rambling." She closes her eyes. "I ramble."

"It's alright," I say. I'm speechless at the vulnerability I see on her face.

"Thank you," she says again.

"You're welcome." I want to say more, but I don't know how.

I quietly leave the intimate confines of the changing room.

Sissy stands outside the room, arms folded over her chest, a smirk on her face.

"Who's handsy now?" she asks.

I shake my head and drag her and her dress to the checkout.

While we're there she sees Bert and his friends on the sidewalk.

"It's Bret," she says.

"Go on," I say. She rushes out.

I'm signing the receipt when I smell flowers and snow. I turn. It's Miss Drake. Still in the knock-out little black dress.

"I'm going to wear the dress out," she says. She blushes. I come to a quick realization that the reason she's still wearing it is that she had no one to unzip her. And maybe no one to zip her back in once she's home. Unless, of course, she's expecting her fiancé to do the unzipping. A shot of irritation hits me. I bat away the why of that feeling.

"Please, put it on my tab," Daniella says to the woman at the checkout counter.

"Of course, Miss Drake," says the woman.

Daniella starts to walk out the door. I grab Sissy's dress and rush after her.

"Hey. Hang on," I say. I suddenly realized that this might be the last time I see Miss Drake. I don't like that thought.

Maybe I still have a chance to win her over. Not under false pretenses. I've decided I'll be upfront about the project.

Right. The project.

That's why I'm rushing after her. That's all. With that in mind... "Let me buy you some ice cream. I was about to take my sister, but..."

She raises an eyebrow. "No, thank you. I'm meeting my fiancé for dinner. He's expecting me."

I push down a flash of jealousy. Not over the fiancé, but over the fact that she's not having dinner with me.

I hold open the door for her. As we exit, we bump into a couple on their way into the shop.

"Shawn?"

Daniella is looking between the man and the woman. A sinking sensation fills me. Yup, slick suit, shiny shoes, too-narrow nose. It's the fiancé. I watch as he drops his hand from the woman's back.

"Daniella, hi. What are you doing here?"

Daniella's face drains of color. She doesn't respond. I don't think she can.

Shawn continues, "I was out with Tammy. She's been a comfort since the news..." He trails off. I'm sensing that Daniella was *the news*.

Daniella takes a deep breath. "Hello, Tammy. Nice seeing you again." Her voice is strained politeness. She holds out her hand. Tammy gives a quick limp shake.

Shawn looks at his watch. "Look, Daniella, Tammy and I were heading out to dinner."

Dang it.

How is Daniella still maintaining her composure? She has epic restraint.

Then something clicks. Prim Miss Drake was misleading

me. She didn't have plans with her ex-fiancé, and most likely she also still doesn't have a place to live.

Her shoulders are drooping, and I have a sinking suspicion she might be about to cry. Not okay.

I step forward and put my hand to the small of her back.

"Ready to go?" I ask her.

She looks up, startled.

Shawn and Tammy study me in confusion. Apparently they hadn't noticed me.

I give them my cat's got the cream smile.

"Daniella and I have big plans. Dinner at the new Michelin starred place. A romantic evening with a bottle of wine in front of the fire. My baby got all dressed up and I've got to take her out." I take a strand of her hair and proprietarily rub it between my fingers.

Her back stiffens beneath my hand, but I'm hoping she keeps her face placid.

"Who are you?" asks Shawn. His nose looks thinner when he's angry. Good.

"Shawn." Daniella moves to step forward. I pull her back. "It's nothing," she says.

"But my love..." I say. "Daniella and I go way back. She proposed marriage to me once. Stupidly, I let her go. Won't make that mistake again."

"Really?" asks Shawn. He's looking between Daniella and me. Shock lines his face.

"Come on, Shawn, can we go?" asks Tammy. Apparently, she's not impressed with the male territorial behavior radiating off Shawn.

"How do you know each other?" he asks.

"We just met," says Daniella. She tries to shrug my hand off. I pinch her backside. "Ow," she squeaks.

"We just met *again*. Serendipitously. We live together now. Very domestic. Very wonderful. I'm so happy. Ecstatic," I say.

Shawn's brows are lowered. His eyes are calculating. The weasel. He doesn't look one hundred percent convinced.

But Daniella's catching on.

"Really?" he asks. "Daniella? You live with him?"

"Yes?"

I nudge her backside.

"Yes. On Rose Street. It's the sweetest house. The most beautiful kitchen I've ever seen."

"Remember, the first day you told me you loved me?" I ask.

She steps on my toe. I try not to flinch.

"I do." She bares her teeth and smiles at me. I hold her eyes with mine. I love it when they flash.

Shawn clears his throat. "Um, well. Look, Daniella. Maybe we can get together and talk soon?"

She turns to him. Her cheeks are pink and she's looking full of life again. Thank god.

"Okay," she says.

Shawn gives her a long speculative look. Daniella sends him doe eyes. I resist the urge to bare my teeth.

"Bye now," I say.

I turn and steer Daniella down the sidewalk, letting my hand drift up and down her back. I can feel Shawn's stare as we walk away.

"Keep walking," I say.

"What do you think you're doing?" she hisses.

"Saving face and making your fiancé realize what he's missing. Now shut up and act grateful."

She sniffs. Primly.

I grin down at her.

"You're welcome," I say.

She sniffs again.

"The rental is still available. I can pick up your bags tomorrow."

"Don't bother," she says.

I deflate. I thought my heavy-handedness was working for her.

"My driver will bring them round."

Yes.

Triumph. My chest fills with a warm heady feeling. Triumph.

12

Dany

*K*arl drives down Rose Street, ferrying me to my new home. My bags are in the trunk. I fold my hands in front of me and try to calm my nerves. What will it be like living in the same house as Mr. Jones? Jack? My hands shake and I clasp them tighter.

I was fenced in and agreed because...so many reasons.

My mom's hints are becoming blatant requests. Shawn clearly needs more time. Plus, there are no other rentals. I looked. So...I'm moving in.

Maybe on further acquaintance the magnetism I feel toward Jack will fade.

I wonder, what will it be like when he sees me come home from chemo? It's not pretty, and I have a feeling it's going to get worse. Ugly, even.

Karl turns the car. The station is tuned to classical baroque. I hate baroque. It's so ornate and stuffy and restrictedly metered. It's suffocating and confined. I imagine Karl thinks I like baroque since for six years running I played it at my piano recitals. I shudder at the thought.

"Would you turn the station please?" I ask.

"Miss?"

"Never mind. Silly thought." I look down at my hands again.

We've only been in the car for twenty minutes. Stanton's downtown isn't a far drive from Rolling Acres.

I'd like to say that my parents were upset to see me go. Relieved is more likely. Although my father probably didn't realize I'd left. He's in Chicago at a business meeting. My mother was appropriately reserved. *I'm so glad you found a place,* she'd said. *You know how your father needs an uncomplicated home life. You staying here would be too much stress for him.*

Of course, I said. *I understand.*

I did. I do.

I noticed that since the diagnosis, some people, my parents included, look at me differently. With, let's call it, fear. As if what I have is contagious, and if they get too close they'll catch it. Not cancer. They aren't worried cancer is contagious. They don't want to catch misfortune. Unluckiness. Whatever bad karma I have that made a twenty-four-year-old woman get breast cancer. It's like, if they keep me at arm's length, they won't catch misfortune too.

My coworkers quizzed me about my eating habits. Family history. Alcohol use. Exercise. Stress management. Do I meditate? Vitamins? How about water from the tap versus bottled? What about BPA, do I use BPA-free bottles? How often do I dye my hair?

Perhaps they think, if they can pinpoint what I did wrong, why I deserved to get cancer, then they can avoid it.

Because surely I did something wrong, didn't I?

Didn't I?

I squeeze my eyes shut.

Guilt, says Ms. Dribett's voice in my mind, *a stage of grief.*

"Almost there, Miss," says Karl.

"Thank you."

My mother assured me that Karl would come round to take me to and from my chemotherapy appointments.

I study him in the mirror as he pulls up to the curb in front of the house.

He opens the door for me and I step out onto the sidewalk.

"I'll get your bags, Miss."

"Thank you."

We walk up to the porch. I ignore the peeling paint and the weeds. This is my home now. Weeds and all.

Karl presses the doorbell.

His uniform—black leather gloves and a wool pea coat—fills me with a kind of strength. His hair is starting to silver. I look at him from the corner of my eyes.

Back in junior high, when I was grossly unpopular, Karl's crisp goodbye as he dropped me at school and his perfunctory hellos when he picked me up were often the only kind words I heard for days at a time. *Hello, Miss. Goodbye, Miss.* I doubt he knows how much his constancy meant to me.

Means to me.

I smile at him.

He rings the bell again.

I clear my throat.

"Yes, Miss?"

I shift on my feet and look down at the rough planks of the porch. I try to articulate what I'm feeling.

"I was thinking...you've driven me to and from all the important moments of my life. You've seen me grow up," I pause. An awful thought strikes me. "I don't know anything about you."

Suddenly, a shame-filled heat washes over me.

I look into his familiar face. His eyes are warm and understanding.

"Miss. You're a good person," he says.

I shake my head and swallow back tears. I don't feel like one. I've never even wondered about his life, and I've known him nearly twenty years.

Yet, he's always treated me with courtesy, even now. He doesn't seem to be afraid of me since the diagnosis. He hasn't avoided looking at me. I mean, really looking at me. Sometimes, lately, even I'm afraid to really look at myself.

"Have you ever cared about someone who's been really sick?" I ask. It's hard for me to ask the question.

Karl tilts his head and considers me.

"Yes, Miss," he says solemnly.

He doesn't say any more, but I have the feeling that he's speaking about me.

"Thank you," I say.

The door swings open. Jack is there.

An awareness of him settles over me. He fills the doorway and I look up from his long legs to his wide shoulders.

Jack looks between Karl and me.

"Right on time," he says. It breaks the tension. He grabs the bags and pulls them inside. I'm relieved to see the front room is free of construction and the walls are painted a soft robin's egg blue. The floors are newly sanded and the room is bare. He's been busy.

Jack places the bags down.

"Is that everything?" he asks.

"Yes, that's all," I say.

"I'll show you up then."

I turn to Karl. "Thank you. Thanks again. I'll see you at three?"

Karl nods. "Goodbye, Miss."

I smile as Jack shuts the door after him.

There's a long silence as we feel each other out. I'm going to be living with this man. *Living with him.*

Outside, the car engine starts and Karl pulls away.

"Not much for conversation, is he?" asks Jack.

"My favorite kind of man," I say pointedly.

Jack laughs. I follow him as he carries my bags up the stairs. I absolutely, one hundred percent, avoid looking at his backside.

The magnetism is there, stronger than ever.

Fade, darn you, fade.

13

Dany

"Well, girl, you're back, are ya?" Gerry and the rest of the girls are watching as the nurse inserts the IV and plugs me into the chemo.

"Humph," says Cleopatra.

Sylvie frowns. "Now, dears. Dany was merely having a hard time before. It was her first day. First days are always hard. She didn't mean any offense."

"Exactly," says Matilda. She sends me a warm smile.

The tightness in my chest loosens. I was embarrassed about how I spoke to them last week. They hadn't done anything to deserve my anger. All of them are smiling at me now, well, except for Cleopatra, but I haven't seen her smile yet. I give a tentative smile back. I'm still not exactly interested in becoming one of "the girls," but I can be polite.

The cold bite of the medicine hits my veins. I block it out.

To be honest, I was kind of hoping I wouldn't see the girls again. It was awkward last time.

"How is it that you're all here again at the same time?" I ask. Chemo is treated in cycles, and not all the cycles are the same. It can be once every week. A full week straight then three weeks off. Or once every three weeks. The list goes on.

"Sylvie and I have the three o'clock appointment on Thursdays. If you don't like us, change your time," says Gerry.

"Bah, I'm here when I'm here," says Cleo.

"I'm just...I come a lot," says Matilda. "I try to make my time match Gerry's. I like her stories." She fidgets with the hem of her cat T-shirt.

"Dears, did I mention how much I like how they put the recliners in a circle? It's like a knitting circle," says Sylvie.

"No one is knitting," says Gerry.

"I am," says Sylvie.

I smile and decide not to reach for a magazine.

I could change my appointment. If I don't want to see them again. I could change my time. Or maybe the days.

I look around the little room. Today, Sylvie is knitting a... "Is that a scarf?" I ask.

"No, dear. It's a blanket. See, I'm knitting all these flowers in a row."

Sylvie holds up the blanket and I look closely. The light from the window shines through the pattern. There are flowers, little light green stems and yellow petals all chained together surrounded by rows of white.

"It's lovely," I say.

It reminds me of when I used to string together dandelions as a kid. My hands would be stained yellow and I'd wear the dandelion necklace. That was before my mother's final marriage, when I still played outside. I can smell the bitter scent of dandelion. The antiseptic and alcohol smell of the hospital chases away the memory.

Sylvie is talking, explaining the blanket. "I mark important moments in life with knitting. A cardigan and hat for births. A sweater for kindergarten. Socks for graduation—walking into life. A blanket for love."

"Ooh, I like that," says Matilda. "Steve's mama gave us a quilt when we got married. I can't imagine she thought about what we'd get up to under that quilt." Red spreads from Matilda's cheeks up to her hairline. I've never seen anyone turn such a bright tomato color.

"Dear, she was counting on it. Don't underestimate the lure of grandbabies," says Sylvie.

Gerry lets out a loud guffaw.

I smile into my hand.

"I'm not poetic, or a journaler, but I can knit," says Sylvie.

"Who is this blanket for?" asks Matilda.

"Why Dany, of course" says Sylvie.

"Me? Why me?" I open my eyes wide. Oh, that's right. I told them last week that Shawn and I were getting married in a few months, foregoing the postponement.

"Oh, right. The wanker," mutters Cleopatra. "Did he come crawling back?"

Sylvie watches me with a shrewd expression. Her needles click as she knits the blanket.

"I, uh..." I pause and lick my lips. Could I share with them what's happening? I look around the room. Sylvie with her knitting. Gerry with her turquoise track suit and wild makeup. Matilda in a pink sparkly cat shirt. Cleopatra scowling at the window. I glance down at myself. I'm just another woman in the circle of chairs, getting a dose of chemo. All of a sudden, this feels like a circle that hopes can be shared in, without fear. This place is safe. Strange, seeing as we're all being fed a chemical cocktail that poisons our bodies. But there it is. I feel as if I can share.

So, I tell them about how Shawn dumped me when I woke, how I had to find a new place to live, how I saw Shawn with another woman. At the end of my story I look at Sylvie's needles clicking away as she knits my love blanket.

Finally, I say, "The hardest part of it all...a month ago, I knew exactly who I was and where my life was going. I was healthy, happy. My fiancé loved me. Then it's like..." I struggle to find the words. Instead, I snap my fingers. "Gone."

I catch Cleopatra studying me closely. She nods at me. "And..." she says.

I lean forward. "I want it back."

"Why?" asks Gerry.

This is hard to admit. "Because I'm scared. If I don't get it back, does that mean I'll die?"

I don't look up. I stare down at my clasped hands. I admit my darkest thought. "And...if the man I lived with and loved, who I gave all my best parts to for five years doesn't love me... then who will? Who could?"

"Who indeed," says Sylvie.

There's a smile in her voice, so I look up. Her brown eyes remind me again of warm chocolate chip cookies.

"Humph. It's my turn today," says Cleopatra.

We all turn to her. I let go of my fears and prepare to hear Cleopatra's love story.

She scowls at the group of us. "I've heard enough of your syrupy love stories. David, blah, blah, David. I'm going to tell a real love story today."

"By all means, wow us with your romance," says Gerry.

"Humph," says Cleopatra.

I settle back in my chair and raise the leg rest.

Cleopatra scrunches up her wrinkled face and begins.

"When I was seventeen, I fell into puppy love with my neighbor. His name was Robert. Big brute. Hung like a horse. Gerry, you'd like that."

My mouth falls open. I look at Gerry. There's a smile on her bright pink lips.

"My parents were devout Catholics. They saw me watching Robert. He used to chop firewood in his front yard. I would sit and watch and watch. His arm muscles were thicker than my thigh. We never spoke. Not once. But I loved him. I watched him swing that ax. He would watch me watching him. Some days he would wink. That wink. It made me thirsty. So, one day, I went inside and made him a big cup of iced tea. I brought it over to him. He took the cup from my hand. Neither of us said a word. He drank the entire thing in one long gulp. His dark eyes watched me the whole time. Then he took his hand and wiped his mouth. The whole while we never broke eye contact. He walked to the wood shed. I followed. I don't know what I expected. It was rough. It hurt. The whole thing lasted less than a minute. There was no speaking. No kissing. Nothing. When he was done he went back to the wood pile and started chopping again. I cried a little. Then I wiped off my tears and went back to my house."

She stops.

"Cleo, your idea of a romance is as warm and fuzzy as a porcupine mating," says Gerry.

"Humph," says Cleopatra. "It's my romance."

"Go on," says Matilda.

"Four months later, it's obvious that I'm in the family way. My parents suspected Robert. They'd seen me watching him. But Robert had left town. We'd never spoken. We'd never met again after the day in the shed. My parents found me a groom and married me off. His name was Vince."

Cleo puts a hand up to her face and presses the wrinkled flesh beneath her left eye. "Vince was a mean bastard," she says.

I stare at her. At her hand pressing against her cheekbone. There's a wealth of meaning in those words.

I can't take my eyes off Cleo. Her wrinkled face. Her mouth, tilted down in a frown. For a moment, the only noise in the room is the clacking of Sylvie's knitting needles.

"Did you leave him?" asks Matilda.

Cleo drops her hand.

"I didn't. Did you know there were worse things in life than a mean bastard for a husband?"

I let that sink in. It falls like a stone to the bottom of a lake. Dark, heavy, awful.

After a moment Cleopatra goes on. "Finally, my birthing pains started. I begged Vince to take me to the hospital. He wouldn't. We were dirt poor. No insurance. He said he wouldn't pay any money for another man's bastard to be born. He sent me outside, where he didn't have to hear me carrying on. I gave birth to my baby girl in the back garden. She had a cord wrapped around her throat."

"Oh no," says Matilda. "Cleo, I'm so sorry."

"She didn't make it?" asks Gerry.

"No," says Cleopatra. "I passed out. Vince buried my baby girl while I was unconscious. When I woke, he wouldn't tell me where her grave was. Said it was time to forget and move on."

"How nice," says Sylvie dryly.

"It was spring. I got depressed. I'd spend hours outside throwing flower seeds into the wind. The packets had been a wedding gift. I thought I could throw all those gifts away. Funny thing, come summer, there were flowers everywhere. Darn stubborn things. I grew with them. Learned I was strong. Maybe not beautiful. But worthy. I started to love myself. I bloomed. Became me. Once I loved myself, nothing could take it away from me. Not Vince. Not this cancer. Nothing. My whole life has been a garden, full of weeds and flowers. But, let me tell you, the best bit has been learning to love myself. Me. Cleo."

She hits her palm against her chest and leaves it to rest above her heart.

"That's a real romance," she says in challenge.

For the first time, I see her not as a wrinkled woman with a down-turned mouth and a sour expression, but as a thorny flower that has thrived in rocky soil.

"Well done, Cleo," says Gerry.

"Humph," says Cleopatra.

I smile at her. "I want to survive," I say. Then, I'm shocked, because until that moment I didn't admit out loud that I might not. Cleo looks at me with understanding.

"And thrive," I add.

"Throw your seeds to the wind then. From my view, you've been closed up tight your whole life. Try blooming for a change," says Cleo.

I shake my head. "I don't know how."

Sylvie tsks. "Dear, every flower is born knowing how to bloom. You have to trust yourself."

"Follow your joy," says Gerry. "Like I followed my David."

"Oh, blah," says Cleo.

"Steve and I always made lists. You could make a list of the things you've always wanted to do," says Matilda.

"A survive and thrive list," I say.

"The fall in love with yourself list," says Cleo.

We settle into silence. I think about all the things I've never allowed myself to do. I'm lulled by the soothing click clack of Sylvie knitting my love blanket.

14

Dany

When you think about your bucket list, all the things in life you want to do before you die, what's on it?

I can't think of a list of things to do so much as emotions to experience. I've not let myself experience the full range of emotions life has to offer. At six, I put on a mask of placid charm and I never took it off again. I worked at being polite and unobtrusive so hard, that I became those things and nothing else.

I've forgotten what the real me looks like.

Am I wild? Geeky? Boring? Funny? I don't know, because I've never let myself be anything but...but grass. Muted. Utilitarian. Walked all over. Anytime grass reaches or tries to grow it's mowed down.

That's me. Any time I felt or wanted to do something out of the bounds of "proper" I mowed the urge down.

I'm grass.

I stop walking. I made it to the hospital lobby. The exit is ahead. I look around the lobby at the people walking through. I can only see the bustle. The nurse rushing across the hall with a coffee. The mother carrying a crying child. There are a lot of stories here, moving through. I look more closely. There's an older man sitting in a wheelchair. He's facing the window, looking out over the parking lot. Everyone is moving and hurrying, except him.

He turns toward me. He catches me watching him and stares back.

I shift under his look.

Usually, if someone catches me staring I quickly turn away. It's embarrassing. But, hey, I'm ready to experience embarrassment in all its shining glory.

"What's your name?" he asks. He has an interesting accent, a mix of British, American and something else. I can't put my finger on it, except to say, it sounds like adventure.

"Dany," I say.

"I'm Dave. Stuck in this purgatory. Got a spare kidney by any chance?"

"What?" I squeak.

"I'm looking for a kidney. Figured I'd ask. Never hurts."

I laugh and step closer. "You wouldn't want my kidney. It's chock full of chemotherapy drugs."

He holds up his hands and shrugs. His skin is yellow and papery fine. His hair is wispy. But he still has a sort of roguish air. A dapper old man. He's dressed in a gray three-piece suit under a silk robe and has a blue silk handkerchief. He uses it to wipe his forehead.

I smile and am about to say goodbye when he continues.

"At this point, I'd take a kidney from a plague-infested yeti. I saw one in the Himalayas back in '74."

I'm shocked. "A plague-infested yeti?"

He looks at me like I'm crazy. "Yetis aren't real," he says in a loud stage whisper.

"But you said—"

"I saw a kidney."

"Oh," I say. I'm not sure how to respond. "How nice."

He nods. "Lamb kidneys are a real delicacy."

"Oh."

He winces. "Looking back, I don't think I enjoyed it as much as I should have. The symbolism. I turned down the fried brain in China, though. Thankfully."

"You're a really interesting person," I say. Hospitals are chock full of interesting people. Gerry, Cleopatra. Dave.

He hums under his breath. "People are interesting. Sometimes it's obvious, sometimes you have to look close."

I look out at the parking lot and the low, scraggly grass sticking out of the cracks in the pavement. Grass.

"I'd like to be more interesting." I'm embarrassed to admit it.

He turns to me and looks me up and down.

"What's stopping you?" he asks.

The music over the speakers starts to play the eighties rock song about time running out again. My body flinches in response.

"Nothing," I say. "There's nothing stopping me."

Then I start to tap my foot.

Usually, I'd stop myself. I don't dance to music. Ever.

But then, I nod my head back and forth. What if I do? What could happen? I decide that I'm going to dance. I'm going to dance to this freaking awful song.

I'm going to live.

"I like that," says Dave. He wheels his chair forward and backward.

My cheeks burn red. Hesitantly, I start to sway my hips and

dance to the music. Maybe I can do this. Maybe I can beat this. Maybe I can dance.

Dave laughs. He wipes at his eyes.

"Mommy, what's that lady doing?" a young girl in pigtails lisps.

"Ignore them," her mom says. They hurry by.

I look around, people are staring.

I cringe and my steps falter.

Maybe I can't do this.

The hospital security guard walks up and taps me on the shoulder. "Ma'am. This is a hospital, not a dance party," he says.

"Oh. Okay. I'm sorry." I stare at the collar of his uniform. Not able to meet his eyes. "Sorry, sir," I say.

Mortification fills me. I can feel people watching. The security guard walks back to his station at the revolving doors.

The burn in my cheeks spreads over me. Embarrassment is a hot wave. My shoulders hunch.

Maybe the list was a bad idea. Dancing was definitely a bad idea.

"I haven't danced like this since that rain dance ceremony in '82," says Dave. He starts to chortle then he laughs, long and happy.

I look up in surprise. Dave wasn't afraid.

That laughter. It unlocks something in me. I feel it click open in my chest.

I *can* do this. I can step into my life and survive and thrive.

I can.

Confidence, that's what I feel. My shoulders push back again. I don't have to be afraid.

"Dave, it has been an absolute pleasure," I say. I mean it.

He takes my hand and shakes it. "Good luck, kiddo. Let me know if you run across a kidney."

"I'll be on the lookout," I say.

I wave goodbye.

15

Dany

*K*arl is at the curbside pickup. I walk to his window and he rolls it down.

"Hi Karl. Sorry for the trouble. You can head home. I'm going to take the bus."

"Miss?" he asks. He knows as well as I that I have never in my life set foot on a bus.

But ten-year-old Dany always wanted to.

This is it. This is the moment that I decide whether or not I can do this. Can I survive and thrive? Experience life through a "fall in love with Dany" list? The bus is my ticket.

"The bus sounds interesting, doesn't it, Karl?" I ask.

"Interesting, Miss?"

"Yes, interesting," I say. "I've always wanted to ride on a bus. When I was little I dreamed about the smells—vinyl seats, diesel fuel, hairspray and Juicy Fruit gum. Doesn't it sound wonderful?" In my mind, magical things happened on buses.

"Wonderful, Miss?"

"Thank you, Karl. I'll see you next time. Or I might keep taking the bus."

"I'll follow the bus. In case," he says.

"That's okay, Karl. No need." I give him a wave and lift my chin as I head toward the bus stop.

When I get there, there's a woman with a shopping basket and a younger man in scrubs.

"Nice day for a bus ride," I say to the woman. She ignores me.

The city bus pulls up to the curb. The brakes let out a long shrieking whistle and the bus shudders to a stop. The front door opens in a whoosh.

Okay, I can do this. Easy peasy. I climb on. The smell hits me. Air freshener. Hair spray. Body odor. Diesel. Juicy Fruit gum. I was right. I take in a deep breath and smile. The bus is crowded. Not a little crowded, but crammed-in-seats, bags-in-laps, standing-in-the-aisle crowded.

"Good afternoon," I say to the driver.

I scan the bus. There's an empty seat near the middle and two near the back of the bus. I take a step toward them.

"Hey, lady. Pay your fare," says the driver.

"Oh." I stop and turn back to the front. I pull out a twenty-dollar bill from my purse. "How much?"

He looks at the bill then back at me. "Lady. Quarters only. Or a ticket. You got a ticket?" He snaps his gum through his teeth.

"Oh, um..." I say.

Behind me, the woman with the cart is crowding on. She pushes past me and shoves the wheels of the cart against my ankles. Then she sticks her ticket in the machine. It spits it back out. She shoves past me to sit in the seat near the middle.

Right, I need a ticket. My ticket.

"Where do I buy a ticket?" I ask.

"At the ticket machine," says the driver in a slow voice.

The young man in scrubs clears his throat.

"Step aside," says the driver. He snaps his gum.

The scrubs-clad man dumps a load of quarters in the machine at the driver's side. A receipt spits out. His elbow jabs my side as he jostles past. He grabs a hand rail instead of sitting. I turn back to the driver.

"Could I give you this twenty instead?" I ask.

The driver scowls. "Lady. Either pay with quarters, a ticket, or get off my bus."

"Just a moment," I say. I rifle through my purse. There's always a load of change in there.

"Come on, lady. You want to ride the bus or not?" says the driver.

"I do. I really do. Just a second," I say. This is important.

In thirty seconds, that somehow feels like an eternity, I pull out enough change to pay the fare. The quarters clack as they bounce down the change funnel.

I grab the receipt that spits out.

I sigh in relief.

I did it. My ticket.

"Thank you," I tell the driver.

"Have a nice day," he says. He snaps his gum and jerks the bus into gear.

I stumble and nearly fall in a woman's lap. I grab the edge of her seat to steady myself.

"Hey," she says.

"Sorry."

I try to keep my balance as the bus lurches through traffic. Everyone is staring as I work my way to the back of the bus. Fifty, no, a gazillion eyes are on me. Finally, I make it to an open seat. Thank goodness. I plop down.

What the...

Something squelches and warmth oozes under me.

"I sat on your sandwich, didn't I?" I turn to the man sitting in the next seat.

"Burrito," says the large bearded man. He's wearing a tank top and there's thick hair on his back and shoulders.

I raise my rear end enough to pull out the flattened tortilla. The refried beans and sauce are spread across the seat.

"I'm so sorry," I say.

I hand over the flattened burrito. He takes it. Inspects it. Then swipes a finger along the edge and tastes the beans. *Oh no.*

"I could buy you another," I say. I start to unzip my purse.

He glowers at me.

"Or not. That's okay, too."

The bus jostles me with every stop, start, and turn. I try to keep from bumping my seat mate, but it's a losing battle. The beans and sauce make the vinyl seat too slippery to stay still. At the next stop he glares at me then pushes past to move to the seat behind me. Even there, I can still hear him chewing.

A new load of people gets on. I recognize the first one. I look down. *Don't sit with me, don't sit with me. Please, don't...*

"Hey, Dany. Mind if I sit here?"

"Oh, hey Jack. Err, sure," I say.

I move my legs so he can take the window seat.

"Didn't you ride with your driver today?"

I nod and try not to move too much on my wet seat. "Oh, you know. I felt like taking the bus. I *love* the bus. Looove it. Yup. It's one of my most favorite things. The people that ride buses are so friendly. So, so friendly."

He raises his eyebrows. "Do you smell that?"

"Hmm?" I ask. "Smell what?"

"Tacos or chimichanga or something? It's really strong."

I choke back a laugh. "Why are you riding the bus?" I ask.

"Sissy borrowed my truck. Bad idea, I know." He shrugs. "She wanted to go to the movies with her friends."

"Well, next time she could take the bus. It's really a wonderful mode of transportation." I grimace.

"Hey, lady. You forgot my nachos."

I ignore the man behind me. Maybe he'll go away. Get off at the next stop. Something.

"Hey, lady. You're on my nachos." He taps me on the shoulder.

Jack turns around and scowls at him. "Keep your hands to yourself, buddy."

"Lady, give me my nachos."

I shift nervously. Something crunches under me.

I don't want to stand up. There's going to be crushed nachos, melted cheese, refried beans and hot sauce all over my butt. I can feel it seeping through my pants. It's passed through the linen and made its way into my lacy underwear.

"I said, give me my nachos." The bearded man stands and looms over me.

"No," I whisper.

"What did you say?" His hair-lined shoulders bulge.

"No," I say more loudly.

"Buddy. You need to sit down and leave us alone," says Jack. I bury my face in my hands.

"I. Want. My. Nachos."

"Oh sweet sugar," I breathe into my hands.

"Sit down," says Jack.

"Lady," the man growls.

I shake my head. I'm not standing up.

"I want my—"

"No. You can take your nachos and shove 'em where the sun don't shine," I say. Then my mouth falls open in shock. I said that. Holy mackerel, I said that.

"Lady, you already did," the bearded man says, "and I want 'em back."

"Sit down," says Jack.

The man turns, raises his fist. Oh no. He punches Jack in the eye.

I scream.

Jack bounces against the seat. Collapses. His head falls into my lap.

The big man yanks on the emergency handle.

"That wasn't nice." He points at me. "I want my nachos."

The bus screeches to a halt.

I raise my thigh and slowly pull out the carboard container of crushed chips.

"Here you go," I say.

"Thank you," he says. Then he storms off the bus.

Jack is still lying across my lap.

"Are you okay?" I ask him. "Oh no. Your poor eye." I brush his hair away. His eye is already starting to bruise.

He groans.

"Oh no." I smooth his hair. "You're not okay."

He nuzzles his face into my legs. Rubs his check into my belly and strokes my thighs. Then he turns and grins up at me.

"You...you..." I push at him. "You're fine. Get up. Get up," I laugh.

He rubs his cheek against my leg.

"I love nachos," he says. "Mmm. You smell so good. Tacos, chimichangas..."

"Don't be vulgar," I say.

"Can't help it. You bring it out of me."

I brush my fingers over his hair. It's soft at the ends. I decide that I like buses. I do. They're interesting.

"I'm starting a new venture," I tell him.

He still hasn't moved from my lap.

"You want me along," he says.

I look up. The driver is standing in front of me. His arms are folded across his chest.

"You two." He points at us. "Off my bus."

Jack scrambles up.

"But...but...I paid my fare," I say.

"Off," he says. He points at the open door.

"That's not right," I say.

"Aww, get off the bus," shouts the woman that I accidently bumped earlier.

I sniff.

"I'm not driving until you get off my bus."

"Booo," jeers a blue-haired teenage boy.

"Go on, get off," says a man in a Christmas sweater.

Jack chuckles. He stands. He bows and sweeps his hands toward the door in a courtly gesture. "My lady."

I push my lips into a firm line. This is my first adventure and I'm getting kicked out of it? I shake my head.

"Get her off," shouts the woman again.

Jack grins and a wicked light enters his eyes. He bends down and swoops me up. My legs kick out and I'm in his arms.

The driver nods and points at the door. "That's right."

The blue-haired teen starts a slow clap. The rest of the crowd on the bus joins in. I'm getting the slow clap. Unbelievable.

I bury my face in Jack's flannel. But then, as we're about to leave, I decide to own the embarrassment.

This is my ride. My list.

I raise my head and give the people on the bus a royal princess wave and throw them kisses.

"Go on," the Christmas sweater man shouts.

Jack gives a full belly laugh. He steps down to the curb.

The bus door lets out a hiss as it closes and the driver yanks the bus into traffic. We're left in a puff of diesel.

Jack's laugh vibrates through me. It trails off as he looks down at me with bright eyes. I stick out my chin and give a cocky smile. It's a new look for me.

"You're trouble," he says.

Never in my life have I been trouble. I think I like it.

I grin. I'm going to make that list. My interesting, thriving, surviving, loving myself, I'm trouble list.

I reach up and brush my fingers over his bruised eye.

"My hero," I say.

He smirks. "I knew I smelled Mexican food."

I laugh. It feels good.

Thank goodness Karl followed. He drives us back to Rose Street.

As we ride, I watch Jack and I wonder what part he's going to play in my future.

16

Dany

A list. The list.

I chew on the tip of a Bic pen and think. Hard.

I'm curled up on the blue linen couch. The soft sea glass throw is tucked around my legs and a notebook is perched on my knees. I'm freshly showered and dressed in clothes for napping. But first, the list.

I still feel jubilant from the bus ride.

I write a big number one then dot a period.

I have a few limitations. I have to stay in the Stanton area while undergoing chemo. I can't do anything that's beyond my physical limits—fatigue is currently my biggest obstacle. And here are my hard limits. I don't want to do anything illegal. Getting arrested is not on my list. And, more important, I'm not looking for romance, or love. No pity wooing from Jack. No rebound relationships. No friendly kisses that are only about making the poor, dumped, sick girl feel better about herself. Because what else could it be?

There's nothing worse than a pity romance. I can't imagine how horrible it would be if I fell for Jack. Especially if he told me the feeling wasn't returned. That he was only trying to give me a little boost, make me feel better during hard times.

I realize that Jack is a really, really good guy. He cares about people and wants to take care of them. Even strangers or people he barely knows. The way he takes care of his sister—I know he has a big heart. Which is why the only reason he might pretend he cares is out of misplaced concern. To make me feel better.

No matter how appealing Jack is, that would be the worst thing that could happen.

So, no getting arrested, and no romances.

That decided, I circle the number one.

If I'm going to do this, then I may as well start big. What's something that the old Daniella would never, ever do? Ever?

I wouldn't let myself be free, wild, spontaneous, adventurous, or daring.

I stare at the vibrant modern painting on the wall. The colors are slashed together. I can see the speeding movement of the brushstrokes slashed across the canvas. Falling down in riotous colors. The effect is dizzying.

Ah.

The one thing the old me would never have done? Bungee jump off River Bridge.

Whenever I drove past and saw people dangling from a cord over the deep brown river water I would think 'what if?' Even thinking of the jump would send a thrill through me. But then I'd put it away. Because bungee jumping didn't fit in with beige.

I write the words in looping cursive.

1. Bungee jump off River Bridge.

My heart is beating more quickly. Bungee jumping is definitely the opposite of beige. I look down at my camel-colored pajamas.

How about the ultimate in rebellion? No more beige, no more camel, no more taupe, ecru, khaki, or sand. No more muted colors.

I write a number two on the paper.

2. Go on a shopping spree and get colorful, bright, beautiful clothes I feel sexy in.

The sexy bit snuck in there. But I like it.

I think about other things I've always wanted to do. Scotland. That's not a possibility but...

3. Explore a castle ruin.

I know of one not far from here. It was built years ago and then fell into disrepair.

Quickly I write the next items on my list.

4. Skinny dip at sunset.

5. Ride on a bus.

6. Eat whatever food I want.

7. Go to a dive bar and get in a bar fight.

I pause at number eight. Then, I write three X's. For unknown possibilities. Places I'm not ready to let my mind venture yet.

8. XXX

For number nine, I have a big task. I need to find a new career. After college, I took a position at Drake International as a donations coordinator in development. It was what everyone expected, and a compromise to please my parents. But it doesn't feed my heart. It doesn't feel like the right place for me. I admit that now. I never thought about what I wanted to do for a career. I just glided along the laid out path. Lately, that feels wrong. So, I jot down number nine.

9. Find a career I'm passionate about.

The last number, number ten, I go back and forth on whether to include. This item was my dream, my biggest dream, even as the English rose. And I think it's still my dream.

What if, after all this, I can still have it?

Will I still want it?

Heart in my throat, I press firmly on the paper and write out:

10. Have a beach wedding.

Only a short while ago I believed that if I got Shawn back that I'd beat the cancer. Do I still believe that? I don't know.

I sigh and set down the pen.

That's it then.

I take a good look at my list.

1. Bungee jump off River Bridge.

2. Go on a shopping spree and get colorful, bright, beautiful clothes I feel sexy in.

3. Explore a castle ruin.

4. Skinny dip at sunset.

5. Ride on a bus.

6. Eat whatever food I want.

7. Go to a dive bar and get in a bar fight.

8. XXX

9. Find a career I'm passionate about.

10. Have a beach wedding.

I wonder if a few items on a piece of paper can really make me thrive and survive?

Yes, something inside me whispers.

But there's doubt there too, and a little bit of trepidation.

17

JACK

"Let me get this straight," I say.

Dany and I are in the kitchen at the house. Dany wandered down after taking a long nap. She has a pillow crease on her face. Clearly, she showered after the bus incident. She's in a light pink cardigan with pearl buttons and a pencil skirt.

I sit down at the kitchen table across from her. She has a list and a pen. I stare suspiciously at the paper with its neat cursive writing. She hasn't told me all the items, but enough of them to get the gist.

I continue, "You rode the city bus as part of your bucket list?"

"It's not a bucket list." She narrows her eyes and sits up straighter.

I hold up my hands in a peace gesture. "Is this all because of that pencil neck? Is this some sort of crisis because..." I trail off. I realize too late that I sound like a jerk.

"Because I have breast cancer?" Her lips are tight. I watch them and expect them to loosen. They don't.

"Not what I was going to say."

"What then?" she asks.

"I guess I don't think you need to start doing crazy things because your ex showed his true colors."

"Riding the bus isn't crazy." She shakes her head in agitation. A lock of hair falls out of her braid. She holds up her list, "Going to a dive bar isn't crazy. Swimming at sunset isn't crazy."

"Swimming at sunset naked. Naked," I repeat. Then I squash the image that flashes in my mind. I look back at the list she's holding up like a talisman. "And going to a dive bar in this town *is* borderline crazy."

She sets the list down and glares. "Pardon me, but I'm not asking your permission."

I drag my hand down my face. This isn't going well. She came down for something to eat, not for a lecture or my uninvited opinions.

"Sorry, you're right," I say.

Her eyes widen in surprise. She tilts her head and studies me. "That's really big of you. How's your eye?"

I shrug. It hurts like a son of a gun, but I'd do it again. "It's alright. I'm going for that dark and dangerous air."

She laughs and little lines crinkle at the edges of her eyes. I lean forward, drawn to her. I impulsively say what I've been thinking since I saw her list. "You don't need to change. Forget what he said. You're perfect the way you are."

Her laughter cuts off. "Funny thing. I'm tired of being perfect. Perfect is *boring*."

Ah. I hear the pain in that one word.

I let out a long breath and scoot closer. Then I reach out and rest my hand on the table, not far from hers. My fingers twitch to touch hers. But I don't.

How can she be so unaware of her appeal? I wanted her the second I saw her.

"You're not boring," I say. "You're the opposite of boring."

Clearly, my blood wouldn't rush every time she came in the room if she were *boring*. Flipping pencil neck. An idea suddenly comes to me. It feels absolutely inspired.

I don't think too deeply about why I'm so excited by the thought.

"You forgot something on your list," I say.

"What's that?" she asks.

"You need to be swept off your feet. Wooed. Romanced."

"You're kidding," she says dryly.

But I'm warming to my idea.

"Yeah." I nod. "I'll come with you on your adventures. On top of that, I'll woo you."

I tell myself that I'm aiming to get my bid accepted. But really, honestly, I want to spend time with her. I know we won't end up together. I already counted the reasons that won't happen. But is it so wrong that I want to be near her? To see her eyes scrunch up when she laughs. To watch the hair that inevitably slips loose from her braid. I'm in it deep. But as long as she doesn't return the sentiment, as long as it stays casual and fun, it'll be fine.

Her fingers curl into her palm and I watch as her knuckles turn white. Finally, she responds. "You think I'm some pathetic woman that needs a confidence boost, don't you? You want to play pity party to my poor broken little heart? Who signed you up for the role of charity Don Juan?"

I shake my head in denial. Clearly, she has no idea that I fell for her the second we met. Before I knew anything about her situation.

"No," I say. I hold up my hands. "That's not it at all."

Her eyes narrow on me. "You want something, don't you? What's in it for you?" she asks.

Right. I'd already forgotten. I was going to come clean about my project.

Do I tell her that she can get my bid through with her connections? Should I tell her I want to use her to win my proposal? I have a feeling that won't go over well. That she might shut me down and not speak to me again.

The thought scares me more than it should.

So, I hedge.

"Uh, well. You see. I'm raising my sister. It's new. I don't know much about girls. I thought you could help out."

She raises an eyebrow.

"Help out?"

I nod.

"What? Do mani/pedis, talk about our periods, braid each other's hair?"

"Yeah?" This feels like a trap.

"Riiight. I don't think so. You're some kind of creep that gets off on dating girls with an expiration date, aren't you? Oh gee, this ones got cancer. I can date her and in three months she'll be gone. No breakup text necessary. Gee, swell. You've got some real commitment issues, *buddy*."

I can't help it. I grin.

She glares.

"You're amazing," I say.

She shoves her chair back and stands to leave.

"No, you're right. You're right. Here's the truth."

She sinks back into her chair.

"This is important. I need to convince some people to give me a chance on rehabbing a property. If you'd help with this house, see how much I put into my work, maybe talk to some of the people on the committee, it could change my life...truthfully, everything's on the line. You could help." I clear my throat. "I need your help. Please." Even giving this much truth makes me feel uncomfortably exposed. If she learns the full truth, though, that her father is the reason I'm asking for her help, she may say no. She may never want to see me again. The jab of pain that thought brings convinces me to stick with vague explanations.

"You want me to help you renovate? Talk to some committee? So you can keep your job?" She weighs my words.

I clench my hands under the table.

"Yes. I'm asking for your help. To save my career. My dream."

"What kind of renovations?"

"Nothing strenuous, nothing you can't handle."

"And the committee?"

"The Downtown Development Committee, for housing."

I hold my breath.

"You need help?"

I take a breath. "I do," I say.

"And you want to join me in my list."

"That's right."

She looks over at the moon shining through the stained-glass window above the kitchen sink. The silence stretches into a minute. I shift in my chair.

Then, finally, "Yes. Alright."

"Good. Great." I close my eyes in relief. Only now do I admit how worried I was that she'd say no. I want to join her on her adventures.

"On one condition," she says.

"Anything."

"No Don Juan."

"What?"

"You can tag along on my list. Help out if I need it. But I don't want your pity romance."

"It wouldn't be pity. You're amazing—"

"Ah ah." She holds up her hand.

"You are. It could be fun and—"

"Shhh." She shushes me.

"You know, it might be inevitable—"

"No." She shakes her head.

"Alright." I hold out my hand. "I help with your list, you help with my project. It's a deal."

She smiles. A full-on beaming smile that knocks the breath from me. She glows with it. She takes my hand and gives a firm shake.

"Deal."

18

JACK

"I didn't know the list doing would start so soon," I say. It's the next day and we're in a booth at Chet's Bar. The vinyl seats are sticky and cracked. The windows are blacked out. There are peanut shells on the floor. The tangy scent of old beer, cigarette ash and dirty fryer grease permeates the air. The room's dark and the jukebox plays an old country western favorite. This is as dive as it gets in Stanton. If you're looking for trouble, or running from trouble, this is where you come. I don't know which side of the line we fall on. Maybe both.

"I'm hungry," Dany says. "That's rare lately. So I'm going with it." She scans the stained paper menu.

I nod sagely. "What you said earlier..." I pause and consider my words.

"What?"

"Are you really going to...uh, check out in three months?"

She sniffs and sets her menu down. "No. Didn't you read my

list? I'm going to survive and thrive. Starting with a bacon, onion stack, barbeque burger at my new favorite dive bar."

"So you're not—"

"I'm going to live," she says.

"Alright," I say. But I have this horrible feeling in the pit of my stomach that if I get too close to her, or fall in love, she won't.

"What'll it be?" a hoarse-voiced waitress asks.

We place our orders and in five minutes the food is plopped down in front of us.

"Oh wow. Look at the grease," Dany says.

I take a bite of my double bacon burger and chew. Yeah, that's good. "You said you wanted a dive bar. The grease makes it authentic."

She takes a small bite. Her eyes widen as she swallows. "Oh, that's good."

I watch in awe as she wolfs down the burger. Grease runs down her chin. She dabs it away with a paper napkin. Tea party manners for a greasy burger. I smile.

"What's so funny?" she asks. Her burger's already gone.

"I like your enthusiasm."

"I've never eaten a bacon, onion stack, barbeque burger before. I liked it. I really, really liked it." She's progressed to delicately licking her fingers. I watch, entranced as she places each in her mouth and sucks.

I clear my throat and throw my crumpled napkin in my basket.

"All set?" I ask in a choked voice.

She shakes her head. "I'm getting dessert. Did you know, I haven't eaten red meat in almost two decades?"

"Really?"

"Red meat is uncouth. Not fit for proper young ladies."

I wince. "It sounds like you're reciting instructions from some freaky 1950s debutante instruction manual."

She gives me a tight-lipped smile, the devil sparking in her eyes. "My life was a freaky 1950s debutante manual." Cool as a cucumber Dany waves down the waitress. "I'll have the deep-fried Snicker balls."

"Side of ice cream?"

"Double scoop."

She turns back to me. "I love dive bars," she says.

"You're drunk on grease and the second-hand fumes of old beer."

She tilts her head back and laughs. I stare at the column of her neck. It's smooth where it meets the pearl buttons of her cardigan. I flag down the waitress for an ice water.

A few minutes later, I watch Dany down the bowl of fried sugar. She pops ball after fried ball into her mouth and licks the vanilla ice cream from the spoon. She moans in appreciation.

Dang.

"Want some?" she asks.

"No." I shake my head.

"You look like you really want some," she says. She holds out the spoon to me.

I shake my head again. This is the first time in my life I've had a hard-on from fried balls. I shift uncomfortably in my seat.

"What's happening over there?" Dany points to the other end of the bar. There's a crowd of people cheering.

"That's Chet's mechanical bull contest. The longest rider on gets to wear the beer cap crown the rest of the night." I'm talking to myself. Dany's already off the bench. She strides to the other side of the bar.

I throw forty dollars on the table and follow her.

Her eyes shine. "I'm doing this," she says.

Currently, there's a champion on the bull. She has on hot pants and a midriff shirt showing off her six-pack.

"Really?" I ask.

Dany's eyes shift to the bull. She bites her lips. Tilts her head. I think she's going to change her mind. Then she pushes her shoulders back and she mutters under her breath, "You're doing this, Dany. You're living."

When she looks up I can tell she's decided on the bull.

"I'm signing up," she says. She points to the emcee holding a clipboard.

After she's signed in we work our way to the front of the sidelines.

"If I win, I also get a twenty-five dollar cash prize and a bucket of peanuts," she says.

"Heck, maybe I should sign up too," I say.

She elbows my side.

I try to hold back a laugh, but can't.

"Laugh now, buddy. But you won't be laughing when I don't share my winnings." She arches an eyebrow at me. I grin back.

Finally, the pro bull rider is bucked.

The crowd cheers.

The emcee silences them. Then he announces Dany.

"Next up, a virgin rider. We love our virgins here. Miss Dany. She's here to get bucked with a capital F." The crowd hoots. "If any of you boys have the school teacher fantasy, you might try our girl after she's had her bull cherry popped."

Heck no.

I send a glare around the crowd and let them know she's not available for bucking with a capital F.

I look at her. Her face is white. Is she losing her confidence?

"You can do this," she whispers. Then, "Just a minute," she calls. She hustles over to the jukebox and slides in two quarters. When she turns around a 1980s dance song starts to play.

She winks at me and mouths *trouble*.

Wow.

The guys in the bar go wild.

She struts over to the bull. She's nervous, but I don't think anyone else can tell.

She climbs onto the bull and wraps her legs over the saddle. Her pencil skirt rides up her legs. She has on thigh-high stockings with a dark line up the edge and stiletto heels. I've never seen anything more erotic in my life. She rolls up the sleeves of her pink cardigan and sends me a wink.

"Holy shit," I say.

The emcee turns on the bull.

Her body sways to the bucking. She clenches her thighs and rocks. As the music picks up and the electric guitar and drums play, Dany sends one arm in the air and starts doing the lasso. She sends the imaginary rope to me and mimics pulling me in.

Holy...

The bull enters its beastly bucking stage. This is when most riders get tossed. I can tell Dany isn't ready for it. Her arms are up and she's doing, what is that, the sprinkler dance from the eighties?

Oh no.

The mechanical bull bucks.

The guys in the crowd cheer.

You have to give Dany points for class. As she flips through the air, she tucks under and, dang, she makes it look graceful.

"She's bucked," yells the emcee.

"Yeah!" The guy next to me pumps his arms in the air.

Dany bounces off the landing trampoline and knocks into a big guy at the edge of the crowd.

He falls to the ground with an "oof." Dany lands on top of him. His container of cheesy fries and beer are squished between them.

I shove my way through the crowd. They're all cheering and hollering. Dany pushes herself up off the chest of the cheesy fry-covered man. I grab her and help her up. She wobbles back and forth on her feet.

"Hey, I know you." The guy stands up and looms over Dany. "Back up, buddy," I say.

He shoves a finger into my chest. "And I know you, too."

I look up from his cheese-covered belly to his beefy shoulders to his red bearded face. He's nodding at my look of recognition. He hits a fist into his hand.

"Oh yeah," he says.

"Dany," I say. "We should go."

She shakes her head.

"Dany, we need to go."

"I don't feel so—" She cuts off. Then she lets loose a fried onion bacon burger, fries, and a basket of deep-fried Snicker balls all over our bearded friend.

The song has ended. There's dead silence in the bar.

The big guy looks at his cheesy puke-covered T-shirt and roars. He swings a fist in my direction. I'm ready this time. I duck. The guy slips in the mess and crashes to the ground. He knocks a few guys over on his way down.

You better believe all hell is about to break loose. Dany's still standing, staring with horror at the guy rolling on the ground.

"Let's go," I say over the sudden yelling and cursing. The bar fight has begun.

She doesn't hear me. So I do what any good date would. I grab her and fireman-carry her butt out of the bar.

I bust out onto the street and rush to the truck. I toss her into the front seat, jump into the driver's side and lock the doors.

My heart is jackhammering in my chest.

"You alright?" I ask after I've caught my breath.

"No. I didn't get my bucket of peanuts."

I look at her in shock. Then she starts to laugh. "Your face. Your face." She points and starts laughing again.

I try to level a stare, but I can't. It's too funny.

"You've got a little vomit," I say. I touch her hair. "Right here."

"Oh jeez," she laughs. She stops and holds her stomach. Her face turns green.

"Chemo sucks," she says. Then she opens the car door and lets loose everything left in her stomach.

She comes back up after a minute. She closes the door with a snick.

"Sorry about that," she says.

"Don't worry. You alright?" I ask.

"I'm okay. Vomiting's okay. It means I'm still alive."

"Amen to that," I say.

I start the truck.

"Well, Jack Jones. You're signed up now. Official sidekick. Rescuer. Back-gotter." The slang sounds funny mixed with her proper accent.

I chuckle. "That's right. I've got your back."

"I've never had a back-gotter before," she says. There's a small smile on her lips.

I put the truck in gear and pull onto the street.

"Can we go home now?" I ask.

"Absolutely. Have to rest up for tomorrow's fun."

I give her a quick, startled look then turn back to the road. "You're kidding."

"I never kid. It's against the 1950s debutante handbook."

I laugh. Then look over at her again. The headlights behind us illuminate the inside of the truck.

She sits all prim and proper with torn stockings, a cheese-stained cardigan and puke in her hair. And I'm struck. Dumb-struck by the fact that I'm deeply, irrevocably in love with this woman. My heart thuds. She can never know.

I can't...

The truck swerves a little and I pull back into my lane.

I glance at Dany again. Nothing's changed. She hasn't noticed a thing.

I let out a sharp, painful breath.

For the rest of the ride home I avoid looking at her. I ignore her smiles and her hilariously awful humming renditions of eighties songs. Instead, I concentrate on the task at hand. Driving. Building my business. Raising my sister. Daniella Drake as a means to absolution. Nothing else.

19

Dany

I hear crying. It's muffled, but it's definitely crying. The house is inky dark and otherwise quiet. It must be the middle of the night.

After Jack and I got back to the house on Rose Street, I slept. And slept. I slept through the next day, waking up for quick bathroom breaks and glasses of water. And then I slept some more.

List doing takes a lot out of me. Or it's the chemo. Take your pick.

I look at my clock, its 12:05 in the morning. I hear another sob. It's coming from downstairs.

"This doesn't sound good," I say. Sometimes I talk in the dark. It's a hold-over from when I was a kid and afraid of nights alone in my mausoleum-white bedroom. I swing my legs off the bed and touch my bare feet to the cold wood floor.

Brrr.

I wonder if I should wake Jack? No, I'll go see what it is

myself. I tiptoe down the stairs. The crying's coming from the kitchen. I stop at the entry and peek around the corner. It's Sissy. She's at the kitchen table with her face in her hands. The kitchen's dimly lit by the under-cabinet lighting. Sissy's shoulders shake and she lets out another cry.

I don't know if I should stay or leave.

Sissy lifts her head. Her face is streaked with mascara. "Hey," she says.

"Oh, um...hey." I don't think it's polite to ask her why she's crying. I shift my bare feet on the cold kitchen tile.

She shakes her head. "You may as well come in."

I don't know what to say, so I blurt out the first thing that comes to mind.

"I just came down for some, uh, cookies. I've always wanted to make cookies. And I woke up and said to myself, this is my moment. My cookie moment."

Sissy lets out a small laugh. "You are seriously weird."

"Yes," I say.

She grins and wipes at her eyes with her sleeve.

I walk into the kitchen and start randomly opening cupboards. Now that I came up with the idea, I kind of like it. Growing up, chef always made the meals and the desserts. I've never in my life made a cookie. Now's the time. Plus, I am actually hungry.

"Do you know what goes in a cookie?" I ask.

"What kind of cookie? Like peanut butter?"

"What about chocolate chip?" I *love* chocolate chip cookies.

Sissy stands and pokes around in the cupboards. She grabs a bunch of containers then pulls eggs and butter from the refrigerator. She puts everything on the counter next to a mixer, measuring cups and spoons.

"Wow. You must be really good at baking," I say.

"Seriously? I've never baked in my life."

I look at the ingredients on the counter and back at her.

She shrugs. "Did you know I grew up in the back of a car?"

She watches me and waits for my reaction. I shake my head. "Didn't you...I thought...didn't you grow up with Jack?"

She turns and opens the container of sugar. "Nah. I only met Jack like half a year ago. My whole life I didn't know he existed. I lived in a car with my dad."

She's drawing little patterns in the sugar. Stars, flowers, hearts.

"That must've been hard," I say. I think of my childhood home. Then I think of her, living in a car.

"I loved it," she says. She wipes away her doodles and turns to me. There's a deep earnestness on her face.

I shake my head. What do I say?

"Dad figured I'd be more settled with Jack. He's an alright brother."

"So, your dad dropped you off and then...what?"

"It wasn't like that. Dad wanted me to stay, it just didn't work out."

I nod. "Right. Of course."

"Seriously," she says.

"I believe you."

I grab a measuring cup and scoop up some sugar.

"Cream it with the butter," Sissy says. She drops a stick in the bowl.

"Don't know what cream means," I say.

She rolls her eyes and turns on the mixer.

"How'd you learn to bake cookies if you grew up in a car?"

"I binge watch cooking shows. I've seen chocolate chip cookies made about five thousand times. Trust me. We can figure it out."

"Alright," I say.

Sissy directs and I add and mix. I'm pretty sure she's making up half the measurements, but that's okay.

"Done," she says.

I look down at the soupy mixture. "Do you think it needs more flour?"

"Nah."

I poke my finger in. When I pull it out it makes a sucking noise.

Sissy laughs and plunks a cookie sheet onto the counter. I drizzle the mix into little circles on the pan.

"Are you sure it shouldn't be less, I don't know, less...wet?"

Sissy sighs and shakes her head. "Is this your cookie moment or not?"

I put back my shoulders. "It's my cookie moment."

"That's right." She points at me, "it's your cookie moment. No wussing out."

I set the baking sheet in the oven and then clean up the mess. Sissy watches. I start to feel brave.

"Why were you crying?" I ask. "Do you miss your dad?"

Even though I never knew my biological dad, sometimes, when I was little, I missed him. Or the idea of him. Then John Drake became my dad, and that was that.

She leans back on the counter and stares up at the ceiling. "Maybe I was crying because I *don't* miss him."

I turn to her. She's still looking at the ceiling.

"Really?" I ask.

She shakes her head.

"Dude. No. I got dumped."

She wipes at her nose.

"You did?" This, I can handle. "I'm sorry."

She shrugs. "He was a dick."

"You too?" I ask.

She gives a small laugh. "He was, like, pressuring me to get a hotel room on prom night."

"Oh. Ohhh. What did you tell him?"

She shrugs. "That I wasn't super excited about losing my virginity to an inexperienced sixteen-year-old who'd jizz all over me within thirteen seconds of fumbled groping in the dark."

I snort. I can't help it. My hand flies to my mouth and I try to cover my laugh but I can't. "You didn't."

"Dude. I did."

I grin at Sissy. She shrugs.

"I thought thirteen seconds was generous. But he was pretty mad."

"No," I say.

She nods and wipes at her eyes. "Then he said that my chest was flat and I was too tight for a man of his size, blah blah blah, and he said he was going to take Jessie to the prom anyway seeing that I'm not even a woman yet."

"What a dick," I say. I feel liberated saying it.

Sissy nods.

"Seriously," I say. I use her tone of voice.

She looks at me, a glint of humor in her eyes. A grin spreads over my face.

"Seriously," she laughs.

We both crack up.

The oven beeps. "The cookies," I say. I open the door with anticipation.

A huge puff of smoke pours out and fills the kitchen.

"Ack," I say.

Sissy coughs and waves her hands in the air. Within three seconds, the fire alarm starts to blare. I grab an oven mitt and yank the cookie sheet out.

Sissy jumps up and down and waves a towel in front of the alarm. I toss the cookies on the stove and then open a window. Then I grab a towel and start waving. The alarm won't stop beeping.

Over the noise I hear feet pounding down the hall and then Jack runs into the kitchen.

He's in pajama bottoms and his hair is tousled and sleep

mussed. He stops short when he hits the smoke. "Sissy. Are you okay? Dany?"

I drop the towel. So this is what he looks like in bed. *My word.*

Then I take in his expression.

His eyes are wild, his face white. He's pulling in short, harsh breaths.

He's not just scared or startled by the alarm, he's...panicked?

Sissy manages to stop the beeping.

"Hey, Jack. Sorry to wake you," she says.

"You're alright," he whispers. He takes a breath and the wild look in his eyes fades. "You're alright," he says again.

"Dude. What's the deal?" asks Sissy. She frowns at Jack. "It's just a little smoke."

"Right. It's alright," he says. He walks into the kitchen and manages to half hide a wince when he reaches the lingering smoke.

"Are you okay?" I ask.

He nods. "I'm fine."

I clear my throat and change the topic. "We were just making..." I gape at the long rectangular blob with blackened edges.

"What is that?" Jack asks.

Sissy comes over and looks at the pan. "That, my friends, is a Texas chocolate chip cookie bar cake." She stops and her face scrunches up as she tries to restrain a laugh. "*Not.* It's not," she says.

I poke at the glob with a fork. A piece of burnt sugar sizzles. "I'm still eating it," I say.

"Oh yeah. Me too," says Sissy.

Jack looks skeptically at the tray.

"Come on, bro. This is Dany's cookie moment."

He shakes his head, but takes the fork I offer.

I blow on the hot sugary mess. It burns my tongue as I chew.

"It's surprisingly..."

"Awful, it's awful," says Sissy.

"I was going to say...surprisingly edible."

Jack swallows his first mouthful. "Mmm, good," he says. He winks at me. I'm glad that all his color's back, and he looks like he's shaken off whatever spooked him. I smile at him and wink back.

"Here's to surprisingly edible cookies." Sissy tips up her fork and clinks it against mine in a toast. "To my cookie moment," I say.

"Cheers," says Jack.

We all click forks. Then I shove another bite of chocolate chip goo into my mouth.

We eat the whole tray. Even the crunchy burnt bits.

20

Dany

"Let me see this list," says Jack. We're sitting on the brand new couch in the downstairs living room. It's dove gray fabric with lots of black throw pillows. Jack says he picked the colors for Sissy and her monotone love affair.

I pull the list from my pocket. It's creased and worn. I've pulled it out over the past week and studied it, then refolded it and put it in my pocket again. For the past seven days, Jack's been busy working and I've been busy chemo-ing, physical therapy-ing, and looking for a career I'll love.

But tonight, I'm putting all that aside. Jack and I are going to do another two items on my list. I have my backpack packed and ready. It's on the floor next to my feet.

"Ride on a bus," he reads.

"Check," I say. I make a check mark in the air.

"Go to a dive bar and get in a bar fight." He raises his eyebrows. "Wait a minute, you planned that?"

"Double check." I smile at him.

"What else?" He skims the list.

I know it by heart.

"Have a beach wedding?" asks Jack. "You're still focusing on that guy? What's his name?" Jack levels a hard look at me. Out of all the items on the list, he has to latch onto the last?

"Shawn," I say. "That guy's name is Shawn."

He waves that away. "I'm not helping with that one."

I shrug. I don't have to explain myself to Mr. Jack Jones.

"And what's the triple X? Wait. Is that what I think it is?"

I ignore his question. I fold the list up. "Are you ready to go?"

He watches as I put the paper back in my pocket.

"Alright. I'm ready," he says.

At his truck he holds the door open for me. I settle in for the drive. After a few minutes he pulls onto the highway.

"I never knew there was a castle around here," he says.

"It was built by a nineteenth century industrialist as a pleasure hall."

"Pleasure hall?"

I can tell that Jack's interest is piqued.

"Yeah, that's what obscenely wealthy men did back then. They built country houses and filled them with all the things that were off limits in the Victorian Era."

"Like?"

"Oh, pretty much everything. They had a lot of rules. No mentioning words like 'trousers.'"

"Trousers?"

"No eating onions in a lady's presence."

"Really?"

"No enjoying, you know, the act. Conjugal relations were something to be endured not enjoyed."

He looks over at me. My face heats. The phrase "conjugal relations" tastes dirtier than just saying "sex." Suddenly, I'm aware of how close we're sitting. How I could just reach a few inches over and touch his hand.

He clears his throat. "I can see why they built these halls. I'd want to get away too."

"Exactly." I also see the appeal.

"I mean, I love onions," he says.

I laugh and he turns to me. "Really?" I ask.

"Yeah. And I can't go a day without saying *trousers*."

"Trousers," I enunciate.

We settle into a happy silence. I look out the window. We've left the city behind. First there were farms. Corn and soy beans. Now we come to a more forested area. Tree branches hang overhead and the sun streaks though their limbs, flashing light then dark.

"There's our exit," I say.

Jack turns onto a small country road.

It's funny, but I think my life before was a lot like the Victorian era. My family placed a lot of restrictions on me and my behavior. But after I left home, I didn't have any excuse. I restricted myself.

Jack takes a few more turns until we're heading down a washed out dirt road. There are grooves in the dirt and deep ruts. For a half mile, Jack steers over the rocks and potholes.

"Pull over there" I point to an area where the shoulder is mossy and the beech trees are beginning to unfurl their bright green buds.

Jack pulls over and turns off the truck.

I hop out and stretch my arms in front of me. My boots sink a bit into a thick cushion of moss. There are a few birds calling in the forest. There's a sweet descending whistle and a caw. I try to pick out the different sounds and hear a chickadee. Jack shuts his door and his feet crunch on the gravel as he walks to my side.

We stand for a moment, then, "So. Where's this illustrious pleasure den?"

I close my eyes and let the shifting light play over my eyelids. The sun streams through the tree branches and shoots speckled light over my eyes.

I flinch.

It reminds me of the fluorescent lights when I was waking up in the hospital.

I snap my eyes open and turn my face away from the pale spring warmth.

"It's a half mile in," I say. My voice is short and tight. Jack doesn't say anything.

I pick my way across the small ditch and scramble into the woods. I wore boots, which is good. My feet sink into old leaves and my wool dress pants snag on little thorny vines. Spiky brown burrs catch on the fabric.

The forest is quiet except for the chickadee and a cawing raven. I step on a dry stick and the snap echoes through the trees. The woods are open, not dense at all. There's a downed tree with moss spilling over it like a green waterfall. Ferns line shaded areas. A squirrel chatters and leaps ahead of us from one oak branch to the next. As we walk, we kick up the scent of turned over leaves, wet soil, and new grass. I stop walking, close my eyes and breathe it in.

Jack pauses next to me.

He's so close that I have the urge to lean into him. My eyes are still closed but I can feel the back of his hand running over my fingers. His touch is soft, as gentle as the spring wind caressing my skin. The back of my hand feels more awake then the rest of me. All my awareness is centered on the feel of him, touching me there. The electricity spreads over my hand, up my arm, and through my whole body. I uncurl my fingers and let them tangle with his. His long fingers drift over mine and send a throbbing pulse through me. I hear the sharp intake of his breath. I lean toward him and open my eyes.

He's looking down at me. His dark pupils have nearly enveloped the gray of his eyes.

"Dany," he swallows.

"Yes?"

"Look."

He points. A few hundred yards away, mostly hidden by a copse of beech trees, is the castle. Or the ruin. The castle ruin.

"Wow." I grab his hand and pull him after me. His legs are longer though, and he's faster. Soon he's pulling me.

We make it there, out of breath and full of wonder.

"Would you look at that," he says.

There's a rectangular foundation, maybe a foot high, of cut granite. In the far back corner there's a circular stone tower. It's probably thirty feet high. A third of the stones have been knocked away. You can see the stairs spiraling along the edges of the tower. I start to walk forward. Entranced.

"It's like a fairy tale," I say.

"You're not climbing that," says Jack.

I keep walking. It may not have held a princess, but I bet someone looked up from the tower and wished on the stars.

"It's romantic," I say.

"It's a death trap. Not safe—" His words are cut off. The ground disappears beneath him.

"Jack!" There's a loud boom. Then the soft ground I'm standing on caves and I scream as I fall.

21

Dany

*T*he air is knocked from me as I land on hard, cold stone.

"Dani?" Jack wheezes my name.

"Here. Over here."

He crawls over and runs his hands over me. "You're alright?"

I move all my parts. I'm sore. Definitely bruised. But I feel okay. "I'm okay. You?"

"I'm alright."

We look up. We're in a hole about ten feet deep. There are broken rotted wood boards above us. Slits of light shine through. Jack rubs his hands over the rock floor. "I think we're in the cellar," he says.

"Ouch," I say.

I lie back on the ground and try to regain my equilibrium. Jack leans back next to me. I move closer to him and rest my head on his chest. "I'm going to use you for a pillow. No offense."

"None taken." He shifts and pulls me closer.

I look up at the sky. The limbs of the beech trees sway in the wind. The fact that we are all alone out here hits me. The only noise is the creaking of the branches in the wind and the rhythmic beating of Jack's heart.

"So, I'm in a castle," I say. Then I make a little mark in the air and... "Check."

I sense him smile. I shift on him and look up at his face.

"Is it everything you dreamed of, Miss Drake?" His gray eyes are full of mirth.

"It depends." I stretch and feel the bruises starting to form on my back and legs. "Can you get us out of here?" Really, I'd rather not die in a ruined castle's dirty old cellar.

Jack shifts beneath me. "If I said yes, would you forget about your scheme to win back your fiancé?"

"What?"

He sits up. "You don't have to do all these list things to prove to him you aren't boring."

"I know," I say. I sit up too and try to wipe the dirt off my clothes. I smack a little more forcefully than necessary. It stings the newly forming bruises.

He lets out a long sigh. "I'll boost you up, then climb out after you."

"Thank you."

He starts walking the perimeter of the cellar. He taps at the walls and then looks up.

He turns to me. "Then why are you doing it?" he asks.

"Doing what? My list?"

He gives a sharp nod.

I pause and consider my answer. After a minute he comes and sits down next to me. I rest my elbows on my knees. "It's hard to explain," I finally say.

"Try me."

"Okay." I rub at a grass stain on my pants. "Have you ever

wanted something so much that you change who you are to get it?"

He shakes his head, like he doesn't understand.

I sigh. "When I was six, my mom had already had four husbands. She told me if I was good, if I was a little lady, this fifth dad would stick. I really wanted him to stick."

I rest my chin on my arms.

"I used to be a hellion. I was always rolling around in the dirt. Getting into trouble. When I met my father I had on a pink lace dress, and I was sparkly clean. I was so scared that I could only curtsy and say 'how do you do?'"

Jack leans back against the dirt wall. "Come here," he says. He pulls me next to me.

"Mr. Drake. That's my father. He was enchanted. He called me his little lady. From that moment on, I was terrified to be anything else. I put on that mask and never took it off. Until, finally, I didn't know what was underneath. I didn't know how to be me anymore."

He puts his arm over my shoulder and pulls me in tight.

"My father liked me that way. My teachers liked me that way. *Oh, what a treat. What a pleasure. Such a lady.* Even my mom liked me better that way. I met Shawn, he liked me that way. And by that time, I didn't know how to be any different."

I look up at the sky. There are little blue patches and wispy clouds showing through the trees.

"The mastectomy, the cancer, Shawn dumping me. It shattered the mask. So now, this list, it's me trying to figure out who I am without it. Do you see?"

He turns and draws his fingers down my face. "I see," he says. His fingers trail over my lips. His gaze catches on my mouth. I think...I think he's going to kiss me.

I stand up.

"Anyway. It's none of your business what I do or don't do with Shawn."

I turn from him and study the dirt walls. I hear him stand and walk behind me.

"True."

"And I'm not looking for you to give me a rebound relationship self-esteem boost. I told you that already. I don't need that."

"I understand." His voice is full of restrained tension. "But I'm going to say something while you're stuck down here and I don't care if it pisses you off."

I turn around in shock. I start to say something but he holds up a hand. I stop.

"You're so worried you don't know who you are. But it's clear to me," he says.

"Really?" I cross my arms over my chest. "After a few weeks?" My heart picks up speed and beats hard in my chest.

He swallows, and I watch his Adam's apple bob in his throat. "Really," he says.

He studies me. Looks me up and down. He's only a few feet away. Everywhere his eyes land, my body heats in response. Finally he comes back to my face.

"No matter what mask you wear, you're still you. Kind. Considerate. Funny. Mischievous. Brave. Beautiful. No mask can hide all that."

I shake my head. Deny it.

"Was it that fiancé who made you believe you aren't desirable?"

I wrap my arms tighter around myself.

"I'm adding to your list. Before I boost you out of here, I'm adding a number eleven."

"I don't want your pity kisses."

"For crying out loud. I'm not going to kiss you. No kisses. No screwing. Satisfied?"

No, my heart cries. I nod. "Fine. Feel free. Number eleven."

He takes a step forward. I take a step back.

He takes another step forward. I take another step back. I come against the dirt wall.

He bends down and grabs me behind the knees and my back. My stomach dips. He picks me up and cradles me in his arms. I'm pressed against his chest. I carefully loop my arms around his neck. My fingers brush the ends of his soft dark hair.

Maybe I did knock my head in the fall. I'm feeling dizzy. Like the world is tilting and everything is rearranging itself. As if suddenly, everything has been shaken up and flipped and now Jack and I are at the center. Of everything.

I shake my head to clear it. He pulls me closer and grins down at me. There's the spark of a challenge in his eyes.

He's going to kiss me. I just know it.

I tilt my chin up. My lips part a centimeter. They feel full and lush. I lick them. We're breathing at the same time. His chest rises and so does mine. Will he catch my breath with his mouth?

His hand starts a slow caress along my spine. He drags his hand in a slow, teasing circle up and down my back. A liquid warmth flows over me.

He gathers me close. Lifts my face to his. Our eyes meet. His gray to my blue. I'm lost in them.

We're posed there, in the dusty cellar, with a sunbeam dimly lighting the space. His skin looks like honey in the light. What if I licked it? I send my tongue over my lips again.

He lets out a low rumble. I feel the vibration deep in his chest. It spreads over me.

"What are you doing?" I ask.

"Number eleven," he says.

"Number eleven?" I can't remember what that means.

He blinks and his eyes clear. "Number eleven. Sweeping you off your feet."

He nods at me prone in his arms.

Oh. He picked me up. Swept me off my feet.

"Check," he says.

I smile up at him. But the smile is hiding something else. It's a slow dread flowing over me. Something in me actually wants him to sweep me off my feet. Not in play. But for real. Something inside me wants this man. Really, desperately wants him. That terrifies me. I'm only getting myself back now. I'm only seeing who I am these past few weeks. I can't give myself away again so soon.

He smiles down at me and I beam at him. I laugh to cover the fear rolling through me.

I don't want to love another man. I want to have adventures. I want to discover who I am.

He sets me gently on my feet.

"Who's ready for a swim?" I ask. The only thing to do is to go on as if nothing has changed. As if all I want is to finish my list.

Jack can't know.

I'd rather spend my life alone than lose myself wearing another mask trying to please a man.

22

JACK

J stand at the edge of the small inland lake and watch the setting sun. The water ripples reflect orange, gold and pink. The lake's going to be freezing. Hypothermia has never been on my bucket list, but hey, not my list.

I bend down and pull off my shoes. Then my socks.

"What are you doing?" Dany asks.

I unbuckle my belt and slide it from the loops.

Dany's eyes widen and red splotches pop up on her cheeks.

"Skinny dipping at sunset," I say. I push the buttons on my flannel one by one through their holes. She watches my hands as they work their way down. One button, then the next. Then my shirt hangs open. I'm bare to her.

"I'm skinny dipping. Not you. You, you..." She shakes her head and spins her finger in a circle. "You turn around."

I laugh and shrug off my shirt.

She makes a little choking sound.

"You alright?" I ask. "Didn't pencil neck ever strip for you?" I'm trying to goad her, but the mention of her ex sends a strange feeling through me. I don't like thinking of him and her together. Not one bit.

"We didn't..." She pauses and her face goes red again. "None of your business."

"Oh, right." I say, remembering her ex's outburst in the hospital. "Pencil neck blamed his inadequacies on you. Classic."

"We were waiting for marriage." She crosses her arms over her chest and scowls at me.

"He was incapable," I say.

"Just because we didn't pork the pie doesn't mean he couldn't get it up."

"Pork the...? Pork the what?" I start to laugh.

"Pork the pie." She scowls at me. "It's a phrase. It's a term for sex."

I can't stop laughing. "What are you talking about?"

"I'm talking about kinky sex," she says. She stamps her boot in the sand. "What are you talking about?"

"I'm talking about pie. I love pie."

"This isn't funny."

"Apple pie. Pumpkin pie. Pecan pie. Mmm. Peeecan pie."

She covers her face with her hands. "I'm not talking about this."

"Now I've heard of porking," I continue. "And I've heard of pie. But I'm not sure how they come together."

She peeks at me between her fingers. Then her eyes narrow and she throws up her hands. I'm still laughing, I can't help it.

"Peeecan pie."

Dany advances on me. She's spitting mad. Her finger pokes in my bare chest.

"That's enough," she says. "Just because you go porking pies all over the bakery—"

144

"What?" I laugh.

Her finger shoves into my chest again.

"And think that's the only way to achieve sexual satisfaction. By sprinkling your little pecans in every pie around—"

Her finger jams my pectoral muscle.

"Little?" I sputter.

"—around town. Well I have news for you. I've had more satisfaction than you can ever dream of, buddy. Slot A and Tab B are only two pieces of the recipe and if that's all that's in your mix, then I feel sorry for you. So...so, there."

She waves her hand in the air and gives me one final jab.

I stand and stare. Completely speechless.

Wow. *What a woman.*

She whips around and yanks her cardigan over her head. Then her tank top's gone. She has a little band around her chest. She tugs that over her head.

Her back's poker straight. She bends over, kicks off her boots and socks. Then she pulls down her wool slacks.

I let out a long breath. It hurts to let it out because I feel like I've been holding it my whole life. The curve of her back, how her hair brushes along her naked shoulders, the way her stomach curves in then flares out at her hips, and those dimples, those taunting dimples at the base of her spine...she's the most beautiful woman I've ever seen.

Her fingers settle at the top of her lace-trimmed panties. Everything around me, the castle ruin, the trees, the sunset, it all disappears. All I see are her fingers pulling at her panties.

Then she looks over her shoulder.

"Turn around," she says.

"Uhh...umm," I can't talk.

"Turn around, little pecan."

I huff in mock offense and turn my back. "I'll show you little. I'm coming in after you're in the water."

"Mmmhmm," she says.

I hear a splash. I whip around. Her panties are in the sand next to her clothes.

"Dang," I say.

Then she surfaces. Water drops run down her face. Her hair is wet and smooth. She shakes the water from her head.

"Oh, that's cold," she says.

My pants are off in a flash. I push them to the sand. Then dive in with a splash.

"Ahh!" she shrieks.

I come up and she splashes water at me. "You cretin. I'm trying to enjoy my sunset skinny dipping in p-p-peace."

Yeah, the water is what you'd expect from a lake in late springtime. Freezing.

I swim closer to her.

"Don't look," she says. She tries to cover herself with one arm while still treading water.

"At what?" I ask.

"You know what."

I make a grab for her, but she kicks out of the way. "I'm looking," I say.

She glares at me and I think I see the sheen of tears in her eyes.

Not okay.

"You're beautiful," I say.

She tries to swim away, but I grab her.

"Look at you," I say.

"Yeah, I've heard that line before."

Sure, it's what her ex said in the hospital.

"No. I mean *look at you.*"

The sun is dipping beneath the trees on the other side of the lake. The water shimmers like liquid gold. It shines over her, coating her in a warm, gleaming aura.

"Look," I say. I slowly draw my hand across her collarbone.

She looks down. All the water drops on her chest sparkle

like golden orbs. They glint in the setting light. Her shoulders are narrow and delicate. Her collarbone forms an elegant vee beneath the soft bend of her neck. Her chin dips as she looks at her chest. It rises and falls with her breath.

The raised scars are pink and red. Her flesh is mounded beneath it. The dying sun sends a cleansing light over her.

My fingers drift over her heart and circle there. It beats strong beneath the pads of my fingers. "Look at you," I say again.

She lets out a shuddering breath and a tear falls and drops into the lake.

"I see strong. I see brave. I see survivor. I don't see anything to hide," I say.

"Thank you," she whispers.

"You're welcome."

I lean forward. I'm going to kiss her. Even though I told her I wouldn't. And even though I told myself it was a bad idea to fall in love. It's too damn late.

"Jack," she breathes.

"Yeah," I say.

My mouth is an inch from hers. I want her so much.

Then there's a crashing sound from the shore. I jerk my head toward the sound and freeze. *No way.*

Then a man shouts, "Get your hands up. Get out of the lake with your hands up."

Dany shrieks and ducks under water. My hands spring into the air.

It's the police. There are two uniformed officers at the edge of the water.

Dany comes up from underwater and slowly raises her hands in the air.

"Come out of the water with your hands up. You folks are trespassing on private property."

"Oh nooo," says Dany.

"I thought you said you knew the owners," I say to her, out of the cops' hearing.

"I do. It's the Boremans'. I figured it was okay."

"Clearly not okay." Then the name sinks in. "What a minute. Your ex owns this property?"

I stop and look at her.

"Out of the water," the officer says.

"His parents." She grimaces.

We've reached the water's edge. There are two officers. One is older with an excellent gray handlebar mustache. The second is young with red hair and freckles. He's looking down at my manhood and smirking.

"It's cold," I say. I refuse to be embarrassed. That lake was like ice.

The redhead snorts. Handlebar shoots him a quelling look.

"Get dressed, son," the senior officer says.

Neither is looking at Dany. She's throwing on her clothes as quickly as possible.

"S-s-sorry," she says. "I know the owners. It's a a a mis-misunderstanding."

Both officers avert their eyes as she talks. Dang, she sounds cold.

I put on my clothes in hurry.

"The owners called and reported trespassers. We're going to have to take you both in."

"But I know the owners, it's not a a p-p-problem."

"Sorry, miss. We're just doing our job," says the redhead. He flushes cherry red when he looks at her.

They escort us to the cruiser, read us our rights, and duck us into the back seat. When the door slams shut, Dany closes her eyes. Her hands shake in her lap. *Not okay.* When in doubt, cheer her up.

"Remind me, was going to jail on your list?" I ask.

Dany's eyes open and she scowls at me.

"Check?" I wink.

A small smile appears, then it grows even bigger. Hallelujah. Job done. She'll be alright.

But still, it's going to be a long night.

23

Dany

$\mathcal{I}$ get up early to make amends. I run out for coffee and donuts. Chocolate filled long johns, cake donuts covered in cinnamon and sugar, apple fritters, and huge cups of blacker than black coffee. When Jack stumbles into the kitchen, bleary eyed with hair sticking up straight, I hold out the box of donuts as a peace offering.

"Would you care for a thank you, you're amazing, please don't hate me for getting you arrested donut?" I ask.

Jack rubs at his eyes and looks down at the offering. His lower lip forms a pout. "You didn't get sprinkles," he says.

I laugh and set the box on the kitchen table.

"Coffee?" I ask. "It tastes like diesel fuel scraped off a rusty lead pipe."

"Mmmm," he says. "I take it with sugar."

I open the sugar jar and measure a liberal spoonful into his cup.

"How was your night?" I ask. I stir the sugar into the coffee and breathe in the sweet, bitter scent. Then I hand the cup over.

I got home after a short visit at the station. The Boremans were adamant that they wouldn't be pressing charges against their favorite lady in Stanton. Mrs. Boreman even took me aside and told me it was her dearest hope that Shawn and I would patch things up soon. Such a misunderstanding, she'd said. I sigh.

"How's the coffee?" I ask.

Jack has his eyes closed and is taking a long drink. He pulls the cup away from his mouth and looks at me.

"I'd add jail cell toilet disinfectant to your description of its taste. Brings back the memories. Good times." He smiles and takes another gulp.

I didn't hear Jack come in until four in the morning. He must have had a different experience at the station than I did. Apparently, he made it to a cell. I wince at the thought.

"Sorry. Donut?"

He chooses the cinnamon and sugar cake donut. I grab the long john and take a fortifying bite. The chocolate and mass of sugar sends a wonderful jolt through me.

"Are they pressing charges?" I ask.

"No. Your ex wanted me to sweat it out a bit."

"Oh," I say. That sounds like Shawn. He never did like to share, even if what was being shared didn't belong to him.

"Did he say anything?"

Jack shrugs. He pops the last of the donut in his mouth and brushes the sugar from his hands. "The usual. Stay away from the girl. Blah blah blah. I have the world's thinnest wiener blah blah blah. I don't know how to please a woman and I feel so inadequate blah blah blah."

I laugh and roll my eyes. I'm not sure why Shawn cares, since he never contacted me since the kiss-off, but I like Jack's rendition of the confrontation.

Jack grabs the apple fritter.

"You know. Any time you want to get me to do something, lay a trail of donuts in front of me. I'll be all yours." He takes a big bite of the fritter. "That's good."

I sip my coffee and watch as he enjoys the sugar.

When he's done I gesture at the jeans and T-shirt I borrowed from Sissy.

"Well, I'm ready to uphold my end of the bargain. Put me to work, boss."

Jack has been tackling my list with me like a champ. It's time I helped him with his renovations.

"Alright," he says. He downs the rest of his coffee.

I stand and notice he's looking at me with a strange glint in his eyes. It reminds me of yesterday, the moments before we were picked up for trespassing.

"Um, about yesterday..." I say. I shake my head.

He raises his eyebrows.

Exactly. What about yesterday? I'm not sure, myself.

"I, um, appreciated it." I finish lamely.

Wow, Dany. Real stellar with words.

"Anytime," he says.

We stand in the kitchen. A round wooden table and the remnants of donuts between us. And a whole lot of stuff not being said. I would've kissed him if we hadn't been interrupted by the police. In fact, I may have done a whole lot more. I *wanted* to. That scares me.

Jack clears his throat. "I'll give you a tour around the place. Tell you all that I'm doing."

"Okay," I say perkily. Glad for the chance to get moving out of the pregnant tension in the kitchen.

We walk through the finished living room to the library. It's a small, cozy room with built-in bookshelves, wall sconces and a corner fireplace. The dark wood paneling needs polishing, and some of the shelves need replacing, but the room is charming.

There's also an unfinished half bath tiled in 1950s shell pink, a mud room, and Sissy's bedroom and en suite bath.

Next, Jack leads me to a covered porch off the back of the house. I stop at the doorway and hold my breath. It's stunning. I slowly run my finger down the trim. The velvet brown wood is carved with flowers and vines. The porch has thick wood floor planks and wood beams. There are two ceiling fans turning in the breeze. Two rocking chairs, a wood bench, and a low coffee table. A few empty ceramic pots line the wall.

"I didn't know this was here," I say.

Jack gives me a small smile.

"It's purposely hidden away. A sort of secret room. It opens to the back garden."

I walk through the porch and open the screen door to the back yard.

"Oh, wow," I say. "Wow." It's small, maybe a quarter acre. But it's the most beautiful little garden I've ever seen. I walk hesitantly over the grass.

Jack follows. "The garden is the reason I bought this place."

"Really? I thought you were into buildings."

He shrugs. "I am. I saw this place in winter. I knew I could renovate the house. But the garden. It was dead, or hibernating, brown and gray. But there was this anticipation."

"Like it was holding its breath," I say.

"I wanted to see what happened when it came to life again."

A queer feeling settles in me.

"What do you think? Did it meet your expectations?" I ask.

But I don't wait for an answer.

I walk over a gray stone path that winds through the yard. There's a low ground cover between the stones. It's sage green with tiny white star-shaped flowers. Rough barrel-sized boulders are strewn about the yard anchoring the landscape. Leaf green slender stems of lilies and irises bend in the shade. The spring bulbs are blooming. Grape and candy pink hyacinths, fat-headed red tulips, the last lingering creamy yellow daffodils. The herby ground cover is spongy soft under my feet. The garden smells like thyme, sweet blossoms, and sun-warmed soil. Something in the back corner catches my eye.

I weave past a miniature grove of flowering trees with a grassy mat underneath.

There's a thick trail of ivy. Hidden periwinkle blossoms peek out at me. In the center of the ivy stands a stone angel. She's maybe three feet high. Her wings are spread wide, ready to catch the wind and fly. She's glancing toward the sky, longing rapture on her face. The ivy binds her feet.

My chest tightens looking at her caught there, tied to the earth.

I prod at the vines tightly roped around her feet. Then I carefully pull the ivy away. After the clinging vines are cleared, I brush off the dirt. There. I feel better. The knot in my chest loosens.

I stand up and wipe the dirt from my hands. It's caked under my nails and in the creases of my palms. I shrug. When I turn, I see that Jack is watching me.

I ignore the searching look on his face.

"A lot of weeds back here," I say.

It's true. Amidst the blooming beauty of the flowers there are three times as many weeds, climbing and spreading and choking. Another year or two and they'll suffocate the flowers.

"Maybe you can help?" he asks.

I look at him in surprise. "I'm not a gardener," I say.

"Really? You looked like one just now."

Something inside me perks up. The one part of my child-hood home that I truly loved was the gardens. As a girl, I learned all the scientific names of the plants. I longed to go out and dig around in the dirt. There's something about the beauty and the mess that draws me.

"This project will take more than one gimpy amateur. But I'll do what I can." I smile at him.

"Good." He nods. "Good."

I feel like I'm doing something forbidden. Something wonderful.

I let my face open into the wide smile that I'm feeling inside. I'm giddy.

Maybe this is something I can be passionate about.

When I'm out of the ivy and back on the grass I spin in a circle. I let my arms hang wide and I spin and spin.

When I stop spinning the whole world's tilting. I sink to the cool herby ground cover.

"I'll clear out the weeds. They're masking the beauty," I say after the world stops spinning.

Jack settles down next to me and lies back.

"It exceeded them," he says.

"What?" I ask.

"The garden. You asked if it met my expectations. It exceeded them. There's more hidden in its depths than I realized."

My breath catches. "Are we speaking in metaphors again?"

Jack chuckles. He turns toward me and rests on his elbow. "I was going to kiss you yesterday," he says.

My stomach dips and the world tilts again.

He watches me, his eyes ask for my response. I lean my head back and look at the clouds drifting through the sky. Finally, I gather enough courage.

"I was going to let you," I say.

24

Dany

I glance over at his face. It's hard to take a breath. His face is smooth and expressionless, but his eyes, a storm is starting there.

He reaches out and runs a hand over my cheek.

I stay still and let him explore the line of my jaw and the curve of my lips.

"But we agree it was a bad idea," he says.

His thumb plays with my lower lip.

"Terrible. Terrible idea," I say.

His fingers trace over my lips and up my cheek. I suppress a shudder.

"Horrible," he says.

My lashes lower and brush against my skin. I turn my face into his palm. His warmth draws over me. I turn my gaze up to him. He's watching my lips.

They feel swollen and dry. I draw my tongue along them. He stops. Holds completely still.

I let out a shuddery breath.

The breeze ruffles over me, and I smell the crushed herbs beneath us. The soft chorus of morning crickets and birds fills the air.

I let out a sigh.

"I'd like you to kiss me," I say.

"Hell," he breathes.

Then, he rolls over. He puts one leg over me and his hands on either side of my head, until I'm caged beneath him. Cradled between the soft ground and his hard body.

He presses himself lower, until there's only a whisper separating us.

We're not touching, but I feel like we're touching everywhere. I only need to arch up, to shift the slightest amount, and we'll be connected.

His warm wood and leather scent tickles my nose. His eyes crinkle and he leans down until his nose touches mine. I warm at the contact. More. I tilt my face up. My bottom lip brushes against his. Heat pulses through me and I raise my hips toward him.

He growls and then catches my mouth in his.

He tugs on my lip, sucks it and plays with it. I grab his hair and try to pull him in closer. But he keeps his body taut above mine, refusing to press against me. I bite at his lip. He growls and pushes me back to the ground. I tilt my hips up again, catching a little throb as I rub against him. He's hard. Holy mackerel, he's hard. There. Goodness. *There.*

I drag myself against him and little sparks dance over me. I like that. No, I love that. He tastes like donuts, like apples, cinnamon and sugar and the word *yes*...

"Yes, yes. More." I whisper into his mouth.

A low humming in his throat vibrates through me. I open wider to him. His tongue darts over my lips and I take it in my mouth and suck. I draw it in and move my hips in time to the push of his tongue. I rub up against the long hard column of him. He hits me perfectly, in that spot that shoots fire through my veins.

"More," I say. "More."

"Yes. More," he agrees. He grabs my mouth again and swallows my pleas.

He begins to drive against me. The length of him, the friction of the zipper, the wetness of my panties. My god. He... he's...

"More," I cry.

The swell is building. I arch against him. There. *There.*

I grab his shoulders. Pull him to me.

He buries his face in my shoulder.

There.

I convulse up against him. Everything building in me shoots to *that spot* and then explodes.

Oh. Holy. Wow.

I hold on to him and ride the wave.

He's breathing raggedly.

My eyes fly open. Jack's looking down at me. His eyes are open and vulnerable and I see him. *I see him.*

Then I'm pulled out of it. That oneness. I hear the birds chirping and a lawn mower in the distance. I feel the spiky plants beneath my hips.

I collapse back to the earth. My heart beats frantically in my chest. My breath is ragged.

I blink and smile up at Jack.

He looks down at me, his pupils dilated, his expression dazed. Because I'm watching, I catch the exact moment he moves from wonder and openness to shuttered and closed off. I close my eyes and blink back any telling emotion and bury any telling words. Jack isn't here for a real relationship and neither am I.

Who would I become if I let myself fall in love with another man? I can't bear to put the mask back on. I grab at the grass. I can almost feel it growing. I can't cut myself down again. I won't. Not even for soul-shattering kisses. *Goodness*, I orgasmed from a kiss. I squeeze my eyes shut tighter. Don't want to open them.

He rolls off me and lies back on the ground.

I open my eyes when I'm certain that nothing in my face will give my feelings away.

"Dany..." starts Jack. He's going to give me the *it's not you, it's me* speech. I can tell by the tone. I don't want to hear it. I can't.

So, I'll treat this feeling, this something, like a weed and cut it down.

"Dany...I..." Yes, he's definitely about to give me another version of the *that was a mistake* talk.

I can't hear it, I can't.

"Well, that was pleasant," I say in a breezy tone. "Glad we got that out of the way. Thank you."

Jack coughs. Then shoots up. His brow furrows. "Pleasant?" he asks in a dangerous tone.

I shrug. "Sure." The feigned nonchalance is killing me. The look on his face...I take the weed, the feeling, and cut harder. Slash it out.

"Got it out of the way? So, what. Was that triple X? Just another check on your list?"

That cuts. I flinch. "No. Not at all. Like I said before, it wasn't a good idea. You agree, right?"

Say you don't, a small voice cries.

His jaw clenches. Then he closes his eyes. When he opens them, the funny, joking Jack is back. "Right. Can't let anything get in the way of our dreams. I've got my bid, you've got your list."

He agrees with me. So why does it hurt so much?

"I'm going to get to work if you don't mind," I say.

Jack stands. His hands clench and unclench. "Right," he

says. "Let me know if you need anything. The garden tools are in the shed."

"Okay." I nod. "Thanks."

I watch as he strides back to the house.

I stay sitting in the grass for a full five minutes. What the heck am I doing? I rub my hand over my face and lie down on my side. The angel mocks me from the ivy corner.

"What? Like you would've done differently," I call.

We both stare at the sky. Her in longing reflection. Me with the dawning horror that I could give my heart to this man, and I might not be able to stop it, even if I want to.

25

JACK

"So, this is what Jack Jones does all day," says Dany. I like her in her tight jeans, leather boots, and the Carhartt jacket she borrowed from Sissy. It's Dany, construction style.

"Yup. This is what I do all day," I say. I clear my throat awkwardly.

It's been a few days since the kiss.

An excruciating few days. She hasn't mentioned what happened in the garden, so neither have I.

But I keep thinking about it. Every time she comes into the same room I *think* about it. When I hear her working in the back garden I *think* about it.

At night, when I'm tossing and turning, I *think* about it.

All that thinking and not doing is making me cranky.

"Impressive," she says. "I never knew how much work went into this kind of thing. All the planning and organization, permits, codes, managing contractors. I mean, you have to do more and know more than any of the project managers at Drake International and I always thought their job was difficult."

We're on site at one of my projects. It's a 1950s Cape Cod that fell into disrepair. I purchased it because it's on the border of one of the neighborhoods I concentrate on. Downtown areas that have fallen on hard times but still house working families. I want to make sure the people in these communities have safe homes.

There are major foundation issues. I had a meeting with a structural engineer today about the repairs needed. Dany asked to come along. She said she wants to learn more about why I do this and see how she can help me with the committee.

"To uphold our bargain," she'd said. Which had me thinking again. About the kiss.

So, I brought her. Because she's right. I know she's right. None of this is about feelings. It's about her finishing her list, and me winning the Creston warehouses bid.

"How many houses have you rehabbed?" she asks.

We climb back into my truck. "This'll be my sixty-third," I say.

"Wow," she says. "That's...that's amazing."

"Thanks," I say. I smile over at her. We're cocooned in the small bubble of the truck's cab. Just me and Dany. *Dang.*

She reaches over and hesitantly puts her hand on my arm. A current jolts through me where her fingers press. I grit my teeth and try not to think about that kiss.

"I could tell how much you cared about making that house safe, not cutting any corners. Your dedication is amazing. I already knew you could make a house beautiful, but this...I was really...I was impressed."

I do this because I care, and I know that the end product will be making people's lives better. The fact that she's impressed, though, it fills me with glowing pride.

She pulls her hand away. I watch as she sets it in her lap, then twists her hands together. The air in the truck is thick with tension. The ease we had together before the kiss is gone. I need to do something to get it back.

"So..." I say. "Now you know."

She turns and looks at me. "Know what?"

"That I really know how to screw," I say. "My Phillips head gets lots of use."

"What?" Her eyes widen, she holds back a laugh, then she can't anymore. "No way," she laughs. "No way."

She punches my arm. I chuckle with her.

The tension's gone.

For now.

No more *thinking*. I turn on the engine and the radio starts to play a country music song.

"Can I change this?" she asks.

"Sure."

She twists the knob until it lands on a best hits from the eighties and nineties station.

"Do you want to see some of my finished houses?" I ask.

"I'd love to," she says.

I drive her through the neighborhoods that I work in and point out all the homes I've helped create. She likes the Edwardian style best. I try to take her by the houses I think she'll like the most. Every time her eyes light up at one of my rehabs, I get a jolt of pleasure.

"I liked the one with pink trim. Also, I can't believe you painted with pink," she says.

"It's a Victorian," I argue. "And it's salmon, not pink. It's an architecturally appropriate color."

"Uh huh," she says.

I shrug. "No worries. I'm solid in my masculinity."

She laughs again.

"One more," I say. I've thought of another home, one of my

favorites. I'm imagining the way her face will glow when she sees it.

I pull down Oxford Street and follow it down. "I've done a few houses on this road. But this one up ahead is my favorite."

I pull to a stop.

Dany lets out a short huff. "Wow. Just wow." She lifts her hand to the window. "It's gorgeous."

It's a small English-style cottage, it has an arched doorway, two round windows, and a brick chimney. But the best part is the stone fence and the overflowing English garden full of spring blooms.

"You did this?" she asks.

I shift in my seat, embarrassed at the awe in her voice.

She turns to me. "All this?"

I nod. "When I first saw it, it was falling down. It was marked as a tear down. But I couldn't let that happen. I saw the potential. It was a long road getting her here." I shrug. "That was quite a few years ago."

I sit in watchful silence as she takes it in. The garden is bursting with spring blooms, a riot of color that spills over the stone wall.

Finally, she turns to me, her face solemn.

"So, you specialize in taking on projects that no one else wants? Rehabbing the broken and unwanted?"

I nod, but it feels like a loaded question.

She gestures to herself. "Is that what this is? You see yourself as my rescuer?"

The pain on her face hits me in the gut.

"No," I say. "Not at all. Are you kidding?"

She won't look at me.

"You said I wasn't your pity project. But look at all this. I'm the human version of one of your houses," she says.

"No. Hey." I rub my knuckles down her cheek. "Dany."

She looks at me.

"You don't need fixing," I say.

She tilts her chin down. Swipes at her eyes.

"You don't need fixing," I say again. My hand lingers at her lower lip. I run my fingers over it and then use all my willpower to pull away.

She takes a breath, then. "Sorry, I got a little emotional. I'm fine now. Forget about it. Okay?"

I want to tell her again that she's perfect the way she is, but I don't think she wants to hear it.

"Okay, alright," I say.

And because I think she needs a change of topic..."I'll take you by the warehouses, show you my vision. Got to win my bid."

"Right. Exactly. You'll win your bid and I'll finish my list."

My gut clenches. I'm starting to dread that list, because when she's done with it, is that the end of us too?

"Yup," I say. "Sure."

I drive us to the warehouses and share my dreams.

26

Dany

"My hair is falling out," I say. I'm hooked up and receiving chemo. Everybody is here.

Sylvie puts down her knitting. Matilda and Gerry stop their conversation.

"Wait until your nails fall out. And the eyelashes," says Gerry.

"Humph," says Cleopatra. "It's called chemo. That's what happens."

"I know that," I say. Annoyed. Then I feel tears. I blink as hard as I can but they won't go away. They start to fall.

"What's wrong?" cries Matilda. "Oh no. Don't cry."

"She can cry if she wants," snaps Cleopatra.

"There there, dear," says Sylvie.

"I'm sorry," I say between hiccups. I sniff and wipe at the tears and my running nose. "I don't know what's wrong with me."

I swipe my hair back from the wetness on my face and another handful falls out.

"Oh!" I cry. I push at my hair and long strands stick to my hands.

This makes me cry even harder. I look down at my fallen hair and sob.

"S-so-sorry," I cry.

"Bah. Sorry is for losers and wusses," says Cleopatra.

I cry harder.

"Mine's been falling out, too," says Sylvie. "Not in big clumps like yours. More slowly. But I thought about collecting it and knitting a hat."

"A hat," cries Gerry.

I choke on a surprised laugh and start to cough.

"You've lost your marbles," says Cleopatra.

I beat on my chest and try to suck in air.

"Oh no, Dany, are you okay?" asks Matilda.

"Of course she's not. Hannibal Lecter over here just offered to sew her a hat from her own hair. What's wrong with you?" Cleopatra is in a real lather.

"Not her hair. My hair," says Sylvie. She throws her hands in the air.

"Excuse me. It wasn't Hannibal Lecter. I think you mean Buffalo Bill," says Matilda. "It was Steve's favorite movie. And Buffalo Bill sewed with skin, not hair." She shrugs.

Everyone is silent a moment. I stare at Matilda's apologetic expression.

Then Gerry turns on Sylvie. "Why in the world would Dany want to wear your hair? It's gray. It would make her look old. Dany has straw-colored hair. She doesn't want a geezer hat."

"Straw?" I ask.

"She doesn't want your creepy hair hat at all," says Cleopatra. She bangs on the side of her chair.

"The hat is for me," says Sylvie. She glares at Cleopatra, then at Gerry. "Me."

"Humph. Then don't offer it to Dany and then quick as a blink take the offer back. Rude." says Cleopatra. "Rude and off your rocker."

"What's wrong with a hair hat?" says Sylvie.

"Same as what's wrong with a skin suit, I'd say," offers Matilda.

I cough and beat at my chest until finally I can breathe again. Then I swipe at my eyes.

Everyone watches me. I look down at the shed hair on my cardigan and pants and a small bubble of laughter bursts from me.

"A hat?" I hoot. "A hat?"

Then Sylvie starts laughing and Gerry and Matilda and even Cleopatra join in.

Finally, we settle into short bursts of mirth and then a happy, comfortable silence.

"Thank you," I say. I smile at each of them.

Matilda reaches over and squeezes my hand.

She has a wrap around her head. Maybe she's started losing her hair too.

"I don't know why it hit me so hard." I twirl a strand. "Losing my hair feels worse than losing my breasts."

"That's because hair is a woman's identity. Her power," says Gerry.

I look at her in surprise.

"Really?" I ask.

Gerry nods. "That's why through history woman have covered their heads. Sometimes all day, every day. Sometimes only in holy places. A woman's hair is her source of strength, her power, her identity as a woman. Think of all that medieval erotica written about hair."

"Bah," says Cleopatra. "Ridiculous."

"If it falls out, does that mean I'm losing my power?" I ask. It feels that way. I feels...awful.

"No," cries Matilda.

"Of course not, dear," says Sylvie.

"Do *I* look powerless?" asks Cleopatra. She yanks off her knitted hat to reveal her gleaming head, covered with only the finest wisps of jet black fuzz.

"Well?" she asks.

I stare. Cleo doesn't look powerless. She looks like a five foot nothing, ninety pound giant that could whoop butt every day of the week from sunup to sundown.

"Well, do I?" she asks.

"No," I say. "Not at all."

"Humph," she says. But there is a small, satisfied curl to her lips. I've made her happy.

"Why don't we have a party?" asks Matilda.

"I'm not knitting a hair hat," says Cleo.

"No. A hair cutting party. We don't have to wait for it to thin or fall out in awful clumps. We can drink a ton of wine and shave it all off." Matilda's cheeks are glowing.

"That's wonderful, dear," says Sylvie. She takes a deep breath. "I'll do it."

"Me too," says Gerry. "I never pass on a party."

"You've all lost your marbles," says Cleopatra.

"But you'll come?" asks Matilda. She's so sweet, not even Cleopatra can resist.

"Humph," Cleo says, which this time means yes.

"I'll host," I say. "You can all come after chemo."

"Bah. I'm exhausted after chemo."

"Yes, but I don't want anyone backing out," I say. Now that I've settled on the idea of shaving my head, I don't want to lose my nerve.

27

Dany

our women stand before me bald as badgers. Their heads gleam in the kitchen light. Now it's my turn.

"Should I be this nervous?" I ask.

Matilda gently pushes me down into the kitchen chair and wraps a towel around my shoulders.

"Nerves are for losers and wusses," says Cleopatra.

I wink at her and she scowls back. Warmth fills my chest at the wonderful familiarity of that scowl.

Sylvie is in charge of the razor. It's an electric shaving device that we picked up at the drug store on the way over.

She comes toward me and the razor starts its low droning buzz. I swallow a mouthful of wine.

The room is delightfully fuzzy around the edges, with a happy muted glow. There's a pile of hair at my feet, all different shades. Sylvie's mahogany with streaks of steel gray. Matilda's honey brown. Cleopatra's jet black. Gerry's silver-tinged white.

My hair will soon join. I take a deep reinforcing breath and another swallow of wine.

Then I lift my wine glass. "To us. To bald heads and friendship."

"To friendship," says Matilda.

"To baldies and friends," says Gerry.

"Bah," says Cleopatra.

"To us," says Sylvie.

We all clink glasses. Well, except Sylvie. She's holding the razor.

I take a drink, then set my glass down.

The razor tickles as Sylvie runs it along my scalp. I watch as my straw-colored hair, wavy and fine, drifts to the floor. It circles and spins and floats. I'm mesmerized watching it fall away.

Matilda turns on music.

Heavy beats start pumping from her phone.

"You have got to be kidding," I say.

Matilda gives me a sweet, mischievous smile. Her hands come up in small fists and she starts pumping her arms in front of her. Her feet glide across the floor and she does the moonwalk.

This is one of my favorite eighties songs of all time. The heavy bass and drums are irresistible.

"Oh yeah," says Gerry. She's in a baby blue sequin velour tracksuit. She turns around, puts her hands on her hips, and starts to shake her behind.

"I'm not drunk enough for this," says Cleo.

Matilda dances up to her. "Come on, Cleo." She pumps her fists and circles around her.

Sylvie sings the lyrics in a high soprano. She runs the razor over my head and the last of my hair falls away. She whips off the towel and shakes it out. Hair flies over the room. Sylvie bends over and picks up the pile of hair and throws it in the air. It flies around us like confetti.

I start to laugh. Then sneeze. Then laugh.

Sylvie jumps up and down.

Matilda moonwalks past me.

Gerry bumps her swinging hips into Cleopatra.

"Humph," says Cleo. "Have it your way."

The girls stop as Cleopatra begins to dance.

Her mouth is pursed up. She's glaring at each one of us. Then her shoulders start to rise in time to the music. She puts a hand behind her head and bends her elbow back and forth. Her other arm she sends out and points around the room at each one of us. Her feet are tapping. Her hips are swinging. Then she breaks it down and she does...I don't know what she does...but she's dancing like I've never seen anyone dance before. She's a rock star.

There's no movement except Cleo and the falling hair.

Then we're released from our shock.

"Yeah, Cleo" says Gerry.

Matilda laughs and the girls begin to dance.

I sit in the chair watching. And I realize, this is it. I see my life before, and I see it now. Before, I'd never dance in front of people.

Now...

I'm not dancing in front of them, I'm dancing with them.

It's like my whole life has been building toward dancing to eighties music with the people I love.

I jump up and start rocking the Cabbage Patch.

We're kicking up hair, jumping around the kitchen like lunatics. I grab Matilda and we swing around in a circle. Gerry and Sylvie are doing the jitterbug, and Cleo is rocking down the house.

The kitchen is full of music, laughter, and I realize this is one of the happiest moments of my life. It wasn't on my list. It just popped up. Spontaneously. And I'm so grateful.

The music ends.

"You know what this means?" I ask.

"More wine?" says Gerry.

"Group hug," I say.

Cleo groans as I grab her, Matilda, Gerry, and Sylvie and pull them in.

"I love you guys," I say.

"Humph," says Cleo.

I burst out laughing.

Then, all that dancing and bouncing and wine and chemo... "I think I need to vomit. I'll be back."

After I do, I wash out my mouth and come out of the shell pink half bath near the kitchen. Matilda is waiting in the hall.

"Are you okay?" she asks.

She's wearing another of her fanciful cat T-shirts and black leggings. "I don't think I've ever been better," I say.

She nods and we sink down to the wood floor of the hallway and rest our backs against the wall.

I take her hand. She's skinnier than when I first saw her.

"Are you okay?" I ask.

She looks over at me and smiles. There is warmth and mischief in her eyes. "Oh, yes."

We sit against the wall in silence. Just holding hands.

"Is Steve alright with all this? Did he take it well?" I ask, wondering how Matilda's husband took her diagnosis. Surely not as badly as Shawn did. Was he more like Jack? Hmm, Jack.

"Oh, he was wonderful," says Matilda. She's quiet and her eyes go slightly unfocused. Too much wine. "He's the love of my life. Did I tell you we're going on our second honeymoon when all this is over?"

I'm staring at a crack in the opposite wall, tracing it up and up. "What? Oh, right. You did. I'm so happy for you."

She squeezes my hand.

I smile down the lump in my throat.

"It must feel amazing to have someone love you so much," I say.

"I'm glad you're my friend," she says. She rests her head on my shoulder. "Sometimes, life's worst moments bring the best..." She drifts off and I realize that she's crying.

I shake my head. "Don't cry," I say. "Don't cry."

"Humph," she mimics Cleopatra. "I can cry if I want to."

I laugh and squeeze her hand back. A warmth rushes through me.

"I'm glad you're my friend too," I say.

And I am. So glad. I can't imagine if I kept myself closed to them like I wanted to that first day of chemo. If I stayed closed up I wouldn't have my friends. I wouldn't have any of this.

Finally, I stretch my legs. I'm cramping up on the hardwood floor.

"Come on, let's go to the kitchen. We have to make sure Cleopatra doesn't murder Gerry." I pull up Matilda and we walk arm in arm back to the party.

Jack is seated at the kitchen table.

He's facing off against Gerry and Cleopatra. Even Sylvie has her arms folded across her chest. The tension is thick.

Oh no. It's a clash of my two worlds and it doesn't look like it's going well.

"What's your answer?" asks Gerry. She jabs her finger at Jack. I close my eyes, worried

I'm about to witness some carnage.

"We're waiting, punk," says Cleopatra.

Oh my gosh. What the heck happened in here? I was gone maybe five minutes.

I look at Matilda. She widens her eyes and shakes her head. She has no idea.

"Guys," I say, attempting peacemaker.

Sylvie shushes me.

"What?" I ask.

Jack looks at me and winks. I realize this is the first time he's seen me without my hair. Bald as a baby. He gives me a bedroom smile and it hits me down low deep in my belly. I bet he doesn't even realize he's doing it.

I shoot him a Cleopatra scowl.

"Come on already, Jackie-boy," says Gerry.

"I can visualize a niche market for the uniqueness of the product," says Jack.

What? What is he talking about? I look around the room in confusion.

Sylvie is nodding in agreement, while Gerry is shaking her head no.

Jack continues, "However, I would say that the return on investment would be too low to market human hair hats."

"I told you," says Cleo. She jumps up and does a quick chicken dance. "In your face."

"Phooey. I thought you were a nice young man," says Sylvie.

"Sylvie, you're off your rocker," says Cleo.

"Therefore," says Gerry, "by impartial judge, the hair goes in the garbage and not in Sylvie's knitting bag." She sweeps the cuttings up and tosses them in the kitchen trash.

"Oh, botheration," says Sylvie, but she's laughing good-naturedly.

I look at Jack with trepidation. What does he think of my friends? What can he think of their uniqueness?

He catches my eye and winks again. He's laughing. Not at them, but with them. With me.

At that moment, while I stand there bald and smiling, I realize that he likes me, even wants me, without my mask, just as I am. He doesn't see anything to fix. He thinks I'm perfect just as I am.

The realization crashes into me. I sit down hard at the table.

"Now the next question," says Gerry.

Jack winces. "Now, now, it's not right to ask a gentleman—"

"Where's a gentleman?" asks Cleo.

"Ouch, burn," Gerry says.

Jack laughs. "Alright," he says. "Although, you are all stunning and it's nearly impossible to choose..."

I realize that they've roped him into saying who looks best with a bald head. Goodness. Poor guy.

"As a big brother, if my sister is in the room, I'm obliged to say that she's the prettiest."

"Aww," says Sylvie.

I turn around. Sissy is wide-eyed at the entry to the kitchen.

"Humph, wily as a fox," says Cleo.

"Sissy," I call happily.

"Seriously, awesome," says Sissy as she takes in the empty bottles and the bits of hair.

"Who wants pizza?" asks Jack. "I'm ordering Jets."

And in one fell swoop, Jack has the entire room in love with him.

"He likes you," whispers Matilda.

I look at Jack from the corner of my eyes. He's watching me. I'm happy. Truly, truly happy.

"I want pepperoni and sausage, no, meat lovers, double cheese," I call. "I usually have salad pizza," I explain.

"Salad pizza?" gags Sissy. "Is that lettuce on a crust?"

I nod.

She fake gags again. "What's wrong with you?"

"Exactly," I say.

I pull up a seat for her at the table and she joins in the laughter.

I can feel the heat of Jack's gaze on me for the rest of the night.

28

JACK

Dany's held up her end of the bargain. She toured the Cape Cod site with me, saw my projects, went to the Creston warehouses.

For the past two weeks, she's even been weeding and cleaning out the garden. She's also helped sand, paint, and shared thoughts on design. She's done everything we agreed on.

I help with the list. She helps with the house, and eventually my bid.

I can't help but feel bitter about it. Her sticking to the letter of our agreement.

My mouth twists. Not once has she mentioned the kiss in the garden. Not once has she looked at me like she wants more.

I would've noticed. Because I can't stop looking at her.

Still, two weeks later, I'm thinking about it.

Pleasant. She said the kiss was *pleasant*.

I growl. I'll show her pleasant.

Then I let out a sigh and release the tension. She doesn't want pleasant. She doesn't want me. That, she made perfectly clear. I've been over this a thousand times.

It's funny, I'm terrified of what I feel around her. I don't want it. But I can't stop trying to get more of it.

She's twisting me up and she doesn't even know it.

I stalk into the kitchen.

She's there, washing a coffee mug at the sink. The morning sun shines yellow over her.

My stomach dives like it's in free fall. Ever since I met her I've been falling and I haven't hit the ground yet. I can only hope when my landing comes it isn't too hard.

She turns and the light catches her smile.

"Morning, you," she says.

Her smile hits me in the gut. Let's be honest, when I hit ground, the flipping impact could crush me.

I wince.

"What? Somebody's grumpy without his morning coffee. It's in the pot." She grabs a mug from the cupboard and holds it out to me.

She's in a sweet flowy flowered top and tight jeans. There's a hot pink baseball hat on her head and pink Converse on her feet. Her lips are glossy and lush.

Dang.

"Wake up, Jack," she says with a laugh.

This woman has no idea what she's doing to me. I grab for the mug and our fingers graze. Electricity shoots through me. Unbelievable. Down below is ready for a tumble from an innocent touch and a smile. What would she do if I grabbed her, pushed her against the sink and...

"I was wondering if you could teach me how to screw today?" she asks.

I drop the mug to the counter. It clatters on the marble. I

grab for it and steady it before it can shatter. My fingers shake as I right it.

"What did you say?" I ask.

She walks over and grabs my mug then fills it with steaming coffee and a spoonful of sugar. A jolt of pleasure shoots through me when I realize she remembers how I like my coffee.

I can't take my eyes off her. Any look, any more encouragement from her and I'll be on her, showing her *pleasant* all over again.

These past two weeks have been torture. Could it be that under her friendly exterior she's been...

I clear my throat.

"Tell me more...about, uh, about what you want," I say.

She presses the coffee into my hands. "Drink."

I take a long sip. The coffee burns on the way down.

"Well, ever since my first day here, I've wanted to screw," she says. She pulls a piece of paper from her pocket. "I've made a list of all the things I'd like you to do with me."

I hold back a groan. Dany and her lists. She's going to kill me.

"I'd like to see some steel erections," she begins.

"Yeah?" I ask. My voice is low.

"Oh yeah. I want you to teach me about butt-glazing and rim joists—"

Wait a second.

"—and weep holes and, oh baby, I've always wanted learn about tongue and groove and —"

She keeps going, throwing out more and more dirty. Her eyes look up at me from her list and they are lit with mischief.

Unbelievable.

"You little she-devil," I say.

She squeals as I grab for her.

She throws her list in the air and runs around to the other side of the kitchen table.

"You think you're pretty funny, don't you?" I ask.

The kitchen table separates us. I move one way, she moves the other. Like a game of cat and mouse.

"I think I'm hilarious," she says.

I fake lunge to the left. She darts to the right. I turn and grab her. She yelps and I pull her around. My hands loop over her arms.

"Hilarious?" I say.

"Yes." She starts laughing again. "Your face. You should've seen your face."

She collapses against me in a fit of laughter. A slow smile spreads first over my face, then I feel it all over me.

Based on her list, I think she's gathered the dirtiest, most innuendo-laden construction terms she could find.

This was payback for the Phillips head incident when she first came here. No doubt about it.

"Are we even?" I ask.

She pulls out of my arms. It's a shame, because I can't stop thinking about tongue and groove.

"You've been all Byron broody for weeks now. I was trying to lighten the mood."

"Did it work?" I ask.

"Not yet," she says.

I raise my eyebrows.

She smiles. "I'm doing number one today."

I scowl.

"Bungee jumping? I was hoping that was a joke."

"Oh, are you afraid of heights?"

"No." *Yes.*

"I could take Sissy if you are," she says.

Dang it. I've been falling for weeks anyway, may as well do it this way too.

29

Dany

$\mathcal{J}$ack and I are standing at the top of River Bridge. It's a long way down. I look over the edge and immediately regret it. Okay, maybe it was a bad idea to include this on my list. But I wanted to do something that the old Dany would never in a thousand years consider.

I squeeze my eyes shut tight.

"Still time to reconsider," says Jack.

"Not helping," I say.

"I'm going to have you re-grout the entire first floor bathroom for this. No mercy," he says.

I look over at him. I think Jack is really, actually afraid of heights. He's determinedly not looking at the edge of the bridge or the water below.

"Hey," I say. I walk over and put my hand on his arm.

He looks down at me and gives a weak smile.

"You don't have to do this."

He gives me a look, like he's disappointed in me. "Dany, Dany, Dany." He shakes his head.

I scoff. "What?"

"What's a little free fall if it's with you?" He winks at me and I warm. Just like that his bravado is back.

"You are such a B.S.er," I say.

He shrugs. My heart does a little flip.

"If we die...tell my parents I love them," I say.

Jack nods solemnly. "If we die...tell Sissy she can have the truck."

"If we die...tell the cancer, screw you, bee-atch."

He lets out a sharp laugh.

The operator walks over. "We're all set," he says. He has a grizzled face with black hair that sticks straight up from his head. It looks like its permanently blowing in a free fall wind. His name is Curtis, and as he said, he's been doing this for twenty-five years with no injuries, et cetera, et cetera.

Jack and I are strapped into our harnesses and the safety measures have been checked and double checked. We've been weighed, we viewed a safety video, and signed the waiver. We did everything we needed to do to prepare for this moment.

"When I call 'go,' you jump," says Curtis.

We're doing a tandem jump, which means Jack and I are jumping off a platform one hundred and sixty feet high —together.

The last few steps to the platform are really difficult. My feet start to drag.

Jack notices. He squeezes my hand. Then we both stand on the jumping platform and look down.

My stomach lurches.

I don't know that I can do this.

I shake my head and start to say something.

Jack turns to me, the devil in his expression. "If we die..." he says, "tell my Phillips head sorry he never got that screw."

"What?" I cry. Then I laugh and punch him on the arm. "You cretin."

But I feel better. He took away the fear.

We stand together, holding hands at the top of River Bridge. It hits me that I'm on top of the world. That my life has never been better. I have four amazing friends. I have Jack. I'm living my life in amazing ways and becoming someone I love. In a strange way, my life has never been better.

I can do this.

"Three, two, one, go," says Curtis.

At the same time, Jack and I dive off the platform.

I scream. In a fraction of a second, gravity kicks in and Jack and I are free falling.

He's whooping and I'm screaming. We're flying through the air together.

It only lasts a few seconds. But I feel so free, so alive, that the seconds are like an eternity. Then the cord stretches to the end. We're near the water, then we bounce up, then down, then up and down until we settle. And it's over. Just like that.

The adrenaline spike, my pounding heart and all the anxiety, it transforms into euphoria.

I hang there with Jack. Both of us breathe heavily while the boat chugs over. Curtis's assistant is on board ready to release us.

Our bodies are close. I think I can feel his thundering heart. I look at him and I can see that he's feeling the same awe I am. We did it. *We did it.*

Suddenly, I'm curious about something.

"If you had a list," I ask, "what would be on it?"

He closes his eyes, then, "I'd go up in a hot-air balloon. It's weird, I know, but that's what I'd do."

"What? Really? Why haven't you done that? There's a company in town."

He looks at me and shakes his head then says in a slow voice, "I'm. Afraid. Of. Heights."

I start to laugh, I can't help it. We're dangling upside down over a river after a bungee jump and Jack is admitting he's afraid of heights. He did this. For me.

When I stop laughing I notice him looking at me. Staring. Like a wolf who's starving. If I could I shift away in embarrassment, I would.

"What?" I say.

He doesn't answer.

"What is it?" I ask.

He brushes my hand with his. "I think, that even though we didn't die, I'm going to take you home and I'm going to strip you down and then I'm going to show you that tongue and groove you're so curious about."

I grin. Euphoria. It has to be the euphoria.

I love this. I never want it to end.

"Y'all ready?" the assistant shouts up.

Jack gives him a thumbs up.

Then the assistant releases us, takes us to shore and item number one on my list is complete.

In the small dirt parking lot, we wave goodbye to Curtis and his assistant as they pull away. We're in the middle of the woods, at the foot of a bridge. And now, we're all alone.

Jack holds the door to his truck open for me. Then, when I'm about to get in, he closes it.

I turn back to him.

He's still looking at me with the same expression as after the jump.

I'm still filled with that deep happiness and euphoria. He walks forward and presses me between the truck and his lean body.

I decide to step out on the ledge again. Maybe Jack and I can have something without masks, without me getting hurt?

"Did you know there's a secret item, hidden on my list?" I ask.

"Is there now?" He leans in and I catch his scent, the same as always, wood shavings, leather, man.

"I've always wanted to kiss in the woods," I say.

"Kiss?" he asks.

I nod.

Then he picks me up and stalks toward the tree line at the edge of the parking lot.

He carries me into the forest to a small grove of blue spruce. The air is full of sap and it smells like Christmas morning. He lays me down on the bed of dried pine needles. They crackle beneath me and poke through my shirt.

"Is this alright?" he asks as he kneels next to me.

I relax back to the ground and take in the moment. "Better than alright," I say.

He smiles. I gaze up into his gray eyes. This is right.

He pulls his shirt over his head. I reach up and run my hands over the lines of his chest and the firmness of his abs. His skin is hot against my fingers. He pulls in a sharp breath as I drift lower.

I drag my fingers over the button of his jeans.

He's so still that I wonder if he's still breathing. I look up. He's watching me with quiet awe.

It's almost too much. I pull my hand away.

"No," he says. He grabs my hand and holds it. Kisses each tip of my fingers. Each time his lips land on a fingertip, an effervescence shoots through my veins.

When he finishes with my pinkie, I pull my hand away and open his button. Draw down his fly. Then I push his jeans down over his hipbones, down his hips. Dark hair dusts his legs. I rub it and feel its coarseness. His maleness.

Jack kicks off his shoes and takes his jeans down the rest of the way.

He's naked, except for a pair of boxers.

I can't help myself. I run my hands over his legs, his stomach, his arms, I want to touch him everywhere. His muscular shoulders. The tapering of his chest to his hips. His strong legs. I'm drunk on the feel of him. Warmth spreads through me and grows, and the more I touch him, the more I never want to stop. He lies still while I explore him.

Finally, I look up. He's quiet and his eyes are questioning. Like he's asking me if all this is okay. If he's okay.

"Yes," I say. "Yes."

That's all it takes.

His stillness disappears. He lunges forward. Piles his clothes in a little bed under me, and spreads me out beneath him.

"My turn," he says.

I reach up to his face and draw my hand over his stubble. "For what?"

"Kisses. And tongue and groove," he says.

Then the torture begins. He circles his hands over an ankle. Slowly he traces my ankle bone and then shackles my leg as he draws off my shoe and my sock. He drags his calloused hand up my calf and then back down. When he grasps my ankle more firmly, I cry out for more.

"Shh," he shushes me.

I kick at him playfully. "Don't shush me, it's my list."

He chuckles. And then, the devil, he starts on my other ankle. Somehow, making the removing of my shoes the most erotic thing that I've ever felt. Until, he starts moving up. His hands climb up my legs, little sparks alight as he runs his hands up my calves, up the inside of my thighs. Up to the buttons of my jeans.

Then he stops.

"Don't stop," I say.

"Shh, this is the groove," he says.

I buck my hips up at him, "I'll show you groove."

But I stop arguing when he tugs up my shirt and starts running his lips over my belly. They're feather light and hot. His lips drift over my skin and brush against me, like a whisper.

Down. I want them down.

I grab at his hair and wrap my fingers in it. Then he begins to unbutton my jeans.

"Thank you," I say.

He laughs again. The devil.

The scratchy material of my jeans drawing down my legs sends electricity over me. He pulls my jeans off and sets them aside. Then he plays with the hem of my shirt.

A flash of fear shoots through me. He's seen my scars already, but...what if...

He pulls the shirt over my head and leaves me bare to him. I close my eyes tight.

"Hey," he says.

I turn my head to the side.

"Open your eyes," he says.

He coaxes my face back up. I open my eyes to him.

"That's better. If I'm going to do the tongue and groove, I want you to watch," he says. He smiles down at me.

And that's when I decide, with a hard pang, that I really, really do love this man.

30

*D*any's naked beneath me. And I, *dang*, I'm in heaven.
When we were free falling from that bridge, I realized that I've been fearing the fall, but there's nothing to be afraid of. There is no crash at the bottom. We made it. Dany and me. And it was amazing.

I've never wanted to make love to a woman so badly in my entire life.

She looks up at me and I see the world in her eyes. She's the bravest, funniest, most amazing person I've ever known.

I lean down and take her mouth.

I wonder if I could make her scream like she did when we were falling. Full throated and passionate.

I kiss her cheek. Along her brow. Down her neck to her collarbone. Her hands flutter and try to send me away from her chest.

"Don't," she says.

Embarrassed?

I growl and draw my lips along the scar.

She shudders beneath me.

"It shows me how brave you are. How strong. Why wouldn't I kiss it?"

I draw my lips over her and she sinks back to the ground beneath me. I pull my lips along her, graze her skin with my teeth. I run my hands along her rib cage and lower to the soft curve of her waist. She shudders. Then I hear a sniffle and realize that she's crying.

I life my head and give her a questioning look.

"It's okay, they're happy tears," she says.

I nod.

I understand.

I kiss each tear. They're salty on my tongue. I press my lips to hers.

Then, she sighs, and it's like she's been released from any worry or fear or hesitation she had. Her hands run along my shoulders and my back. They run over me and pull me lower to rest on top of her. My length against the heat of her. Only the fabric of my boxers and her panties separate us. The rest, our bare skin touches everywhere. And it feels so dang good. I tangle my feet with hers and rub against her.

"I get the groove, but where's the tongue?" she asks.

I laugh into her neck and nibble at her collarbone. Then I flip her over and pin her pert behind beneath me. She gasps and arches up against me. I'm this close to losing control and tearing off her panties. If she keeps rubbing up against me like that, I will.

"Shh," I say.

I rock against her and she lets out a low throaty moan.

Then I catch a glimpse of what I want.

"You have no idea," I say. I run my hands along her spine. Then I trace the path with my tongue. She lets out a long sigh.

"You have no idea how long I've been wanting to do this."

I circle my fingers in the dents at the base of her spine. Those teasing, taunting dimples. They've been haunting my dreams for weeks. I let my tongue circle in them, around them, until I've had my fill. And then finally, I draw her panties down her legs. She flips over beneath me. There's a whole world's happiness in her smile.

She grabs my boxers and pulls them down.

Now there's nothing separating us. I let out a long breath as I nudge her thighs apart and settle between her legs. I hold myself still at her entrance.

I feel like I'm there, standing on that bridge. We're together. I take both her hands in mine and lace our fingers. I watch her eyes, and then...I plunge.

We jump off. Together.

She cries out.

So do I.

It's heaven.

I'm falling and it's heaven.

She's holding me. I'm holding her. And I start to wonder, if maybe, just maybe, I don't ever have to land. If we can keep falling together. Then the world draws in, to this moment and this woman, and I cry out, *I love you*. Except, it's my heart that says it. Because I don't know yet how to say it out loud. Or even if I can.

She contracts beneath me and I ride on her wave until I'm giving her everything. I'm filled with wonder. For her.

When my heartbeat slows I sink down and roll her into my side.

I hear her sniffle. She's crying again.

"Happy tears?" I ask.

"Check," she says.

My heart stumbles to a stop and then slowly starts back up again. Check. I'd forgotten.

Check.

Number twelve, I guess. Or maybe, this was the triple X she had in mind. My euphoria vanishes. Gone as quickly as it came. Dany still has a beach wedding on her list and I have a strong premonition that I'm not the groom she envisions. I never was.

Still, I pull her closer, not wanting to let her go.

31

Dany

It's been a few days since Jack and I made the big leap. Literally. We haven't talked about it. Instead, I weed in the garden and help with painting and grouting. I'm not sure what he thinks about everything. I can't bring myself to ask.

I have a few more items on my list. And more than anything, I want to finish it. I want to see the Dany that I become.

I'm sitting on the back porch overlooking the garden when my phone chirps. It's my mother.

"Hello?" I answer.

She hasn't called much since the chemo began. It's alright though. Like I said, some people don't do well when confronted with their fears.

"Daniella, darling. How are you?"

I smile at her high voice. I guess I've missed her.

"I'm good. The chemo's going well. I'm happy, really happy."

There's a long awkward pause. I watch a bee drone by and land on the lilac bush. Finally, my mother speaks again.

"That's wonderful, darling. Absolutely wonderful. I've been so worried."

"You have?"

"Of course, darling." She sounds affronted. Then, "That's why I called. I spoke with Shawn. He loves you, darling. He wants you back."

I nearly drop the phone. My stomach rolls. Once, when I was little, a boy in my first grade class literally pulled the rug out from under me. One second, I was standing, the next, I was flying through the air, hitting the ground.

This feels like that moment.

The rug has been pulled out from under me.

I take a second to adjust to the jarring sensation.

"Darling, did you hear me? I spoke with Shawn."

"Shawn?" I swallow. Shawn. My fiancé. Ex-fiancé. My...what?

The man I desperately wanted to marry. Who I'd been determined to reconcile with. Who I love...loved?

I realize I'm holding the phone with a death grip. I loosen my fingers.

"Yes, of course. He wants to speak with you. He's sorry. Terribly sorry for what he did. The poor man cracked under the pressure, and now he realizes what a horrible mistake he made. He's absolutely in bits over it. Didn't I tell you this would happen? Didn't I?"

I let this sink in. "No, you didn't," I say.

The air feels hot and closed. I stand and walk out to the garden. I notice a cluster of weeds that I missed near the bleeding heart. The weeds are choking the flower's early blooms.

There's another pregnant pause from my mother. I walk over to the flower bed and fall to my knees.

"I don't know what to say," I tell her.

My mother gushes on, ignorant of my world upending, again. "I expected you to be ecstatic," she says. "He wants to talk with you as soon as possible. He loves you, darling. He wants the wedding. I told him it was poorly done, what he did to you. He knows. He regrets what he did and is wretched without you. He's sorry."

I look at the weeds. Take them in my hand. Start to pull. But, I can't...I don't...

"Darling?"

"Why?" I ask.

"Darling, this is what you want. Aren't you ecstatic? This is your dream. Everything you want. You can have your life back."

My hand clenches the thorny stem of a weed.

"All this will be over. This awful blip. You can put it behind you, darling. Isn't it wonderful?" Her voice is fading to a buzz.

This is what I wanted. It is. Was. Is.

I wanted Shawn back. I wanted my wedding. I believed he was the key to my surviving.

Suddenly, I'm confused. More confused than I've ever been. Because it doesn't feel true anymore.

I don't know what to do.

"I don't...I don't...I have chemo. And the list I made. I want to finish it." I'm groping for something, anything.

I wanted Shawn, and for years I loved him. Am I supposed to throw that away?

I think of Jack. His humor. His strength. His laugh. But Jack doesn't love me.

Shawn does. Right?

I yank the weed from the ground.

My mother sighs. "Oh, lordy, the list? You're still doing that? It's crazy, Daniella. It makes no sense. It's not you."

I throw the weed to the ground. There's red on the thorns. I turn my palm over. Blood from the prickers leaks across my hand.

"What if it is me?" I ask.

"It's not."

"Of course," I say reflexively. A tear tracks down my check. I don't know why I'm crying. I should be happy.

I grab another stem and pull the thorny weed. I toss it aside and wipe my stinging bloody hands on my pants.

"Darling, Shawn loves you."

"I know, Mother."

"You were engaged to be married. You were together for years. He made one tiny mistake. Can't you forgive him? Remember all the family Thanksgivings. The Sunday brunches. Remember when he took you on vacation to his family beach house? You were so happy."

I toss aside the weeds until the bleeding heart stands alone.

"Daniella. I'm your mother. Your happiness matters to me."

"Of course," I say. "Of course."

"And I know you, darling. You're my daughter. Shawn will make you happy. If you don't forgive past mistakes you'll live a lonesome and barren life. Alone. That I promise."

My heart squeezes into a tight little ball.

Will I?

Will I?

A voice whispers, *yes, you'll be all alone.* If I don't put back on my mask, my English rose persona, if I don't go back to that life, I won't have anyone or anything. I won't live. Survive.

I shake my head. Another tear runs down my cheek. I wipe at it.

I don't know what to believe. I haven't considered Shawn, or his place in my heart, for weeks. I pushed that hurt aside.

I've been thinking about someone else...

Jack doesn't love you, that voice inside whispers.

My stomach churns.

"I'm not the same person, Mother. I've changed. I'm not sure Shawn and I fit anymore," I say. What I really mean is, what if I can't put the mask back on?

"Don't be absurd. You're still my Daniella."

"Do you remember what I was like before you married Father?"

I think about the girl I was, the rough and tumble girl.

"Darling, what are you on about?" she asks.

"Never mind. It's nothing."

"Promise me, when he calls, you'll hear him out."

I sink into the grass, lay my head to the earth and stare at the delicate blossoms of the bleeding heart.

"I will," I say. "I promise."

"That's my Daniella. I knew I raised you to be a lady. To err is human, to forgive divine."

A tear falls to the grass.

"I have to go. I have chemo in an hour."

"Oh darling, shall I send Karl?"

A bone-deep weariness cloaks me. Suddenly, taking the bus sounds exhausting. "That would be appreciated. Thank you, Mother."

"Of course, darling. Anything for you."

I hang up and run my fingers through the grass of the garden. It's getting long. I'll tell Jack it needs to be mowed.

32

JACK

$\mathcal{I}$ sit at the kitchen table, Sissy across from me.

She's been suspended. Again.

"One more time. Explain this to me one more time." I say.

The principal warned that one more infraction and Sissy would be kicked out. He gave the barest details of the latest "incident."

Sissy rolls her eyes.

"Bro, seriously. It's not a big deal."

"It is a big deal. You realize, one more of these and they'll permanently expel you. Then, like it or not, you're going to boarding school."

"That's bull," she says.

"I don't get it. Are you testing me? Pushing me? What is the point in these suspensions?"

She folds her arms over her chest. Her mouth forms a mulish line.

"I get it, Sis. After my mom died I had to go live with Aunt

Flo. It wasn't easy for me either. I tested her, too." The tests didn't turn out well. In fact, I try not to think about the miserable years I spent with Aunt Flo. She blamed me for Mom's death and she wasn't shy about sharing it.

"No. Jeez. It has nothing to do with that. Also, Aunt Flo was a witch. Obviously. I could've told you that without ever meeting her. Her name. So accurate. But honestly, I'd rather have my period than spend a minute with that woman. I pity your kid self, bro."

I raise my eyebrows. But I can't argue. When Sissy's right, she's right.

"What then?" I ask.

"It wasn't right," she mumbles. She looks down at the kitchen table.

"The principal said you made a scene at prom. One worthy of suspension."

Red stains her cheeks.

"Yeah. Um...I may have...sort of...used the confetti cannon to shoot a hundred condoms at Bret."

I choke on my coffee. I cough and wheeze for a minute.

Then, "You did what? Why?"

"Turns out Bret was a douche. He told the whole school I was a slut and that he dumped me because I'm diseased...down there."

My fists clench, "I will kill Bart."

"Dude. It's Bret."

"I don't care. Bret is done."

"Nah. I took care of it, bro. I covered him in an avalanche of Trojans. The extra-small size. I'm a hero at school. I got voted student body president today." She tilts her head back and there's a wicked glint in her eye.

I start to laugh and I can't stop.

"How did you...how did you fit condoms in a confetti canon? Jeez, Sissy."

She blows on her nails. "I've got mad skills."

I shake my head, then somber.

"Sis. You can't keep breaking the rules."

"Yeah. I know," she says. "It's hard. All these rules. You realize I used to go to school on a computer in the back of a car, right? Most of my math practice came from running long cons with Dad."

I sigh. "Yeah. Good old Dad."

"It was okay," she says. She shrugs.

But I can see again how vulnerable she feels. That she needs me to be a better brother.

I look down.

"I'm going to do a not-so-subtle topic change to shift the attention off my suspension," she says.

"What?"

"I like Dany."

"Okay," I say slowly. This is not something I'm going to discuss with my sister.

"Don't mess it up because you have some weird hang-up over your crappy kidhood."

I think about how Dany and I haven't spoken about *us*, and how I can't seem to form the words of how much I care. How I love her.

"Drop it, Sis. Dany and I are just having fun."

"Right," she says. "And the condoms I confetti dropped over prom were really just party balloons."

I laugh. "Go on. Go study or something. I've got work to do. Stay out of trouble."

"Sure. Stay out of trouble is my middle name."

I scrub my hands over my eyes. I feel like I'm in over my head. The more I care, the more I feel certain that something will go wrong.

33

Dany

I don't mention the phone call to the girls. Nor the bungee jumping, nor the complications with Jack, or Shawn.

The girls are happy and laughing about the hair cutting party and Cleopatra's aptitude for dancing.

"Let's hear another story about David," says Matilda after they've all settled in.

"Bah. Not David," says Cleopatra.

"Oh, yes. It's been ages," agrees Sylvie. She picks up her knitting needles and starts work on the blanket. It has three different-colored rows of flowers now. Purple, red and yellow.

"Hmm, yes...David Crestwood. Where were we?" asks Gerry.

"He was shipwrecked in Russia," says Matilda. She leans forward with her hands folded in her lap. Eager as a kid in a kitten store. She has on a sweater with a cat talking on a telephone.

"Humph," says Cleopatra.

Gerry begins, "When I arrived in Leningrad—"

"Bah, if you've you were in Leningrad during the Cold War, I'll finally let that old coot Gregory take me to the dance hall."

"Ooh, who's Gregory?" asks Sylvie.

"No interruptions," says Matilda.

You can tell it hurt her to say it, because clearly she wants to know who Gregory is too.

Gerry continues. "As I was saying, when I disembarked, I immediately began asking the locals if they had any news of a shipwrecked American. I had a small picture of him. For weeks, I searched. I was followed and watched by officials. No one had any news. No one would speak to me."

"Because you weren't there and he doesn't exist," says Cleo.

Gerry shoots Cleopatra a stern glare. "Finally, when I was moments from giving up, a washer woman found me. She told me that a local crime lord took David prisoner and sold him to work in the diamond mines of Siberia. My hope restored, I hitchhiked a ride with a gypsy caravan traveling eastward."

"Bah, I can't take it. Fast forward to where you find him."

"No interruptions," says Matilda.

"Dear, you do realize that your story is stretching the bounds of credibility?" asks Sylvie.

Gerry sticks her tongue out and gives Cleopatra and Sylvie a raspberry. Then she smooths her sparkling, hot pink track suit and continues.

"After two months of travel adventures, which I will not relate..." She meaningfully looks at Cleopatra. "I arrived at the diamond mine. I dressed as an eccentric wealthy foreigner and asked for a tour. David was not there."

"Of course he wasn't," mumbles Cleo.

"He'd escaped. All the guards were talking of it. The American who had overpowered them and daringly led a rebellion. They believed he'd made his way to Finland."

"Did he?" asked Matilda.

"No," says Gerry. She closes her eyes. Her eyelids are coated in bright blue eye shadow.

"Then where did he go?" Matilda asks.

"China," says Gerry.

"China," breathes Matilda. "Steve and I always said we'd go to China."

Gerry smiles at Matilda.

The nurse comes in. Chemo is finished. I'm free to go.

"See you girls later," I say.

They say their goodbyes.

Even though I didn't talk about my troubles, I feel more centered.

I don't have to make any decisions right away.

I can work on my list and keep on with my life.

Shawn hasn't called.

I'll keep to my bargain with Jack.

Finish my list.

Survive.

34

JACK

I look up as the changing room door opens. We're doing another item on Dany's list.

"What do you think?" she asks.

She spins around in a little ballet move. I clear my throat as all the blood leaves my head and goes southward.

"It's good," I say. My voice is a low growl. "Good," I say again.

I've been losing sleep over this woman and she doesn't even realize it. This moment is going to haunt my dreams.

She's in a fluttery yellow dress. The front is held together by ribbons and the shoulder straps are tied in little bows. She looks like a present. For me. A present for me. I could tug in exactly three places and the dress would fall to the floor. Do women realize that ties and buttons are enticements to fuel men's imaginations?

"I'm getting it then," she says. She spins again and the dress poofs out. I catch a glimpse of lace underwear. I groan.

"Pardon?" she asks. She's wearing a floral head scarf and little hoop earrings. Wedge shoes. Lots of bracelets and color. She looks nothing like the prim and buttoned-up woman I met all those weeks ago.

But I still feel the same draw. No matter what she looks like. I still feel drawn to her.

I close my eyes. I know I'm fighting a losing battle. What am I going to do when she gets to the end of her list? It's like a big, glowing clock ticking over my head. A countdown to when I'm going to lose her. Except I don't even have her.

And I can't have her.

"What did you say?" she asks.

"I said you should get them all. They all looked good."

After she's bought half the store. I carry her shopping bags onto the street.

"Let's get lunch. I want to go back to Chet's," she says.

I flinch reactively. "No way. No more bar fights."

She laughs. "Kidding."

I shake my head.

"We could get street food. I've always wanted to—"

"Try street food." I finish for her.

"Am I that predictable?" she asks.

"Predictable?" I think of her surprise announcement outside my truck after bungee jumping. I swallow. "Never," I say. "You terrify me with how unpredictable you are."

"That's good," she says. "I wouldn't want to bore you."

Then she frowns. Suddenly, I can feel her sadness. It's a strong current below a deceptively smooth surface. I don't know how I missed it before. When did this happen? Why?

I curse Shawn. I remember as well as she does that he called her boring. It hurt her. A lot.

"It's not possible for you to bore me," I say.

She looks down at her shoes.

"You alright?" I ask. I nudge her with my elbow.

"When I finish my list..."

My throat tightens. That ticking clock threatens.

"When I finish my list, what if I go back to being who I was? I won't always be running around, being spontaneous. I might go back to being what I was. Back to being...I don't know." She shakes her head.

It's not only sadness. There's distance there. A chasm opening between us.

My shoulders tense. I want to reach out and shake her, grab her and pull her across the drop. Pull her to me.

Instead, I say, "Let's go to the kebab stand on the corner of Fifth and Main."

She looks at me. I feel my face burn under her scrutiny. I dropped it. I dropped the ball.

She tucks away the question. "That sounds amazing."

"Alright."

We walk down the street, our shoulders brushing, the back of our hands touching. I want to reach out, pull her around and kiss her. Tell her she never has to finish her list. That she can keep on being the Dany I know. That she doesn't ever have to be anything she doesn't want to.

That I love her.

Good lord, I love her.

I'm terrified of it.

Too scared to admit the truth. To myself or to her.

"Why do you like renovating buildings so much?" she asks, oblivious to my struggle.

I take a moment to pull myself back together. To wrap up those feelings and hide them down deep.

"Do you want my pat answer, or do you want the truth?" I ask.

She looks over at me and lowers her brows. "Why do you have a pat answer?"

"Because most people don't want to hear the truth. It's

uncomfortable. It's not really appropriate for every day."

Her mouth purses into a little pink peach.

"I get that. But I want the truth. You won't make me uncomfortable," she says.

I look down at the cracked gray sidewalk. Funny thing, I've never shared my true reasons with anyone.

It's harder to draw it out than I thought.

She reaches over and gently takes my arm. We start walking, moving forward together. The city moves around us, cars driving by, stores open, restaurants serving lunch. We're in our own bubble.

"When I was young, I lived with my mom on the west side of Stanton," I begin slowly.

"Across the tracks?" she asks.

"Yeah. We lived in the Redwood Development."

"Oh. Ohhh," she says. Her voice cracks.

I almost stop my story there. She knows what's coming. Everyone knows what happened at Redwood.

She doesn't press, she doesn't say anything more.

After a while I continue. "My mom worked three jobs. I didn't know my dad yet. I didn't know about Sissy. My mom. She..." I stop. This is hard to say. "She hated being a mom."

"No," says Dany.

"It's alright. I understand. She didn't hate me. She hated being a mom. I wasn't what she wanted. I made life hard."

"It's not your fault she had you," Dany says. She sounds angry in her defense of me. I smile.

"No, I got it. I was a hellion. I didn't help around the house. I wasn't good at being part of a family. As long as she had me around, she suffered."

"Is that what she said?" Dany asked.

I shake my head no. Not until the end. I just knew, like any child knows when their parent doesn't exactly want them. I'm not cut out for family life. That's always been clear.

"Anyway. When I was ten, my mom was upset that I wasn't pulling more weight around the house. She wanted me to stay home and clean up while she slept. Instead, I snuck out to bike around town and smoke the cigarettes I'd shoplifted."

Dany stays quiet. But she keeps holding my hand and pulling me forward.

"I was mad at her, so I stayed out longer than I should have. When I got back—" I choke on the word.

"It's alright. I know," she says.

Of course she knows. Everyone knows.

But I have to say it. It feels necessary to finally tell someone the truth.

"When I got back, the first building had already collapsed and the fire had spread to the rest of the complex. Fifty of the seventy-one people that died were already dead. My mom was on the pavement. I found her, choking on the smoke in her lungs."

"Oh no," says Dany.

"I begged her to be okay. For the first time in my life, I told her I loved her. With her dying breath she said, 'You did this. Your love is suffering.'"

Dany stops. When she looks up at me, there are tears in her eyes.

"That's horrible. She's wrong. That's wrong," she says.

"It's alright." I pretend to shrug it off. "My aunt took me in. It was fine. Now you know. I renovate buildings so families, poor or otherwise, never have to die because of shoddy building practices. I build so that a kid like me doesn't have to lose"—I clear my throat—"lose anyone he..."

"Loves," she says.

"Sure," I say.

A tear falls down her face. I lift my finger to wipe it away. When I do, I realize that I'm crying too.

Good god. I've never cried over the fire. Never. Not during. Not after. Not at the funeral. Never.

"Sorry," I say. I clear my throat and wipe at my face with the back of my hand. I choke the tears back.

"Don't," says Dany. She catches my hand in hers.

"What?" I ask.

"Don't. You can cry if you want," she says with a wistful smile. "Tears are truth."

Then she moves closer and wraps her arms around me. Her head rests over my heart.

I put my arms around her as well and we stand there in the afternoon sunlight in the middle of downtown Stanton holding each other.

After a minute she looks up. Her eyes are clear. I think mine are too.

"How about that kebab place?" she asks.

"I'm starving," I say. Glad that I don't have to talk more about the fire.

I wonder. Would Dany understand that her helping with the Rose Tower bid will finally allow me to get the absolution I need?

If I had come home earlier, I could've saved my mom. I've been making up for that mistake my whole life. If I can build this development, a safe home for working families, maybe my penance will finally be complete.

My shoulders relax.

We start to walk again, and I decide maybe I can tell Dany that I want more. Not a family. Not marriage. Not anything about love or feelings. Not yet. But more. We could continue on as we have been. Having fun, making love, living each day as it comes. So that what we're doing doesn't have a looming expiration date.

"Guess what?" she asks.

I stop. There's something in her voice. I turn. Her eyes are lit up.

"What?" I ask.

She smiles. "The doctor says I only need two more treatments of chemo. Then I'm in the clear."

"What? That's amazing." I whoop. Pick her up and swing her around. She laughs then beats at my chest.

"Put me down. Put me down."

I grin and set her on her feet. She beams up at me. This is the best news.

She's going to live. *Live.* I didn't realize until this moment how scared I was that she wouldn't.

"That's amazing," I say again. "We need more than kebabs. We need a celebration dinner. Champagne. Cake. Deep-fried Snicker balls. Whatever you want to—"

I cut off. There's a man hurrying toward us.

It's Shawn.

35

JACK

*W*hat could he want?

At my expression, Dany turns. Shawn waves her down.

"Daniella." He's out of breath and takes a second to compose himself. He pulls down the sleeves of his designer suit and straightens his tie. "Daniella, my word. Look at you. You look amazing."

She tilts her head and smiles at him. Her soft smile, directed at him, hits me in the gut.

I have an overwhelming urge to take her away. Throw her over my shoulder and run. Not hear what he has to say.

Then it's too late. He grabs her hands. She lets him.

"I'm so happy to see you. You look wonderful. You look amazing." He looks like he's about to pull Dany in for a hug.

"Hello, Shawn," she says. Her voice is breathy.

I don't like the way he's looking at her. Like he's starving and she's an all-you-can-eat buffet. He squeezes her hands and they look into each other's eyes.

Holy crap. They've forgotten I'm here.

I clear my throat.

Shawn's nose narrows as he shoots a glare my way.

"Look, Daniella. May I speak with you privately for a moment?"

"No," I say.

Dany frowns at me.

"Now?" she asks.

"Please. Only for a minute."

She's going to relent. I can tell.

"Okay. For a moment," she says.

I don't know why this makes me feel like hitting something. He was her fiancé. She needs to clear the air to move on. Let go of baggage. Tell pencil neck she doesn't want to see him again.

She turns to me. "I'll be right back."

I close my mouth in a tight line. I tell myself that she may be walking away with him but she's coming right back to me.

I watch as they have a short animated discussion a few doorways down. Shawn gestures widely. He looks unhappy and desperate. Dany shakes her head and steps back. Shawn grabs her hands. He gets down on his knees.

What the...?

Dany pulls him up. She's shaking her head again.

Then she says something that settles him down.

The hair on the back of my neck stands on end.

Finally, after a few minutes of heated conversation, Shawn gives Dany a kiss on her cheek.

My chest feels like it's about to explode.

Shawn quickly walks away without looking back. Which is good, because at that kiss I really wanted to knock his head against the brick wall.

I give Dany a minute. She's still leaning against the wall in the alcove. Finally, she heads back to me.

"Alright?" I ask.

She nods.

"Do you mind if we head back?" she says in a quiet voice. Her hands are trembling.

"No celebration? We were going to..." Then I can't avoid it any longer. "What did he say?" I ask.

"He proposed. Again. He wants to marry me. In Hawaii. On the beach. In two weeks—"

I stop. There's pounding in my ears. I don't know if she's still talking. She keeps walking. After five or six steps she realizes I'm not with her. She turns around.

"What?" she asks.

I shake my head.

She walks back to me, but she's careful not to touch me. Dread fills me. She doesn't get close enough to touch me. I reach out. She pulls back. The pounding in my ears gets louder.

"What did you say?" I ask. There's a tight clenching in my chest.

"Nothing." She won't look me in the eye.

"You said nothing? It looked to me like you were saying a lot." I realize my voice is getting louder.

"Well, you know..."

"I don't. That's why I'm asking. You told him no?" *Please say you told him no.*

She shakes her head. "No. Yes. No."

"What is no, yes, no?" I don't like the desperate feeling coursing through my veins. That countdown clock may have hit zero.

"I told him I need some time."

"Are you kidding?" I burst out.

She looks stunned. "No. I need to think."

"Why? He's an ass. He dumped you after a mastectomy. Do you remember what he said to you? If not, I do. I can reiterate."

Her face loses color. I'm immediately sorry I said it, but more than that I'm angry. And scared. Which makes me even more angry.

"You can't possibly consider his offer," I say. My throat is tight and hot. *Please tell me you won't consider his offer.*

"Why?" she asks.

"What?"

"Why not? Tell me why not." She's pushing me. I can tell.

I shake my head. "Because he's a jerk. Because you can't be yourself with him. He doesn't love you."

She steps toward me. "And you do?"

I'm speechless at the question blazing in her eyes. Then what she asks sinks in.

This is it. She threw the challenge between us. I can pick it up. Tell her I do love her. That I knew I loved her the second I first saw her.

But I can't. I don't know how to say the words. Get them past the fear.

"Do you?" she asks again, in a small voice.

The words are screaming in my chest, but I stay silent.

What if I tell her I love her and then she dies? What if she says...*you did this, your love if suffering?* What if she leaves? What if...

She steps forward. "What if I told you that I want to have kids? That someday I want to get married and have a big, huge family. I want to be surrounded by love. That all that is on my list. What would you say?"

She reaches out a hand. The question hangs in the air. *Will you do this with me?*

But the minute she mentioned kids, family, love, everything in me shuts down. I can only see all the families that died, the kids and babies and moms that burned, all of them lost.

I look down at my clenched hands. It's funny, when you tell someone the truth about yourself, they can use it against you. Did she know what mentioning family would do to me? Is that what opening up about my past comes down to?

"I don't do families. It's not on my list," I say.

The chasm I sensed before widens. She drops her hand.

"Even if it's with me?" she asks.

"I can't," I say.

"But why?"

The lump in my throat falls down into my chest. It burns an angry, hurting heat. Why is she pushing this?

"I see what this is," I say. I feel like the devil is pushing me forward. Hurt, it says, hurt. "You know you'll be better soon. All this will be in the past. You can forget about me. About the new you. You can go back to your nice cushy life. Like you always wanted. I was the rebound. I should've listened the first time you told me you didn't want a rebound relationship. Stupid me for not taking you seriously. Congratulations, you get to finish your list. Number ten, have a beach wedding. Check."

She doesn't contradict me. She doesn't say anything at all. She looks at me with a pale, sad face. The distance between us widens and I don't think I can do anything to stop it.

Then, because I'm a sucker for punishment and there's a cold misery spreading through me, I plead, "Don't consider his offer. Don't run from the life you're making. Don't."

"Why? Tell me why," she says.

She wants to hear me say I love her. She wants me to tell her that I'll marry her on the beach, that I'll give her a family. And I want to. I want to tell her. But I can't.

"Dany..." I shake my head. There's burning in the back of my eyes. "Can't we keep on like we are? Having fun. No complications? What's wrong with keeping things as they are?"

She sighs, a weary defeated sound. "I'm tired. I want to go rest," she says.

I stay quiet. Hoping this isn't the end.

She waits. Her expression growing more distant.

"Alright," I say. "Okay."

As we walk back to the truck, our steps heavy, she says in a small voice, "It's funny, you saying you don't do families."

"Why?" I ask, even though I don't want to know.

She shrugs. "Because you already have a family. One that loves you."

Sissy. I lower my head. Stare at the ground. Shame, that's what I feel. I haven't done right by Sissy either. I keep pushing her away.

We walk back to the truck in painful silence.

From the way Dany sits, and the expression on her face, I know we're done. It's all over.

When we get back to the house, she goes upstairs and shuts her door. I don't stop her.

36

Dany

$\mathcal{I}$ only have two more treatments left. This part of my life, the chemo, the list, all of it is coming to a close. I look at the women around me. Gerry with her lime green velour tracksuit. Cleopatra with her pinched, sour face. Sylvie with her knitting. Matilda with her sweet smile and love of horrible cat T-shirts. I'm so grateful for them all.

I wouldn't have done all that I have if it hadn't been for their support and inspiration. We'd been talking about going out for a celebration dinner. A girls' night out.

I decide to take a plunge and share what's happened with Shawn. I don't want to think about Jack.

"How do you all feel about a wedding in Hawaii?" I ask. I'd like to hear their thoughts.

I haven't responded to Shawn yet. I haven't talked to Jack either. On both fronts, there's been silence. Shawn, giving me time. Jack...I don't know.

It's been harder not speaking to Jack. I can hear him moving around the house. Brewing coffee. Sanding. Painting. Making a home. But it's been quiet too. It's as if I can feel his pain.

But it was his choice. He doesn't want me. Not even the new me. He doesn't want any of me. Not if it means commitment. Or love. And I won't accept that.

So, the silence.

Which is funny, because all the girls have gone silent too.

I clear my throat. "So, uh, Hawaii?"

They all start talking at once.

"Bah," says Cleopatra. But she is saying it in a happy way with a strange, pinched smile on her face.

"Oh, my dear, I'll have to finish your blanket right away," says Sylvie.

"I knew it, I knew it," says Gerry. She claps her hands and her neon plastic bracelets clink together.

Matilda reaches over and squeezes my hand. "That's so romantic. I told you he liked you."

"Oh. No. No, no, no," I say.

The laughing and excitement dies.

"No?" asks Matilda.

"I'm not marrying Jack," I say.

"Who else is there?" asks Gerry.

"Shawn," I say.

They all give a blank stare.

"Who the heck is Shawn?" whispers Gerry.

"My fiancé," I say.

"That wanker who gave you the cancer kiss-off?" says Cleo.

"You can't be serious," says Gerry.

"I am *not* giving that ogre my blanket," says Sylvie. She drops her needles.

"Oh, Dany. That's an awful idea," says Matilda.

I look around at each of them. I don't see understanding or sympathy, I see judgment.

"Have you gone off your rocker?" asks Cleopatra.

Gerry shakes her head and frowns at me.

Sylvie gives me a disapproving grandmother stare.

Matilda drops my hand. "What about Jack?" she says.

I look down and see the IV pumping chemo into me. It stings, feels cold.

"What *about* Jack?" I ask. My voice is laced with the hurt and anger I feel.

Matilda flinches back.

"Rude," says Cleo. She shakes her head at me.

I defend myself. "Jack doesn't want me. He only *wants* me when I'm a short-term item on a list. When I'm fun. He doesn't want *me*." My voice cracks. I hold my breath to stop from crying.

Sylvie lets out a long sigh. "Dear heart, just because Jack is being a nincompoop doesn't mean you should make bad decisions, too."

Gerry pipes in, "Getting married in Hawaii would be the stupidest, most chicken-shitted thing you could do."

"Humph, Hawaii's for losers and wusses," says Cleo.

I turn to Matilda, "Anything else to add?" I ask.

She runs her fingers over the iron-on cat on her shirt. "Do you think, maybe, you're afraid?"

I shake my head in denial. What is she talking about?

"It's safe going by a list—"

"I went bungee jumping, and got in a bar fight and—"

"But when did you risk your heart?" she asks.

"I was learning to love myself," I cry. And I risked it with Jack, didn't I?

She shakes her head no. It feels like betrayal. Matilda has always been my closest friend in this group.

"You said you used to hide behind a mask. This list was another one. More fun. But still a mask. Not once have you risked letting someone see you. Love you just as you are. You haven't even let yourself," says Matilda.

She's so petite, a tiny, gentle, unassuming person. Except, she just packed a punch. It hit hard.

"She's right, dear," says Sylvie.

I look at her in shock. They're turning on me.

I fight at the tears clawing up my throat. It's really important that I don't cry. I don't want them to see me cry.

"I thought you were my friends," I say.

"We are," says Gerry.

I shake my head. "No. You're not. Friends wouldn't do this. You're just four women, who happen to be stuck in this god-awful crap hole at same time as me. We were all just unfortunate enough to get cancer and be trapped here together."

There's a bitter, astringent smell in the air. I hate it.

"Now, dear," says Sylvie.

"That's not fair," says Matilda.

Over the sound system that awful eighties love ballad begins to play. Again. I hate this song. Loathe it. Something in me snaps.

"Do you know what's not fair?" I point my finger at Matilda.

She shakes her head warily.

"That you have the perfect husband. The most perfect Steve who dances with you in the kitchen and loves you just as you are and wants to take you on a second honeymoon. You don't have to risk anything, because everything is perfect for you. Life must be easy for you, Matilda, knowing your husband will always be there."

"That's enough, Dany," says Sylvie. Her tone is stern.

I ignore her. "You're always so happy. You think everything is so romantic. How nice. Matilda and her perfect love life. It's not the chemo making me nauseous. It's you. You and Steve."

"Be quiet," says Gerry.

"Don't tell me what to do. Admit it. She can't say anything because there's no risk in loving a paragon like Steve. And he must be, to stay with a wife who only wears cat T-shirts. Am I right?"

Matilda has her head down. She won't look at me.

Suddenly, I feel awful. Sick to my stomach.

"Apologize, dear," says Sylvie.

I look up and see her censure. My heart feels small and cold. "You, Sylvie, are a fraud, too. You act like a sweet grandma, always knitting presents for grandbabies. But you never go and see them, and they never come see you. Maybe it's because they don't like you. Because in real life you're awful."

"Rude," says Cleo. "Don't make me get up and whoop you."

I laugh. "Can't. We're all penned down with IVs. You say you found love with yourself, but then, why is it you look so sour and unhappy all the time?"

The room has gone silent. They're all watching me like I've completely lost it. I don't care. I turn to Gerry.

She starts in, "You're being horrid. Also, if you get married in Hawaii to that slug, I will fly there and make hell—"

"Oh, right, because you travel around the world on great adventures. How'd that work out with David? It didn't, right? Because he's not real. And if he were, he didn't sail away to make a fortune. He sailed away to get away from you. Which is why he never ever came back."

I stop talking. And that's when I realize how it feels after a bomb has been detonated. There's the explosion, the wreckage, and the silence when everyone's ears are bleeding and they can't believe what happened.

It feels like that.

I want to rip this IV out of me. I need to get away. I have to get away.

"I think next time you're here, dear, you'll feel sorry for what you've said," says Sylvie.

I shake my head. I close my heart to them.

"I only have one more treatment. Maybe that's why you

don't want to see me get married in Hawaii. Because just like Jack, none of you want me to move on. You'd rather I be stuck in a cancer chair like you than move on and be happy," I say, adding one last bomb to the wreckage.

Matilda sniffs and wipes at her eyes. She looks at me, her face pale.

Matilda speaks. "One thing. It's important for me to say. Life isn't always easy. Not for anyone. But I'd rather be happy than bitter. I'd rather laugh than cry. And yes, I'd rather dance through life, with Steve or without him, than do anything else. That's all."

Nothing more is said.

37

JACK

I've been in a foul mood for days. Dany's avoiding me. Sissy's in a funk. I don't know how to fix any of this. And that wedding date in Hawaii looms like a descending blade at the butcher's block. Has she told him yes yet?

But why? Why would she?

There's a knock at the door.

I answer it and nearly shut it again.

"I'd like a word," says Shawn.

"Dany's not here," I say.

"I know. She's at chemo. Look, I came to speak with you."

Why? I hold the door open and lead Shawn to the library. It's still under construction, but I don't want him in my living room and I sure as hell don't want him in the kitchen where I have so many memories with Dany.

He sits on a low wooden bench. I stay standing.

"Shoot," I say.

Shawn stands up. He paces the length of the library, his wingtips clicking on the floor. Finally, he stops in front of me.

"I don't know what you have with Daniella," he says. He gives me a searching look. I don't let my face give anything away.

He continues, "Look. I'm asking you to let her go. We had a hard go of it. But she loves me, and I love her. As a man, I'm telling you I made a mistake. I'd like you to step aside so that Daniella and I can go back to the way things were."

He stops talking. I consider him. He's in another designer suit. His hair is perfect. His shoes are shiny. He looks like the perfect match to the woman Dany was. She would fit him perfectly in her pink cardigan, pearls, and pencil skirts.

I imagine them having a family together. Spotlessly clean kids in khaki pants and polo shirts. Is that what she wants?

Shawn watches me closely. "She had a crisis. Her mother says she did a few crazy things to get through it. But now it's over and I'd like her to move on," says Shawn.

There's only one question I need an answer to.

"Did she say yes?" I ask.

"She will," he says. Confident. "Look, Daniella and I want the same things. I'm asking you, man to man, step back. She needs to move past this." He looks around the room, it's dirty and covered in sawdust. His face pinches into a frown. His nose narrow. "You can't give her what she needs."

Although he's talking about the state of my home, maybe my finances, he hits the nail on the head. Dany needs a family. A man who can tell her he loves her.

"You're right," I say.

He smiles and puts out his hand to shake.

I don't take it.

I may not be the man she needs, but that's her decision to make, not Shawn's.

"But the Dany I know is fully capable of making her own decisions."

His face screws up and he drops his hand.

"I thought it might come to this," he says.

"Alright," I say. I'd like to escort him to the door.

"I hear you're interested in developing the Creston property," he says.

I don't like his tone. Or the fact that he has that information.

I remain silent.

He smiles and nods. "If you keep on your current course with Daniella, I will make the project die a long, drawn-out death. Then I will make sure you never win a development bid in this city again."

"I'd like you to leave," I say. Cold rage is burning through me.

"Look, Jones. You're not good for her. I am. Trust me, I'll do anything to clear the way for her well-being."

He smiles a shark smile and shows himself out.

The door bangs behind him.

"Don't let the door hit your ass on the way out," says a voice from the living room.

I turn and see Sissy standing in the hall.

"What did you hear?" I ask.

"Oh, only just a little...basically everything. Male posturing, douchebag tactics, business blackmail." She ticks the items off on her fingers.

She smiles at me and flops down on the couch.

"What happened with Dany?" she asks.

I shrug and sit next to her. "Dany makes her own choices," I say.

"Seriously, bro. It's like you're a women's liberty champion. Proud of you." She punches me on the arm.

I roll my eyes and lean my head back on the couch. Moroseness settles over me. Sissy leaves.

After a while, I fall asleep.

None of it matters. Dany will be on her way to Hawaii in less than two weeks.

~

J wake to my phone vibrating in my pocket. It's after eleven at night.

"Hello?" I answer.

"Really, Jones? Sending a girl to do a man's job?"

"Who is this?" I ask.

There's a long, drawn-out sigh on the other end. "I caught your sister breaking and entering. I'm going to call the police and have her arrested unless you show in ten minutes."

My sleep-fogged brain is not catching up. "Who the hell is this? Where's Sissy?" I ask.

"It's Shawn Boreman. Remember? We spoke earlier today. Sissy, your brother is not the most intellectually astute."

I hear an angry response in the background.

"You have ten minutes to come to Boreman Group Headquarters on Second Avenue, or I'm calling the police."

"I'll be there." I'm wide awake now.

I drive over the speed limit, rushing to downtown. What has Sissy done? I clench the steering wheel. God only knows, the little con artist.

I pull into a parallel parking spot and then rush to the office building. The lights are on. I see Shawn at a desk. He buzzes me in.

I yank open the door.

"Where is she?" I ask. I don't know if I'm angrier at Shawn or Sissy.

Shawn points. Sissy sits in an office chair. She scowls at Shawn.

"Someone tell me what's going on," I say.

"Oh, so you really didn't sanction this act?" asks Shawn.

I fold my arms over my chest.

"Sissy, tell me," I say.

She lifts her chin.

"Tell him. Or I will," says Shawn.

"Fine. I broke in —"

"You broke in?"

"The alarm system was amateur. What do you expect?"

I have no response to that. None.

Shawn waves his hand in the air, gesturing for her to continue.

"I lock picked the head office and went through the filing cabinets. I was looking for why the douchewad cares about the Creston property. Also, that whole thing has been shady from the beginning."

I look over at Shawn. He shrugs.

"He's in the second stage of approval for a boutique mall and a parking garage," she says. Then she stands. "He wants to take you down because he doesn't care about affordable housing. All he cares about is parking for his shopping malls."

I don't like the condescending smirk on Shawn's face. I keep a cool head.

"What do you want?" I ask him.

"Jack, did you hear me? He's killing your project for a parking garage," says Sissy.

"I don't want anything right now. Perhaps in the future. Please remove your sister from my place of business," he says.

It's hard for me to contain my anger. He doesn't want anything *right now*. How is he going to use this? Hold this over me?

"Come on, Sissy," I say.

"But it's bull," says Sissy.

"Let's go," I say.

"But, Jack..."

"Miss Sissy. If you prefer, I can call the police. I'm sure you'd enjoy your stay in juvenile detention. Or perhaps a military boarding school? Would your brother like that?" asks Shawn.

I look over at Sissy. The second Shawn mentioned boarding school I sensed a change. Sissy sits poker straight and refuses to look at me.

She knows, this is my opportunity to send her away. To not have to face the pain of opening myself to her.

Sissy sniffs. She's crying.

Finally, she looks up at me.

"I was trying to help you. I wanted you to have everything you wanted," she says.

"It's alright," I say.

I recognize the truth. Dany was right. Sissy's my family. She always will be. She's more important than protecting myself. Sending her away will hurt her more than keeping her with me. This moment, where I can show Sissy that I care about her more than my own backside, it won't come again.

I lost my chance with Dany, but I've got a chance here with my sister, and I'm not going to let her down.

"Come on, Sis," I say.

I walk over and hold out my hand.

Her bottom lip trembles.

"You're not letting him call the police?" she asks.

I scoff, "Are you kidding? Like I'd unleash you on military school. Can you imagine the fallout?"

She looks at me in shock.

"You're stuck with me. No boarding school. We're family," I say.

I grin as Sissy takes my hand.

We walk out of the Boreman headquarters, shoulders back.

"Don't ever do anything like that again," I say.

"I won't," says Sissy. "Thanks, Jack. Love you, bro. Seriously."

My chest clenches.

"I know."

38

Dany

*W*hen I lie down the sky is ugly gray and full of rain clouds. I stay inside my bedroom, buried under a stack of heavy blankets. I don't remember the food I ate or what I did. Three days later, when I come up from the dark funk I descended into, it's still raining.

I go to the bathroom and catch my reflection in the mirror.

I stop and stare at myself. I don't recognize me. There's no Dany there. I touch the dark hollows under my eyes and the sharp, too-skinny jut of my cheekbones.

I've lost Jack. I've lost my friends. And I realize Matilda was right. I'd never found me.

I stare at the blank-eyed woman in the mirror. She terrifies me. Who would love her?

A ringing chime sounds from the nightstand by my bed.

It's my phone.

I walk to the table. The caller ID says Sylvie.

I close my eyes and almost don't answer. But on an impulse I do.

"Hi Sylvie," I say.

"Dany, dear," she says.

Then she starts to cry.

"What is it?" I ask.

"Dany, we've been calling and texting. Where are you?"

"I'm at home," I say. Why is she so worked up? I look at my phone display. Sixteen missed calls. Twenty-three text messages.

"Sweetheart," she says.

My skin runs cold. I don't like the note in her voice.

"No," I say. I don't want to hear whatever it is she has to say. I don't need to know what the sixteen calls and twenty-three texts are about. I don't want to know. "No."

"Sweetheart. It's Matilda."

"No," I cry. I fall to my knees. They crack against the wood floor. A low keening noise rises from my throat. "No."

"Dear, I'm sorry. Matilda's dead."

I'm shaking my head back and forth. It's not true. It's not.

"That's not true," I say. Matilda was getting better. She was going on a second honeymoon with Steve. *She was.*

"I'm sorry," says Sylvie.

"No," I say again.

"She died in her sleep three nights ago."

That was after chemo. After all the things I said to her. All the horrible, ugly, awful things I said. That I can never take back. God, what did I say? What did I say to her? I let out another cry. Something inside me cracks. Like an egg smashed against the side of the bowl. A sob crashes out of me, ugly and pained.

"Oh, sweetheart," says Sylvie.

"No," I say again. "I don't want to. I don't want to." I don't know what I'm saying. It doesn't make sense. I'm on my knees.

Like I'm praying. I'd pray on my knees for months straight if I could go back in time. If I could just take it back. I want to take it back. What did I say? What did I say to her?

"Her funeral is tomorrow. At the Grace Funeral Chapel. The service is at one. We'll all be there."

My sob is muffled now.

I'm lying on my side on the floor.

"Matilda would want you to come," says Sylvie.

I swallow. My throat is raw and sore.

I'm numb now. There's no feeling left inside. It all fell out when I cracked open.

What had I said to her? She died with my horrible words in her ears. I am an awful, horrible, awful person.

"Are you okay, dear? You'll be there?"

"Yes," I say. I don't know to which. Neither? Both?

"Okay, then. See you tomorrow."

Sylvie disconnects. I keep the phone pressed to my ear, listening to the silence. The dead tone. Tears fall down my face, but I don't feel them. I don't feel anything.

There's a knock at my door. "Dany. Are you okay? I heard crying. Are you alright?"

It's Jack. He's worried, I can tell, but I feel nothing.

"Dany?"

I squeeze my eyes tight and tears fall out. I can't see him. All my masks are off, and I see who I am. It's ugly. Scared, judgmental, prideful. I can't...I don't want him to see me.

"Go away," I call.

"Do you need anything? Can I do anything?" His voice is worried and kind.

I don't deserve kind.

"Please. Go away."

I listen. After minutes of silence he turns and walks away.

I lie on the ground for the rest of the night. Not moving. Not sleeping. Not thinking. Alone. In the dark. Just. There.

39

Dany

*M*y mother comes in the morning. Jack called her because he was worried. My mother cuddles me, showers me, dresses me and pops me into the back seat of the Jaguar. She gives Karl directions and in no time at all we're at the funeral chapel.

"Darling, you don't have to go in," she says.

I haven't spoken since she found me. I've only nodded yes or no. I'm afraid if I speak, either I'll cry or more ugliness will come out.

She reaches her hand to touch my face and I flinch back.

"Right," she says. "Well, at least we look fabulous. Never say I didn't raise you to be a lady."

I'd like to say otherwise, but I don't. She takes in my expression and sighs.

"Darling. Please. Be happy. It's always been my greatest desire. I want you to be happy."

I look down at my hands.

Karl comes round and opens the back door. My mother climbs out and I follow. We're in black from head to toe. Black silk funeral scarves and black hats. Black.

"Miss," Karl says. He tips his hat.

I walk into the chapel.

It's the smell that hits first. The pungent odor of embalming fluid and lilies. My stomach churns. Why do funerals have to smell sweet? That sickly, unnatural sweet?

"Do you know those ladies?" my mother asks. She's gesturing to Gerry, Sylvie and Cleo. Sylvie is discreetly waving to me from the front row of chairs by...I block out the word, then force myself to think it, by Matilda's coffin.

"Darling, would you like to sit with them?" she asks.

No. Yes. I don't know. The last time I saw them wasn't my best moment.

The hushed whispers around the room are starting to aggravate me. Someone comes into the chapel behind us. I turn. It's Jack.

He pauses when he sees me.

He clears his throat. "I came to pay my respects," he says.

I nod. I can't do this with him. I turn and drag my mother to the front row.

She walks next to me gracefully, nodding politely at a cluster of people as we pass. I've never been more grateful for my socially conscious mother in my entire life.

I slide into the seat next to Sylvie. Gerry is next to her, then Cleo at the end. My mother sinks down next to me.

There's a board with pictures of Matilda. Images of her as a child. Of her at her wedding. Of her in one of her awful cat T-shirts. There are flowers behind the baby blue coffin. Then, finally, I bring my eyes to where I'd been avoiding looking.

Her body is done up, full of makeup and fake color. It hits me hard. It's not her. There's no Matilda-ness left. No smile. No gentleness. No grace. It's an empty shell.

Matilda is gone.

I look at the photos again. Of her on her wedding day with Steve.

I look back around the small chapel.

There's Jack.

A couple near the back.

The funeral director.

A family with three teenage children.

I turn to Sylvie. She gives me a reassuring smile and pats my hand.

Then something strikes me as odd. Doesn't the family usually sit in the front row at funerals?

I crane my neck around the girls. The front row on the other side of the casket is empty.

"Where's Steve?" I whisper. My voice is dry and hoarse.

"What, dear?" asks Sylvie.

"Where's Matilda's husband. Steve?"

Is he too overcome? I imagine him sobbing in the other room. This has to be hard for him. Losing the love of his life.

Sylvie watches me. She shakes her head.

"Where?" I ask. I look over the room again. I don't see him.

"Steve died," she says.

My heart stutters. I didn't hear her right. "What?"

"Sweetheart. Steve's been dead for fifteen years."

I shake my head. This doesn't make any sense. I stand and push away from the chair. I walk up to the picture board. There's Steve. There's Matilda. They are getting married. And there's Steve and Matilda dancing. She's grinning at the camera. And she looks...twenty-five at most. I scan the board. There aren't any pictures of Matilda and Steve from recent years.

Sylvie joins me at the board.

"I thought you knew," she says.

"How would I know? She was always talking about him.

Always saying they were going on their second honeymoon when this was all over."

Sylvie nods. I look past her at Matilda's body.

"When it's all over," I say.

"Yes, dear," says Sylvie.

I start to cry. And I hate it. Matilda *knew*. She *knew* that she was going to die. And she was telling us all that she was going to see her love again when she died.

I wipe at my eyes. Cursing the tears.

"Her second honeymoon was in death?" I ask. Appalled.

Sylvie nods. "She told us her story the week before you came."

I look away, bitter at the loss of Matilda's story. "She never told me."

"Let's sit down. The service is about to start," Sylvie says.

I blink my eyes and walk back to my seat.

I don't hear what the minister says. I can't hear it.

I had everything so wrong. Everything I thought. Everything I believed. Wrong.

Matilda was right. I've been afraid. I've been afraid nearly my entire life that if I show anyone my true self they'll turn away. Reject me. So I rejected myself first. I didn't love me. I didn't let anyone see me.

A tear falls from my cheek to my hands.

The officiant asks if anyone would like to share a story about Matilda.

The woman who was part of the couple stands. She shares a touching story about Matilda volunteering at the animal shelter.

The family stands. Matilda was their neighbor. The children loved her.

But where is her family? Didn't she have any?

I sniff back more tears.

Sylvie is crying next to me.

Gerry sobs quietly into a handkerchief.

Even my mom is crying.

"Anyone else?" asks the officiant.

I hear a rustling and then Cleo stands.

I look up at her. Her face is pinched and if possible she looks more sour and angry than usual.

"I have something to say," she says.

The officiant nods and Cleo walks up to the podium.

"Bah," she says in a low growl. She waves her hands at all of us. "Bah at you, and bah at you, and humph."

I hiccup back my tears. I look around. Gerry has the handkerchief halfway to her mouth. Sylvie stares at Cleo in shock.

"I don't know why you're all blubbering." She pinches her face down and then blurts out, "Here's what I'd like to say—"

Cleo fumbles for a moment and then pulls her phone from her pocket. She gives each of us a sour look.

Next to me, Sylvie's eyes are wide. My mom is staring at Cleopatra like she's never seen anyone like her in her whole life. Gerry shakes her head, back and forth.

Then Cleo looks at me and winks.

I sit up straight.

"This is for Matilda. Dance, girl, dance," Cleo says.

She holds up her phone and presses the screen.

Then the chapel microphone picks up the beat of the most inappropriate song in funeral history. Heavy bass. Thumping, beating drums. Cleopatra drops her phone beneath the microphone and struts out next to the podium. She puts one arm behind her head and her other arm swings around as she points at each of us.

Her black pants flare out and she starts to shake her hips.

"Let's go," shouts Cleo.

It's Matilda's song. From the party. The bass cranks out.

"What the shit," says my mother.

I stifle a horrified laugh.

The officiant's mouth drops open and he rushes toward the podium.

By the look on his face, he's going to put a stop to it.

No way.

No. Freaking. Way.

I jump up and moonwalk my way across the floor. I block him out. This music isn't stopping.

"Ma'am," he says.

I shake my head and start to Cabbage Patch Dance around the stand.

"Ma'am, this is a funeral chapel, not a dance party."

I do the robot and the sprinkler dance. Every bad eighties move I know.

There's no way I'm letting this music stop. No way.

Cleo sings as loud as she can. She points at the front row.

There is one more second of stunned silence then Gerry jumps up. She bends over and drags Sylvie to her feet.

"Dance," Gerry laughs. "Dance, girls."

The officiant backs up. He knows a losing battle when he sees one.

We're dancing. This is our moment. Matilda's too. We're not stopping.

"Daniella," my mom cries, "what are you doing?"

I slide up to her. "Dancing, Mom. I'm dancing."

She shakes her head. "But a lady—"

"I'm not a lady, mom."

She looks me over and something shifts in her expression. She nods. "Okay."

I stare at her in shock.

Okay?

Then my mother, in her four-inch black Jimmy Choos, starts to tap her foot to the music. She smiles at me and gestures for me to keep going.

My friends cheer.

Gerry grabs my hands and spins in a circle. Sylvie does a little shuffle. Cleo, once again, is moving like she was born on the stage. Her face is transformed from pinched and sour to radiant.

Suddenly, everyone has joined us at the front. We're all dancing.

Every single one of us.

I feel it then.

Matilda's here.

And she's dancing too.

She's swinging around and around. Laughing and dancing. And Steve is here. And they're on their flipping second honeymoon.

I smile and blow a kiss in the air.

We dance and dance.

I'm free. Free of all the masks. All the fear. Matilda was right.

I'm just me now, dancing with my friends.

Something strikes me then. Where's Jack? I look around the chapel.

The music fades.

He's not here. He's gone.

40

Dany

*a*fter the burial, I stand with Sylvie, Gerry, Cleo and my mother at the graveside. The drizzle that began days ago is finally starting to clear. A little ray of sun twinkles on the pink and white of the granite headstone. Matilda is resting next to Steve.

"Darling, how about your friends come over for early dinner?" asks my mother.

She twists her hands together and has a hesitant half smile on her face.

"That's really nice, but what about..."

"Your father?"

I nod.

She shrugs then tilts her face to the sky.

"He's in Chicago," she says. She closes her eyes and her shoulders sag.

"Why is he in Chicago?" I have the urge to reach out and

take her hand. She doesn't look like my formidable mother. She looks lost.

"He left me weeks ago, darling. Your father decided that I was an old hag with neck wrinkles and he'd rather be with his twenty-two-year-old intern."

I shake my head and stare at her in shock. "But you said I couldn't stay because you were having a second wind. Boinking on the printer—"

"Fax machine."

"Fine, making dirty on the fax machine."

"That was your father and the intern. That's where I found them copulating."

I thread my fingers through hers. I had no idea.

"Why didn't you tell me?"

"I was embarrassed," she says.

"What? Why?"

"He's right. I have neck wrinkles. Saggy breasts. I'm a tacky sixty-year-old attempting to look like a twenty-something—"

"Mother—"

"He said I embarrassed him. That everyone but me knew I was over the hill. That makeup can't hide old."

"Mom—"

"Darling." She turns and takes both my hands.

I look at her pristinely applied makeup, her perfectly sculpted brows, her dyed blonde hair. I don't see tacky or old, I see my classy mom.

"He's wrong," I say.

She shakes her head and drops my hands. "He's right. My whole life I've put on my face in the morning, made myself the picture perfect wife, just so he wouldn't leave. So you would have a father."

"Oh, Mom."

She presses a tissue to her eyes. "I've spent nearly twenty years being Mrs. John Drake. Designer clothing, makeup, cock-

240

tail parties, concentrating on pleasing him. Daniella, I don't know who I am if I'm not...I don't have anything else. I don't know who I am if not his wife."

She drops her head and sniffs into her tissue.

I sigh.

I understand. Oh boy, do I understand.

It looks like my mother passed down more than her hair color.

I hold out my hand to her.

She looks up and frowns.

"Hello," I say.

"Pardon?"

"Hello, I'm Dany. I like to dance, sing to eighties music, be spontaneous, and garden. I just lost a good friend, but I've gained friends too."

My mom tilts her head and her lips wobble. Then she reaches out and shakes my hand.

"Hello, I'm Bernice. I hate makeup and tight dresses. I love tacos, reading trashy books, and cooking. I just lost my husband, but I hope I'm gaining my daughter."

There is such an air of hope. It's like the spring morning before the first bulb pokes its green leaves through the cold ground. I take a breath.

"Nice to meet you," I say.

A smile blossoms on her face.

"Nice to meet you, too."

Then we're hugging.

Thirty minutes later we're all in the kitchen at my childhood home.

"Who knew? Dany is little miss money bags. Did you see the bathroom? The soap has 24 karat gold flecks in it. Tell me, do you wipe your tush with dollar bills?" asks Gerry.

I choke on a laugh.

"Rude," says Cleo.

Gerry shrugs. "Truth is rude."

"Sit down and eat," I say. I point at the long butcher block table. On one side there's a low bench, on the other, comfy upholstered chairs.

My mom's at the stove. She brings over tacos, five cheese nachos, and guacamole.

The kitchen is French farmhouse chic. To me, it always felt cold. Until now. I guess what it was missing was friends.

"Tell us the rest of the story, Gerry. We want to hear about David," says Sylvie.

"Humph," says Cleopatra.

I reach for a chip and dip it in the tomatillo salsa. "This is really good," I say.

My mom beams at me. For the first time in my memory, she's in jeans and a blouse.

I turn. The girls are all looking at me.

"Oh, sorry. No interruptions."

"Wait, who's David?" asks my mom. She's at the stove again plating up enchiladas. She's a cooking wonder.

"A figment of Gerry's imagination," says Cleo.

"He's the love of Gerry's life. She went searching for him across the world," I say.

"Ooh," says my mom. She plops the enchiladas on the table, then slides onto the bench.

Karl brings a tray in from the bar full of drinks. I grab the glass of watermelon agua fresca.

"Have a seat," I say.

"Thank you, Miss," says Karl.

"Enough interruptions," says Sylvie.

Gerry begins.

"From Finland, I traveled to China. I traced David to the Tarim Basin in Northwest China. There, I learned of a foreigner who was working on a peach plantation. I was certain, absolutely certain that I'd found my David. I arrived at the plantation during harvest time. I ran down the rows of trees. Searching the faces of the men and women picking. Finally, at the end of the day, when dusk arrived and the sky turned as dusky orange as the fruit on the trees, I found him."

"He's real?" asks Cleo. Her mouth is a perfect O of disbelief.

"No interruptions," says my mom.

I laugh. It's like Matilda is still here enforcing the no interruption rule.

"Slowly, I made my way to him. His hair was glinting bronze in the setting sun. All my dreams had come true. My David. Thousands of peach trees. They're considered the fruit of immortality in China. A good omen. I called out to him. He turned. He was happy to see me. Of course he was. An American man in China meeting an American woman. But...he wasn't David."

"I knew it," says Cleo.

We all shush her.

"Bah," she says.

"David's trail was cold. Any whisper of him had disappeared. As dead as a peach pit in winter. I went home. And gave up my search."

"Ugh," I say.

"This one doesn't have a happy ending?" asks my mom.

"Oh, it does," says Sylvie.

Gerry nods. "It does. I met and married my husband Russ. He owned the Five and Dime here in Stanton. We had thirty-eight fabulous years before he passed."

I crunch down hard on a tortilla chip. "Why didn't you start with that?" I ask.

"Because chemo is painfully boring and I like stories."

Sylvie snorts, "Take up knitting."

Gerry's eyes twinkle. "And I wanted to show that every apparent tragedy brings an equal or greater opportunity."

"Bah, fortune cookie blather," says Cleo.

"You never heard from David?" I ask, not quite ready to let it go.

"Never," she says with a smile. "But if he popped up today, I'd marry him. I'm too old to bother with preliminaries. I want the juicy bits right now."

"Humph," says Cleo.

"So that's how the story ends," I say. I sigh. I really wanted Gerry to find her David.

"Wasn't real," says Cleo.

I start to laugh. Then everyone joins in.

We stuff ourselves with nachos, tacos, and enchiladas and talk into the night.

41

J<small>ACK</small>

"*H*ow was the funeral yesterday?" asks Sissy.

I kick my boot into the shovel and turn up a pile of dirt.

I'm in the back garden clearing the last of the weeds. The garden's in full bloom. Dany upheld her end of the bargain. It's gorgeous back here. I kick the shovel into the ground again and dump another clump of weeds.

"Wow. What'd those weeds ever do to you?"

I sigh and turn to her. "I left early," I say.

"Why?"

I shrug.

"Was Dany there?"

I nod.

"Seriously, bro. You've never been one for loquacious sibling chats, but give me something here."

"Sis, I'm not going to share my internal struggles with you."

"Ooh, somebody's in looove. I called it. I knew it. You're in looove. I knew it the second Dany proposed in the hospital and you got that stupid look on your face. Jack's in love, in love," she sings.

I throw a shovelful of dirt at her.

"Hey," she squeaks.

"Watch it," I say.

She chortles evilly. Then she makes calf eyes and kissy faces at me. What have I unleashed?

I let out a long-suffering sigh.

"Anyway. Why aren't you riding after her on horseback with sword drawn and a bunch of flowers?" she asks.

"You have a weird idea of romance," I say.

"Call her. Apologize for whatever stupid thing you did."

"I didn't—"

"Doesn't matter."

I run my hand over my face.

"Ew. You smeared dirt all over," she says.

"Go away, Sis."

"Call her," she says. She holds a hand phone up to her ear. "Call her and tell her you looove her."

"It's not that simple," I say.

"Why not? You've got manstipation? Constipation of your emotions?"

A laugh is startled from me.

Then I sober. "She's better off without me."

"Dude. Not this again. I'm going to shoot straight because clearly you need it. You were a kid. Whatever you think you did, it wasn't your fault. Your mom was unhappy. Then she died. Aunt Flo was a dick. Dad, clearly, is still a wad. It isn't your fault. None of it is your fault. There's nothing to make up for. You've got me. And Dany, if you can get over your manstipation and go after her."

I punch the shovel into the ground again and dump another load of dirt.

"Yeah, yeah," I say, mimicking her favorite phrase. I hear what she's saying but can't believe it's that simple.

I decide I'm done in the garden. "I'm going to get cleaned up. I have to figure out how to win the bid over Boreman's shopping mall."

"Sorry again, about that. Let me fix it," she starts.

"No. No way," I say.

"But it's not right. He's a creeper. And shady. There were some weird files in his office. I could dig up some dirt. Hack—"

"No hacking." I say.

She blows out a long breath then concedes. "Okay. I'm sorry, I really was trying to help." She looks down at the ground, the picture of humble contrition.

"I know. Next time you help though, stay within the law."

"Seriously," she says.

I can't help but smile at her.

"You think Dany will marry the dick?" she asks. She toes at the pile of dirt. Doesn't look at me.

I pick up the shovel and start digging again. Slicing it into the ground.

"I don't know," I say.

"Yeah," she says. "Bummer."

"Yeah," I say.

Sissy goes inside and I finish up.

When done, I head back in.

The house is completely renovated. Done.

I avoid looking at the walls Dany helped paint, the molding she sanded, the decorations she picked out.

The outside is being painted next week. It's all ready. I realize now that I was preparing it for my family. That even if I hadn't admitted it, deep inside I knew.

I was building a home.

42

Dany

I walk into the hospital for my last day of chemo.
I made it.

I survived.

I hope that I've thrived.

I see Dave in a wheelchair by the window. He waves me over.

"Found me a kidney yet?" he asks.

I hold up my hands. "Nope. No kidney."

He shrugs, "Oh well. Such is life. Where's that friend of yours? The sweet woman that liked cats."

"Matilda? She died." I say.

"I'm sorry. I liked her. Sweet as a peach."

I smile. "That she was."

He looks over the parking lot. "I had a girl like her once. Best time of my life."

I stand next to him and look at the cars all lined up in their parking spots.

"Maybe after you get your kidney, you can go and have another best time," I say.

"You bet. I'll go to New Zealand. I've always wanted to dive with the great whites there."

Talk about lists.

"Wow. Well. This is my last day of chemo. So, I won't be seeing you. Good luck with everything."

"Thank you. You as well," he says.

I wave goodbye then head up to the chemotherapy lounge.

The girls are all there. And surprisingly, so is my mom. She's sitting in Matilda's spot. Funny enough, that sends a happy warmth through me.

She smiles at me sheepishly as I sit down in my chair and get hooked up.

"I hope you don't mind. I thought I'd come and support you," she says.

"Of course," I say. And for the first time "of course" is not just the right thing to say—it's what I want to say. I'm so glad she's here.

"Well, this is it. Your last treatment," says Sylvie.

"I'm in the clear," I say.

For a bit we chat about our future plans. Cleo has decided to join Gregory in a dance troupe. Sylvie is going to take a cruise with her grandkids. Gerry is considering traveling the world. I'm planning on taking classes in landscape architecture. I've found my career.

Then, "I saw your young man at the chapel," says Sylvie.

Yeah, I'd been giving that a lot of thought. *A lot of thought.*

Shawn's left a dozen messages asking me to call. Yesterday, I did. I told him politely that I couldn't marry him. He took it surprisingly well.

"About that," I say.

All eyes turn to me.

"Remember my list?" I ask.

"Yes," says Gerry.

"Bungee jumping," my mom huffs disapprovingly.

"Well, I have one item left...a wedding on the beach."

"If you say with Shawn, I will take this IV pole and throw it at you," says Gerry.

"What?" I say.

"Darling," says my mom. I look over at her. She's leaning forward earnestly. "If you follow my horrible, awful, stupid advice to pursue Shawn, I will order a tray of red hospital Jell-O and dump it on your head and then ground you for a month."

"Ground me? I'm twenty-four. And what's with you guys thinking I want Shawn?"

"Well, dear, there was that bit about Hawaii," says Sylvie.

"Bah, Hawaii," says Cleo.

"Granted. I had a moment. I was scared. I'm not anymore," I say.

I look around the room at my friends, my family, and I smile.

"You guys showed me that I was afraid of being me, even showing anyone who I was. I'm not scared anymore. There's no mask. There's just me. I love myself just as I am, in this moment. Right here." I press my hand to my heart. It just happens to be beneath my mastectomy scar.

"Finally. She gets it," says Cleo.

I laugh. "So here's the deal. I want to finish number ten on my list. I want to marry Jack."

My heart lurches when I say it out loud. Because the thing is, I'm not certain he'll say yes.

There's a general gasp. Then everyone talks at once.

"On the beach?" asks my mom.

"Has he asked you?" asks Gerry.

"That's wonderful, dear," says Sylvie.

I address each statement, "Right. Thank you, Sylvie. And yes, on the beach. And no, he hasn't asked me."

"My experience, Miss, is that a man likes to propose."

"That's true," says Gerry.

Who said that? I look around the room. Karl nods at me from a folding chair in the corner.

"I brought Karl," my mom stage whispers.

I shake my head in amazement.

"Okay," I say. "Hi, Karl."

"Hello, Miss," he says. He tips his hat to me.

Warmth fills me at his familiar words. I say something that I've never said. "Thank you, Karl. You know. For always being there," I say.

"My pleasure, Miss," he says.

I turn back to the girls. "Okay. So, here's the thing. I have to try. I have to let Jack know how I feel. The way we left things, I wasn't completely honest with him. I didn't tell him how much he means to me. You see, he and I made this deal. I'd help him renovate his house, help convince this committee to approve his project, and he'd help me finish my list. I'm going to hold him to our bargain. I'm going to marry him."

"You're off your rocker," says Cleo.

I shrug. Sure, I might scare him off. He may think I'm crazy and reject me. But then again, this is me, who I am, and I'm going to take a chance and invite Jack to come along for the ride. I'm not scared to show my true self anymore.

"It makes perfect sense to me," says Gerry. "I love a woman who pursues a man."

"David's not real," says Cleo in a long-suffering voice.

Gerry rolls her eyes.

I sit up straighter in my chair and clear my throat for attention. It feels like a grand speech sort of moment. I look at everyone and start.

"Thank you all for being there for me. Your friendship means so much. And right now, I'm asking for your help. It's sort of crazy, and maybe a little romantic. I need your help getting Jack to the beach. There, he can make his decision."

"My word," says Sylvie.

"Who are you and what have you done with my daughter?" asks my mom.

I grin at her.

My mom doesn't take any time to consider. "Darling, I'm in. I'll do whatever you need."

"Bah, I'll do it," says Cleo.

"Yes," says Gerry. She claps her hands in glee.

"I'll drive if you need, Miss," says Karl.

I send him a grateful salute.

Sylvie is the last to respond.

"Dear, are you sure? He might say no. It could hurt. Rejection can be heartbreaking," she says. She looks down at her knitting.

I see the pinch of sadness in her eyes.

I look around the room at each of my friends.

"I'm sorry for what I said to all of you the other day. I can't tell you how sorry I am. Sylvie, I bet you're an amazing grandma. Cleo, you are the most funny, fiery lady I know. Gerry, I know you've lived a wonderful life. Please forgive me."

"Bah, stupid girl, we forgave you the minute you said it," says Cleo.

"Really?" I ask.

They all talk at once, assuring me.

I feel buoyed by their support.

Finally, Sylvie says, "Dear, you're sure about Jack?"

I am. I've reached the point of no return. A firm decision. It feels right. Crazy, but right.

"I have to try. I know who I am now, and I know that I won't forgive myself if I don't at least try."

Sylvie nods. "Then I'll support you, my dear."

A slow grin spreads over my face.

"Okay. Then here's what we're going to do..." I lay out a plan that requires mad knitting skills, six dozen sprinkle donuts, a hot-air balloon, a wedding coordinator, and a cat.

"I've booked the pavilion on the beach for tomorrow. We have twenty-four hours. Think we can pull it off?" I ask.

"Do peaches ripen in July?" asks Gerry.

I shake my head.

"Jeez, bah," says Cleo.

Sylvie shakes her head. "No one knows, dear, no one knows."

"Yes, the answer is yes," says Gerry.

"Oh, good. Then let's do this," I say.

There's a cheer.

My team is assembled. We've got a wedding to create and a groom to kidnap.

43

*I*t's D-day. Decision day for the Downtown Development Committee. Dany's father is here. Mr. Atler slaps him on the back as they chat about golf. Shawn's here. He's talking with Ms. Smith and looking self-assured.

For weeks I tried to contact Dany's father to pitch my proposal, but he was always out of town on business and not returning calls. I sent emails and called his offices, I met with local engineers, builders, and every mover and shaker I could think of. Nothing came to fruition. So, I'm here to try one last time to convince the board of my vision, based on nothing but my hard work, passion, and the belief that I'm doing what's right.

Shawn walks over and crowds my space.

"I have the votes. I'm going to win," he says. He has a satisfied smile on his face.

I don't doubt it.

It's funny, I came into this project hoping for absolution and pushing away love. Now, I won't have either.

I turn my head away from Shawn's gloating. I relax my hands and roll my shoulders.

"Would you believe that I envied you?" he asks. He rocks back on his heels and puts his hands in his pockets. We both look at the committee members mingling in the last few minutes before the quarterly meeting begins.

I remain silent.

"I admit, it lacked foresight when I let go of Daniella. I didn't realize how crucial she was to me." I move to walk away. I don't need to hear this. But Shawn holds out his hand.

"She said no," he says.

I stop. Shocked. "She said no," I repeat.

"We both know why," he says. "Look, Jones. I have an offer for you."

"Excuse me?"

He gives me a shrewd look.

"I'll give you everything you've ever wanted. You can win your Rose Tower Project. Here, today. I know it's personal. I've heard how much it means to you." *He knows about the fire. He's talking about absolution.* "I'll make you the most successful developer in the state. Back you. Fund you. I'll even help your precocious little sister get into the Ivy League of her choice. I'll give so much, for so little. All I ask is that you walk away from Daniella. Tell her goodbye. Never speak to her again. Let her come back to me."

Blood thunders in my ears. I don't understand.

"Why?" I ask.

Shawn steps toward me and lowers his voice.

"Because I love her. Is that so difficult to understand? I love her and I want her back." He's breathing heavily and pointing his finger at my chest. I look down at his hand.

He clears his throat and steps back. He loosens his tie.

"I'll give you everything you desire. Just step aside."

I shake my head, but he cuts me off.

"Or, you can keep after her." He looks down at his watch. "With the knowledge that in a short time, she'll realize you can't give her the life she wants. You can't give her what she needs. She'll leave you. Eventually. And I'll be there. If you keep after her, I'll make sure you never build in this city again. All your rehab projects, finished. Your bids, rejected. I'll block your building permits. I'll slow your bank loans. I'll call in favors and cover you in red tape."

"Bull." Anger and desperation sizzle through my veins. "You don't have that kind of power."

A slow smile spreads over his face. "Yes, I do. I'll also show the recording of your sister's little adventure to the police. Poor criminally minded Sissy, breaking and entering carries a sentence of up to five years in our fair state. My friend the judge won't be inclined to leniency. Do we understand each other?"

Understanding coats me like smog-polluted air. I see the two paths before me. Never has making a decision hurt so much.

Leave Dany and get what I always thought I wanted. Forgiveness. Absolution. Building homes for the city's most vulnerable. I can finally go back in time and fix what happened. And Sissy...do I really want to go up against Shawn's connections and political power?

So. Leave Dany. Never tell her I love her. Never ask for a life together. And with that, all of my old dreams can come true. I'd have developments around the state, homes for countless families, and my career will be a success. Or I can tell Dany I love her, beg her to have me, and then Shawn will send Sissy to jail.

Shawn smiles.

He sees realization dawning on my face.

"One more thing," he says.

"Yes?" I ask in a choked voice.

"In case all this wasn't enough to tempt you to the first option...if you go to Dany, I'll tell her the truth about you."

I go cold. "What are you talking about?"

"That you've only ever been interested in her for this bid. That you were told to *woo her* to win this bid. You don't really love her, you're a manipulative bastard only out for your own good. Mr. Atler, her father, they both know the truth and will back me."

I stumble back. "That's not true."

"But who will she believe?" he asks. "Do you really want to take that chance? Chance your project, Sissy's future, just for Daniella to realize you're a two-faced manipulator who she can never love? Like I said, you aren't good for her."

I press my hand to my heart. It hurts.

I think of Dany. Her smile. Her love of life. The way I feel when I'm with her. How much I want to build a life with her. Is that potential future we could build together worth more than decades of striving for absolution? Of hundreds, maybe thousands, of families having safe, affordable homes? Is it worth Sissy going to prison for years?

My heart once felt whole and hopeful. Now it feels broken.

Shawn smiles. "What's your choice?"

44

Dany

*E*xactly twenty-two hours later The Plan is in motion.
And it looks like we really might pull it off.

My mom's at the beach pavilion. When I left her twenty minutes ago she was wrapping every vertical structure in tulle and twinkly lights. There are flowers, folding chairs, a sound system; and this is where she really shined, there's also a pile of hors d'oeuvres and a three-tiered white chocolate raspberry wedding cake.

I'm in a lace and tulle beach-style wedding dress.

My walkie-talkie crackles.

"The donuts are in place. Repeat, the donuts are in place," says Gerry. She's loving the four-way video feed walkie-talkies that Karl scored for us.

I'm currently in the basket of a hot-air balloon in a vacant parking lot a quarter mile away. Karl is parked in a Hummer limo half a block down from the house on Rose Street. I can coordinate the plan from the balloon, yet not be seen by Jack before the big moment.

"Roger that. Sylvie, Chloe, go ring the bell and get Jack. Gerry stay with the cat. Leave the walkie-talkies on. I'll monitor," I say.

I watch on the video feed as Sylvie and Chloe start sneaking toward the bushes at the side of the house.

"Meow, this is one feisty cat," says Gerry. I hear grunting and a scuffle. "Got it, got it. Don't you worry."

Sylvie finally busts through the bushes and Cleo falls into a somersault and pops back up. Then they ruin the special ops vibe by giving each other high fives.

They're going to get grass stains all over their wedding outfits. I shrug. Oh well.

They climb up the front steps to the door.

"Here we go, dear," says Sylvie.

Cleo jabs the doorbell. I hear the chime over the walkie-talkie.

I hold my breath. The door opens.

It's Sissy.

I breathe.

"Um, hey guys. What's up?" she asks. I'd forgotten she knew them from the hair cutting night.

"Humph, where's your brother?" asks Cleo.

"Hello, dear, we're looking for Jack," says Sylvie.

"Seriously? Is Dany okay?" asks Sissy.

She stands on her tiptoes and tries to look around them.

"Yes, dear. Of course. We need Jack's help. See our sweet little kitten climbed up the tree in your back yard and we need Jack to climb up and get her down."

"Your kitten?" asks Sissy. She doesn't sound like she's buying it.

"Bah, go get your brother," says Cleo.

"Uh, what's with the donuts?" she asks.

There's a long trail of six dozen sprinkle donuts leading to the back yard.

"And the special ops comm devices? Seriously," she says.

"Never mind that, get your brother," huffs Cleo.

"Dudes. Jack's not here. He's at City Hall having his dreams crushed by the dick."

Then, over the walkie-talkie Gerry yelps. "Cat, hey, cat. Not so high."

But...Jack is, he's...what? There's only one dick I know of that could be crushing Jack's dreams.

"Hang on," I say over the device. "I'm coming."

"I'll be back," I tell the balloon operator. The short man gapes at me, but I hired him for the day and I'm counting on him to wait.

I jump out of the balloon. Then I kick off my high heels and run as fast as I can to the house on Rose Street. My feet sting. My sides pinch. I'm out of breath when I bound up the steps.

Sissy is nibbling on a donut. Sylvie and Cleo are arguing about what to do.

"What'd you say?" I ask Sissy.

She looks me over. Her eyes widen. "You're getting married?"

I wave away her question. "What did you say about Jack?"

She frowns. "He's at City Hall for his housing project bid. But your *fiancé* is going to get it instead. For his parking garage." Her shoulders slump then she looks at me and scowls. "So, you're marrying the dick, huh? Figures."

I stomp my foot. "What is with everyone thinking I'd marry Shawn?"

"Well, dear..." says Sylvie.

"Yeah. Douchewad was going to send me to jail but Jack saved me, cause we're family and all. I'm sure he's being all noble, giving up his dreams, but I say it's bull. Didn't think you'd be dumb enough to marry the dick." She sighs and looks at me with disappointment.

"Wait. What?" I ask. Jack did what?

"Ladies," Gerry calls over the walkie-talkie. "The cat's gotten a little high."

I point at Sissy. "I'm not marrying Shawn. We're trying to kidnap your brother and take him to *his* wedding. To *me*. Also, we want him to follow the trail of sprinkle donuts, climb the tree in the back yard, save a cat so he can feel heroic, and then we can catch him in Sylvie's yarn trap and fly—"

"Did you say 'yarn trap'?" asks Sissy.

"Um. Yes."

"Seriously?"

"Yes." I nod.

"And you want to marry Jack?"

"Yes," I say.

"You are so freaking—"

"Crazy?" asks Cleo.

"Awesome," says Sissy.

"Thank you," I say.

There's a shriek from the back yard.

We all sprint around the house.

Gerry is sitting at the bottom of the tree, tangled in yarn, with the cat in her arms.

"Humph," says Cleo.

"You guys seriously thought this yarn donut cat trap thing was going to work?" asks Sissy.

Gerry is scratching the cat under its chin. I think I hear a purr.

"I'm adopting this cat. I'll name her Herbert," she says.

We borrowed the cat from Matilda's animal shelter friends. Clearly, Gerry's smitten.

"Change of plans," I say.

I turn to Sissy. "Explain to me again what is happening with Jack?"

So she does.

"Alright, we're going to the committee meeting. This was part of our bargain. I *should* be there. We'll see what I can do. Also, clearly, we're still planning on grabbing Jack and taking him to the beach. Got it?"

Everyone nods.

"Sissy, are you in?" I ask.

"Heck yeah. I just need to grab some stuff."

"Meet us out front." I say.

The girls, Sissy and the cat go with Karl in the Hummer.

I'm at the hot-air balloon.

After a few minutes of convincing, and a *substantial* monetary donation, the balloon operator agrees to make an unexpected stop outside City Hall.

45

JACK

"What's your choice?" asks Shawn.

I look down at my hands, clenched in fists, and I realize that there's no choice at all.

"I don't want your support," I say.

"Listen, Jones —"

"No. I don't want your backing, I don't want your money or your contacts. I get this bid on my own merit, or not at all."

"Not at all then."

I nod. Probably. Then I make the choice that hurts most. Sissy was right, walking away hurts as much as someone leaving, it just hurts sooner.

"I can't let you hurt Sissy."

"Good choice."

I stare at the closed door of the conference room. Then, "If you agree to leave Sissy alone, erase the video, sign a binding agreement...if you leave Sissy alone, I'll do what you ask. I'll never talk to Dany again."

"Very good, Jones. Very good."

He wins.

Then I shake my head.

Try to clear it, because I can't believe what I'm seeing.

Dany walks into the conference room. But...she's in a wedding dress. A white, strapless, glittering wedding dress.

The breath is knocked from my lungs. She looks beautiful.

"Dany?" I say. What's she doing here?

"Daniella, you look amazing," says Shawn. He steps forward to kiss her on the check. She side-steps him. Searches the room and stops when she sees me.

A smile lights her face.

Sissy pushes in after her, followed by Dany's friends, Gerry, Sylvie and Cleo.

"Daniella, what in God's name?" We all look to the booming voice across the room. It's Mr. Drake. Displeasure radiates from him.

Shawn sends me a slanted look. His message is clear. *Step aside.*

"What are you doing here?" I ask.

She wrinkles her nose and gives a grin. Then she points out the window.

"I thought I'd swing by to help you win your bid. Then maybe get married."

I look at the window. My mouth falls open as I see what she's pointing to.

A hot-air balloon.

A red and yellow striped hot-air balloon floats outside the window.

"Be careful here, Jones," hisses Shawn. "Your choices have consequences."

I look between the hot-air balloon and Dany.

She did this for me. Her gesture couldn't be clearer. She loves me.

She *loves* me.

She wants to have a life of adventure together.

Starting now.

"Be careful. Your career, your sister," Shawn whispers.

Right.

He wins.

No matter how much I love Dany, or how much she loves me, I can't let him ruin Sissy's life.

"I can't," I say to Dany. "I'm sorry." She'll never know how much.

Dany looks at me and I see shock and pain in her eyes.

"What?" says Sissy. "Bro, don't be an idiot."

"Are you crazy?" says Gerry.

I look out the window at the hot-air balloon.

The torch in the hot air balloon, the blazing fire that lifts it catches my eye.

I'm taken back again to the smoke, the coughing, the dying, the shame...I'm caught in it. Except, then the torch flickers. The balloon sways in the wind, pulling at the weighted ropes. And it hits me. Fire can burn and destroy. It did. But it can also lift you up. Take you to new beginnings.

"Daniella," begins Shawn, "Jones is no good. I want you back. Look, I made a mistake. I'm sure your mother told you—"

"Shawn," says Dany.

"Yes?" he asks.

"Stop talking."

Then she walks over to me and puts her hand on my heart. "Do you love me?" she asks.

I swallow and I can't not tell her, even if I'll never be with her. "Yes," I whisper.

She nods. "That's what I thought."

Then she walks to the front of the conference room. She has the attention of the entire committee.

"Members of the committee," says Dany. "I apologize for the

interruption. If you could give me a moment of your time. Today, you have an important decision to make. You have two bids before you. The first is from a man who has integrity, passion, and heart. He looks at buildings like they're people. When a building needs a little TLC, or is past its prime, he loves it and fixes it up and helps it become beautiful again. Or if it's a warehouse, he helps it find a new purpose in housing families. When he looks at a building he sees worth and value. He doesn't tear things down or throw them away. He cares."

I watch as Dany speaks to the committee, but whether they say yes or no to my bid doesn't matter anymore. Because I hear what she's saying about me.

"The second man tears down. If he sees an older building, or a building that needs rehab, or one that's not bringing in enough revenue, he tears it down. He demolishes it and puts up a new structure, until eventually he either sells that or tears that one down too. He doesn't value. He doesn't care. If the building makes him money, he's satisfied. If it becomes a bother or stops pleasing him, he demolishes it."

Dany looks at Shawn and he shifts under her words.

"Choose carefully," she says, "a man who values, or a man who tears down."

"Hear, hear," says Sylvie.

"I implore you, Mr. Atler"—she nods at Rick—"Ms. Smith, Mr. Rudolph, Mr. Polinski, Mrs. Hirsch..." *Does she know all the committee members?* "I implore you to choose the bid that will give the city what it needs most. Heart."

"Now, now, Daniella," says Mr. Atler. "You don't understand."

"See here. We've already decided on the proposals. The Boreman proposal is best for the city," says Mr. Polinski.

Dany frowns. "That's a shame. I think that you're making a mistake."

Joy fills me. She believes in me.

Shawn looks between Dany and me. A calculating gleam enters his eyes.

He steps forward. "Look, Daniella. I didn't want to have to tell you this, but Jack's been manipulating you."

"Pardon me?" says Dany.

"Jones here. His entire purpose has been to get close to you so that you'll attempt to swing the vote in his favor. Looks like he succeeded admirably. Woo the Drake girl to win the vote. Wasn't that his plan, Rick? John? From the beginning?"

Mr. Atler's face reddens and he looks away from me. "Sorry, Daniella," he says.

"I didn't want to tell you," says her father.

Dany looks between us all, confused, hurt.

"If you could get a vulnerable woman to love you, you could get her to do anything, even further your business ambitions. Right, Jones?" says Shawn.

"No," I say. I'm shaking my head. But my heart is in my gut. Dany looks between Shawn, Mr. Atler, her father, and me.

"Step aside," says Shawn. He's reminding me of what's at stake.

The torch from the balloon flickers again. Fire.

It's your fault. Your love is suffering.

"Is that true? Were you using me?" asks Dany. She looks small. Confused. I want to go to her and tell her that it isn't. That I never would've done anything like that. But I can't.

"It's true," I say.

Her face leaches of color.

"I started with the intent to use you. I'm sorry."

She shakes her head and a single tear falls down her face.

"Gentlemen, ladies, can we resume our meeting? Histrionics outside," says Mr. Drake.

Dany closes her eyes.

"But it stopped being that way. Dany, look at me."

I walk to her and take her hands in mine. She lifts her face.

I want to get lost in her eyes. I use them as a bridge to tell her everything I've been scared of.

"I couldn't woo you, because you wooed me. From the second you mentioned a Phillips head, and your list, everything about you pulled me in. I fell in love. I love you. Remember when you asked about the rest of your list? The list that lasts the rest of your life? I want that. I want to be there with you."

"Jones. Do this and you kiss your career goodbye. Kiss your criminal sister goodbye," says Shawn.

He wins.

Then Sissy steps forward.

"Dude. Committee dudes. I found some interesting papers you might like to see. Now, I'm only an innocent and naïve kid, but these papers I found, ahem, belonging to Boreman Group, look like, um...embezzlement," says Sissy. "These are copies. Take as many as you want."

My heart stops and then starts up again. My brilliant, wily sister.

The members of the committee crowd forward.

The room is in a state of shock. I want to hug my sister. She's finally using her con artist skills for the power of good. It looks like Shawn, not Sissy, will be the one spending time in the criminal justice system.

I look at Dany...does this mean? She winks and I have the overwhelming urge to take her in my arms.

"Do you need a yarn trap?" whispers Sylvie.

"Daniella, this is unacceptable. Escort your"—Mr. Drake waves his hands—"friends outside. We'll discuss your wedding attire at the conclusion of the meeting. Shawn will be ready after."

Dany shakes her head, "Why does everyone... Father, I'm not marrying Shawn. Also, your recent life choices are extremely questionable."

"Daniella," he says.

"Daniella, please," says Shawn at the same time.

She turns and points at him. "No. No more. Leave me, leave Jack, and leave Sissy alone. Don't you dare try anything. You and I are done."

The girls clap and cheer.

Dany smiles. "Father, Shawn, members of the committee. If you'll excuse me, I have a hot-air balloon to catch." She turns to me. "You coming?"

Joy fills me. "We're doing this?"

"Oh yeah," she says. "Sylvie, now it's time for the yarn trap," she calls.

Sylvie throws a big net of yarn over us.

Then Cleo hoists a 1990s boombox over her head and hits the play button.

"See you fuddies later," Cleo says.

Dany and I are marched to the hot-air balloon to the music of an old-school beat. We're thrown in the basket.

"Thanks for waiting, now we're ready," says Dany.

The man gets to work sending the balloon into the sky.

"Where to?" I ask.

I feel like the whole world is laid out before us.

"A beach wedding," she says, in a half question, half statement.

I let out a laugh.

"Dany, a man likes to propose."

"Told you, Miss," says a crackly voice.

"Is that a walkie-talkie?" I ask.

Dany laughs and turns off the device.

She leans into me. I put my arm around her as we rise into the air. There's no one in the world I'd rather be doing this with.

"Jack." She looks up at me, her eyes serious, "I wanted to do something big. I wanted you to know that I've been wrong and scared. I love you. I don't need to be the Dany of the past. Or the Dany from a list. I just need to be me. I'd love it if you'd come along for the ride."

These are the best words I've ever heard.

"I love you," I say. "I've loved you from the moment I saw you. I'm sorry it took me so long to learn how to say it out loud."

I lean forward and take her mouth. She tastes like home. My home. My future.

I run my hands over her bare shoulders and down to the soft fabric of her wedding dress.

We float on the wind, toward the shore.

Thought returns. I pull away. Her wedding dress.

We're headed toward the beach. To number ten, have a beach wedding.

"Dany," I say. I shake my head and run my hands through my hair. "Are you taking me to our beach wedding?"

"Maybe?" she says.

I let out a long laugh. "You are incredible."

"You like the idea?" she asks.

I shake my head. "No."

"No?"

I reach out and run my hand over her lip. Her shoulders tense. She's scared. She doesn't need to be.

"I want to marry you. I want to spend the rest of my life with you. But I don't want to be a number on a list to be checked off. Will you still have me, will you still marry me, even if it isn't on the beach, as a number ten?"

Her eyes fill with tears. She reaches forward and sends her arms around me.

"Yes," she whispers. "Yes, yes, and a thousand times more, yes."

I kiss her again. I'm lost in her. I don't want to take my mouth from hers. Too soon the balloon starts to set down at the beach. I see a wedding gazebo, chairs, a string quartet, a cake...

"Wow," I say.

"Yeah," she says.

I start to laugh.

"Sad to waste a good beach wedding. Could've finished my list." She sighs, then starts to laugh.

"How about we make our own list together?" I ask. "I've always wanted to see the Himalayas."

She cocks her head. Then her eyes widen.

"Oh, holy mackerel. That's it."

46

Dany

*J*ack and I hold hands as we rush into the front entrance of the hospital. This is the first time I've come here with anticipation and excitement. It colors the whole place differently.

On the way here, Karl drove like a speed demon. I texted my mom to let her know I was thirty minutes behind schedule, but to keep everything in place. Karl had already dropped the girls and Sissy at the wedding.

I drag Jack to the windows where Dave usually sits.

It's empty.

There's no one here.

I turn in a circle. Scan the lobby.

A nurse bustles through. A young couple carrying flowers walks toward the elevators. I stare at the empty space in front of the windows.

"He's not here," I say. All the hope that had been rising like a buoyant balloon pops. "He's usually here in the afternoon." I let go of Jack's hand.

I thought Dave would be here. He'd been in this exact spot every day I came in for the entirety of my treatment. And now...

"Come on," says Jack.

He pulls me to the information desk. "Excuse me," he says. The sharp-eyed woman behind the desk frowns at him.

"May I help you?" she asks.

Jack gives her a flash of his dimples and the corners of his eyes crinkle. "Yes, ma'am."

Her eyes narrow.

He points at the windows. "We're looking for the gentleman who sits by those windows."

The woman purses her lips.

Jack continues, "his name is Dave—"

"He's in his late seventies. Looking for a kidney. He sits in a wheelchair and has—"

"I can't help you," she interrupts.

"We'd just like to know if he's been in today," I say.

"I can't help you."

"Or if he's been in this week?" asks Jack.

The woman shakes her head. "Sorry. Next," she calls.

A woman in a business suit steps forward.

"No wait," I say. "Please. If you've ever been in love, if you've ever loved someone so much that you'd search the world for them, then please tell us if he's been here, if he's still..." I trail off. If he's still alive, is what I can't say.

"Ma'am," says the hard-eyed woman.

"Yes?" I ask.

Her gaze softens. My hope rises again. I lean forward.

She lowers her voice. "I started here this morning. I can't help you."

"Oh," I say. It comes out as a small puff of air.

"Thanks," says Jack.

He takes my hand. We turn away from the desk.

"So, this Dave guy. He had gray hair?"

"Sure," I say.

"And did he wear three-piece suits and wingtips?"

"Yes?" I say.

"And did he wave at you whenever he saw you?"

I turn to look where Jack is pointing.

"Yes," I say.

I run over to Dave and surprise him with a hug.

"You have no idea how glad I am to see you," I say.

Dave pats my back and returns my hug.

"Nice to see you, too," he says.

He looks healthier than the last time I saw him. A lot healthier. There's a twinkle in his eye.

"Did you get your transplant?" I ask.

"I sure did. All recovered, too."

"That's wonderful," I say.

"It's my final checkup. I'm heading to New Zealand at the end of the month."

I look at Jack. He raises his eyebrows.

"This is Jack. My fiancé." I step closer and Jack puts his arm around me.

"Congratulations," says Dave. "When's the wedding?"

Jack coughs to cover a snort.

I clear my throat. "I have a question," I say. I tense in anticipation of his answer. "Are you, by any chance, David Crestwood?"

Dave tilts his head. "No."

"Oh," I say. My shoulders sag.

"Not anymore."

"What?" says Jack.

"I changed my name to Dave Creston forty years ago," Dave says. "It's actually a funny story, I was in the Ural Mountains and —"

"Hang on," I say. "So you're David Crestwood."

"Well, yes," says Dave.

"From Stoutsberg?"

"As you see," he says.

"And did you once know a woman named Geraldine Bloom?"

"Gerry?" he asks. He smiles and his face looks twenty years younger.

"She went to Russia to find you. And China."

"Gerry did?" he asks.

"I could take you to her if you'd like," I say.

He stands. "I'd like that very much."

"Wait a minute," says Jack. "Did you say your name is Dave Creston? Did you by any chance own the Creston warehouses downtown?"

~

We pull up in the Hummer. The string quartet starts to play.

Cleo, Sylvie, Gerry, my mom and Sissy are gathered at the front of the gazebo. Somehow, my mom also managed to invite about fifty of our closest family friends.

"This looks like a wedding," says Dave.

"Absolutely," I say.

Jack winks at me.

The gathering of people notice our arrival. They stand and turn to watch our approach.

Jack, Dave and I walk down the aisle toward the gazebo.

When we are ten feet from the front, Gerry steps forward.

"David?" she asks.

"Gerry. My peach," says Dave.

"He's real?" squawks Cleo. She falls back into her chair with a thud.

"Oh my word," says Sylvie.

"Dude. You're seriously getting married?" asks Sissy.

"No," I say.

"Not today," says Jack.

"Yes," says Dave.

"Yes?" says Gerry as she steps toward Dave.

He pulls a silk handkerchief from his pocket. When he opens it, there's a lock of gleaming brown hair tied with a blue ribbon inside.

"I kept this all these years. You remember giving it to me in the orchard?"

"I do," says Gerry.

"Unbelievable," says Cleo.

"Shhh, no interruptions," I whisper.

Gerry reaches out and puts her hands in Dave's, around the silk handkerchief.

"Gerry. Marry me. I've waited nearly sixty years. I don't want to wait a second more."

Gerry's face breaks into the most radiant smile I've ever seen.

"Yes, absolutely," she says.

"Check?" I whisper to Jack.

He grins down at me, then laughs long and loud.

It's a wedding on the beach. Just not ours.

Then he takes me in his arms. I gaze up at him. In his eyes I see our future. There's adventure, and love, and building a family and a home. It's a whole lifetime of lists and love. I'm not afraid. I'm not scared at all. I'm only happy to be here in this moment, in his arms.

"If you don't stop looking at me like that, I'm going to kiss you in front of all these people," says Jack.

"Well, then do it already. Because I'm never going to stop."

So, he does.

EPILOGUE

I climb out of the deep sleep of anesthesia. It's a thick fog blanketing my awareness. I'm floating in a waking dream. I lift an arm and place my hand on my chest.

It falls on a pair of new breasts.

Hello, bonjour, hola. I say hi to the new girls. The reconstruction surgery is over.

This is it then. The journey is done. I survived and I thrived. *I did it.* I did.

I try to peel open my eyes. The fluorescent hospital light sends sparks over my eyes. They look like twinkle lights. The twinkle lights at a wedding.

There are people around me. I can sense them in the room with me. Jack should be here. He said he would be here.

"I love you," I say. I float a bit more and the room spins. A sense of déjà vu overcomes me.

Jack should be here. Why isn't he answering?

"She's awake," I hear someone say.

"Bah," someone else says.

I open my eyes.

Jack smiles down at me.

"I love you, too." He leans down and brushes his lips over mine.

"You aren't going to leave me, are you?" I ask. I hate coming out of anesthesia. It makes the world jumbled and confused. Jack grabs my hand and squeezes. I hold tight.

"When I married you, I did it for life," he says.

A warmth flows over me.

"Husband," I say.

"Wife," he says.

"Bah, off your rockers," says Cleo.

She's been saying that ever since we said our vows while bungee jumping.

"Dudes. Seriously. Enough with the lovey dovey. Does anybody have anything to eat?" asks Sissy.

"I made an enchilada casserole," says my mom.

"Here, you look chilled. I finally finished your blanket." Sylvie lays her love blanket over my lap.

"Jack, I got a call. The Rose Tower development broke ground on schedule," says Dave.

Dave decided to back Jack's community development company. They're partners in the new venture. I'm officially the lead of their landscape architecture department.

"No interruptions," says Sylvie, channeling Matilda.

"That's right," says Gerry. "Let them kiss. After the recovery time these two love birds are going to go at it like—"

"Rude," says Cleo.

"Truth is rude," says Gerry.

Jack chuckles and then leans down to take my mouth again.

"I love you," he says against my lips. "Tell me you love me."

I smile against his mouth, "I love you."

He kisses me. And I'm filled with the warmth and the love of all my family, my friends, all the people that I love and that love me.

My mom takes out a picnic basket.

Cleo props her 1990s boombox at the end of the bed and pushes play.

"Dude. This isn't eighties music," says Sissy.

"That's Dany's jam. I'm rocking the nineties," says Cleo.

The room fills with the sound of music and laughter.

Dave takes Gerry in his arms and they start to dance.

Sissy covers her eyes.

Sylvie laughs and pulls Cleo into a groove.

Jack laughs and kisses me again.

Déjà vu is no more. This is a whole lifetime away from the last time I woke in the hospital. This time, my life is filled with laughter, dancing, and love.

Sure, the future may not be rosy, hard times will definitely come, but when they do, I know what to do.

Jack, my mom, the girls, they helped me figure it out. When hard times come, surround yourself with love. Then laugh, and live, and dance.

"Who wants an enchilada?" calls my mom.

"I do," says Sissy.

I settle back into the bed. Jack climbs in next to me and I rest my head against his beating heart.

"Looks like tonight you're getting lucky," says Gerry.

"I already am," says Jack.

He kisses me.

"Humph," says Cleo.

I laugh.

Jack catches my laughter with his mouth. The warmth and the laughter enfold us. Jack and me, our friends, our family, we're all together, and we have the whole world and all our lives in front of us.

*T*HE END

GET DANY & JACK'S WEDDING STORY - FREE -

Want more Dany and Jack? Read their wedding story - an exclusive bonus short story for newsletter subscribers only.

When you join the Sarah Ready Newsletter you get access to sneak peaks, insider updates, exclusive bonus scenes and more.

Join Today!

www.sarahready.com/newsletter

ABOUT THE AUTHOR

Sarah Ready is the author of *The Fall in Love Checklist*. She writes contemporary romance, romantic comedy and women's fiction. Her next book is coming in 2021. You can find her online at www.sarahready.com.

Made in United States
Troutdale, OR
08/05/2023

11810741R00181